DESIRE
OF OUR
HEARTS

OTHER BOOKS
BY SARIAH S. WILSON:

Secrets in Zarahemla

DESIRE
OF OUR
HEARTS

A NOVEL

SARIAH S. WILSON

Covenant Communications, Inc.

ACKNOWLEDGMENTS

A big thank-you to my publisher, Covenant Communications, and to my editor, Kirk Shaw (who always makes sure that I say what I really meant to say), for their hard work and support.

A special thank-you to Melody Salisbury and Elizabeth Salisbury for their ideas on the manuscript.

Thanks to Daniel Rona for describing the flora and fauna of the land surrounding the City of Nephi to me.

And as always, thank you to my wonderful family, especially Kevin, for their love and encouragement.

CHAPTER ONE

Alma, high priest of King Noah, was expecting to have a dull evening.

This was certainly not the first feast that the king had organized to find his next wife or concubine, the choice of the woman's status depending entirely on the king's mood. Alma was the youngest of the king's priests and despite having only been in service for the last eight months, he had seen more than his fair share of the king's debauchery.

He had enjoyed it at first. What young man wouldn't? The constant influx of the land's most beautiful young women parading around the throne room for the king and his priests, the maguey wine that flowed without stopping, the revelry that lasted into the early hours of the morning.

But eventually one feast seemed to bleed into the next. The festivities made him feel old, tired. He always had a vague sensation of a huge weight pressing against his chest the morning after. And a sickening, bitter taste in his mouth that he couldn't get rid of.

And then the king had asked Alma to bring his fourteen-year-old sister to a feast. The weight on his chest grew into a mountain. Alma knew what these men would do to his sister, what horrors the king himself could inflict on her.

He used his status as the king's favorite priest to avoid the request, to flatter and turn the king's thoughts away from his sister. But it had changed how Alma looked at the women gathered in the room in front of him. They were not merely playthings for the king. They were someone's daughter, someone's cousin, someone's niece, someone's granddaughter.

Someone's sister.

Alma slowly chewed the piece of chicle gum in his mouth, surveying the scene. The king had ordered, as he always did, that the choicest maidens in the lands of Lehi-Nephi and Shilom be rounded up and brought to the palace for his selection of a new companion, sometimes against their will. However, many of the women in the room seemed happy to be there, trying to catch the king's eye as they laughed and twirled in flashes of color. Their gaiety seemed forced to Alma because of the oppressiveness of the increasingly stuffy room. The air hung heavy with the scent of smoke and sweat.

The light from candles and fires highlighted the opulence of the room, the intricately carved lintels that supported the roof overhead, the precious metals that seemed to flash from every corner, inlaid in every wall. At the center of it all, King Noah lounged on his throne, a masterful work of fine wood, silver, gold, and jade with a jaguar pelt laid across the seat. The stuffed head of the jaguar peeked out from underneath the king's backside. Alma had to choke back a laugh at the image.

Fortunately, no one noticed Alma's amusement at his ruler's expense. His fellow priests were too busy picking through the women that King Noah had not shown an interest in. From watching them, Alma knew why he had been chosen to be the king's priest. Alma was a descendant of Nephi, of a noble family. He was young, fit, handsome, and intelligent. Just as most of the other priests were. Just as the king used to be and apparently still believed himself to be.

Alma shook his head at the disloyal thoughts that filled his mind. He had been selected to serve King Noah, to teach the people the truths of the king's church—not to make judgments about his ruler. Certainly not to disagree with the king either. Men who failed to see things the king's way had a tendency of winding up dead.

Stifling a yawn, Alma stood up from his gilded gold chair on the priests' dais. He wondered if he could sneak out without being noticed. He walked parallel to the length of the breastwork until he reached the end of the dais. He looked about, trying to make certain that no one of importance would see him leave.

The sensation of a cool breeze blowing across the soft hairs on the back of his neck made Alma stop. With a tingling awareness, Alma knew that something was about to happen.

He turned, scanning the room again. Then he saw . . . *her*.

And promptly fell off the dais.

Alma heard rumbling chuckles and dainty feminine trills of laughter at his expense. "Too drunk to stand," someone nearby said. Although he had not touched any wine, Alma did feel drunk. Off balance. Not himself. Alma lumbered back to his feet to find her again.

There. There she was.

His wife.

The thought popped into his head unbidden but, Alma found strangely enough, not unwelcome. He smiled as he considered what the woman would think of him if he crossed the room to propose marriage.

For now it was enough to just look at her. Alma would not have been able to explain the feeling he had watching her, something like recognition. Like he had somehow split into two parts and had finally found that missing piece of himself.

Alma loved her, and he didn't even know her name.

It was not just her beauty, though she was certainly beautiful enough. Her obsidian black hair picked up the candlelight, shining like a halo around her face. Her cheeks flushed with color, but from the expression on her face, he knew it wasn't from excitement. She looked angry, unhappy to be there. Her delicate pink lips were compressed into a thin line, giving Alma a determination to make her laugh, to see what a smile would do to her lovely features. He wished he could see the color of her eyes.

His attraction didn't come from her shining personality. If she had one. It was difficult to tell as she lurked in the shadows, scowling at everyone she saw. He was not captivated by her intelligence either. He had no way of telling if she could put two words together. For all Alma knew, she might be some simpering maiden with all the sense of a rock. He had not heard her laugh, had not smelled her scent, had not kissed her—things that might make a man feel this way.

Aside from beauty, she had absolutely nothing in that moment to recommend herself, but Alma loved her nonetheless.

An urgency pressed upon him, a need to be closer to her. He had to hear her speak. Had to see her smile sweetly at him. Had to get her father's name to seek permission.

Had to learn her name.

He spit his chicle out on the floor, not caring that it landed on an expensive woven rug. "Excuse me," Alma said as he pushed through the throng, never taking his eyes off his beloved.

"Alma! I have the reports on the tower for you!"

Helam, Alma's scribe and aide, stood in front of Alma, blocking his path. As the newest high priest, Alma had been assigned the newest scribe. But Helam was so full of eagerness that Alma had a hard time being stern with him. He forgave things in Helam he would not have forgiven in other men. And Helam did an excellent job. He had the ability to focus on details that few possessed, although it made Helam oblivious to the rest of the world. Like now, when Helam seemed totally unaware that he stood in the midst of a wild, raucous party.

Summoning up his last measure of patience, Alma gently pushed Helam's parchment aside. "Tomorrow. We will go over these tomorrow."

"But . . . but . . . I . . . you . . ." Helam sputtered as he waved the parchment in the air. "You said you wanted to see these right away."

"I know I did. But not tonight. I have to—" Alma stopped. He had let Helam's bureaucratic zeal distract him. He could no longer see her. Where had she gone? Alma's head whipped back and forth. She couldn't have left. He hadn't even had the chance to talk to her.

Alma's throat constricted when he saw her being dragged away by Amulon, a fellow high priest. Alma pushed past Helam, sprinting to intercept Amulon.

He caught up with them in a long hall that bordered an inner courtyard. Alma saw that she hammered at Amulon with her fists and heard her saying over and over, "Not you. Not you. Anyone but you."

"Amulon, I'm glad I found you." Alma put on his best political smile, a warm, inviting expression that didn't quite reach his eyes, meant to lure others into listening and believing. The woman stopped struggling and looked at Alma with an expression of hope.

Alma resisted every impulse in his body that screamed for him to pummel Amulon into the ground. He clasped his hands behind his back to keep them from going around Amulon's throat. "King Noah is looking for you," Alma lied, saying the first thing that came to his mind.

A corner of Amulon's mouth smirked upwards. "Nonsense. The king has already retired for the night with his new concubine. That's why I selected one of the women he passed over for myself."

"You will let her go," Alma said, the false smile sliding off his face.

"Will I?"

"Yes." Alma took a step closer to Amulon. "Or I will make things very . . . difficult for you." The menace Alma felt toward Amulon laced the edges of his threat.

A flash of fear danced across Amulon's face. After a few moments that felt like an eternity to Alma, Amulon released his grip on the woman. Amulon began to walk away, stopped, and turned back toward Alma.

"The king is fickle. His favorites come and go. Your time is waning," Amulon hissed at Alma. "You will not always have his ear. I will see to that."

Alma did not respond to Amulon's challenge. He didn't fear Amulon. Alma knew Amulon's weakness—his darkest fear—knew how to prey upon it. Amulon had no such hold over him. Alma had the higher ground, and he could see that Amulon realized it.

Glaring but saying nothing more, Amulon left. Alma shifted his attention back to the woman. Then he noticed the cuts on her face, bleeding slightly. "You're hurt," Alma pointed at her face. "Here."

Alma reached out to assess the wounds and found her cheek even softer than he could have imagined. "How did this happen?" he asked.

"Amulon hit me when I resisted," the woman replied, trembling slightly under his touch. "He seems to like wearing rings."

White-hot fury lanced through him and he again had to restrain himself from finding Amulon and beating him.

"He . . . he was going to . . ." the woman started to sob. Acting on instinct, Alma pulled her to him. He held her shaking frame close, saying soothing words. He knew he should feel strange holding a woman he had never met before. But holding her felt right. Like she belonged there. Belonged to him and no other.

When her cries had subsided, she began to back out of his embrace. Alma didn't want to let her go. He released her but felt a pang of loss.

"I am sorry," the woman said, her gaze directed down. "I'm not one for weeping usually. It's just been a horrible day."

"I saw," Alma replied. The feeling of caring for her, worrying over her, felt so foreign to him. Her misery cut through him. Despite wanting to prolong his time with her, he had a stronger desire to get her home so she could end this day. It felt somewhat ironic that what was quickly becoming one of the best nights of his life had been one of her worst. Perhaps he could change that. But first she had to be cleaned up. "There is a small kitchen down this hall. May I take you there and wash your cuts?"

She looked up at him and nodded. Alma guided her to the darkened room. He found a jug of water. Alma then located a bowl and filled it with the water. A pile of rags lay folded atop a container, and Alma took one to dip in the water. After he had wrung out the excess, he gently dabbed at the cuts on her cheek. "My name is Alma, by the way," he said.

"I'm Sam."

"Sam?" Alma pulled back to look at her with a bemused grin. "You have a man's name?"

A ghost of a smile played on her lips. "I'm told that my father tired of waiting for a son to pass his name to and decided to give it to me."

Sam. Somehow, it suited her. His heart flipped over in a strange joy that he now knew the name of his wife. Or, more correctly, soon-to-be wife. The formalities would have to be dealt with first.

"There." Alma put the rag down into the bowl of water. "It looks better now."

Sam put her hand up to her face and held it against the scratches. "Thank you."

"It's late. I'm sure your family is worried about you. Do you live here in the city?"

"Yes."

"May I accompany you home?"

She looked flustered. "I can find my way home."

"I am not questioning your sense of direction," Alma said with a teasing grin. "Considering what time of night it is, I think you would be safer if you had someone with you."

Sam appeared to be contemplating Alma's offer. Then she said softly, "All right."

Alma directed her through the corridors and interconnected rooms until they had passed safely out of the palace. The night was as beautiful as any he could have asked for. A blanket of stars hung suspended in the sky above them, and the full moon lit their path. Alma began to ask Sam questions. His mind raged with curiosity about her. It reminded him of the time he had found an ancient book in the king's library, a book he had never seen before. Alma had stayed up all night to read it. He wanted to know everything about the book, just as now he wanted to know everything about Sam.

Sam answered each of Alma's questions, and in a short time he discovered her age, that she was the middle child in a family of five girls, that her favorite dish was her mother's turkey and vegetable stew, that she hated fetching water in the morning, that her favorite color was yellow. He sensed her reservation, heard that halting, hesitating breath she took before each of her replies. She did not ask

Alma any questions in return; he didn't give her the chance. Each answer led him to another question, and another.

He had become so wrapped up in their conversation that Alma didn't notice that they had moved away from the more expensive homes and buildings surrounding the temple and had entered a poorer section of the city. When Sam stopped walking and announced, "This is where I live," Alma had to blink several times.

Her house, if it could be called that, was a poorly constructed hut that Alma wouldn't have even put his peccaries in. Alma touched the fraying ropes loosely holding the sticks that comprised the walls and could only shake his head at the misshapen thatched roof. "You live here?"

Alma realized his mistake too late. He saw her face fall, saw the anger harden her features, saw her stiffen and move away from him.

"There is nothing wrong with where I live."

"No, I apologize. It's just that I—" Alma said in a rushed tone, trying to right the situation, but not knowing what to say about his reaction. How could he explain to her that he imagined such a goddess would live in a palatial mansion? Not a shabby hovel like this one. Sam deserved better. He would give her better.

"I wanted more for you." He hadn't meant to say it aloud, but the words escaped his lips before he could stop them.

"What right is it of yours to want more for me?"

For the first time that night, her shell of perfection cracked for him. Alma had never seen such impertinence from a woman. A woman should not talk this way. Especially if she was going to be his wife.

"Perhaps this is something I should talk to your father about first."

Sam's eyes widened. "Why would you need to talk to him unless . . ." Her words trailed off, and although she did not say it, Alma could see that she understood his intentions.

Her expression was not the joyous rapture he had hoped for. She looked ill.

"I can give you a better life. I think I could make you happy," Alma told her, ignoring the sickening thud of his heart. He had to fix this situation, but these surging, unfamiliar emotions hobbled his usual quick thinking. "I'm a high priest and I . . . ."

The words died in his mouth at her expression. She no longer looked just pained. She looked horrified.

"You're one of them?" Sam said in a voice full of disgust. "I thought you were just a . . . you're one of them."

"I want to marry you." Alma blurted the words out. Now Sam looked like she would vomit. He had lost total control of his ability to say the right thing as he was accustomed to always doing. Sam had made a mess of him in the space of a few minutes. He had to convince her, to show her that marrying him would be the best possible idea. Alma tried to collect his thoughts, tried to think of how to save the situation.

Before he could say a word, Sam spoke. "In a thousand lifetimes, I would never marry you. I despise everything you believe, everything you represent, what your extravagant life costs people like us. Believe me when I say my father will not give his consent. I will not let you speak to him."

"You can't mean that." His voice sounded incredulous, and only he knew that it was tinged with the faintest hint of respect. Alma found he liked that she stood her ground, that she didn't relent. Sam was magnificent in her anger. She was fierce. Rather than deter him, her strength made Alma want her as his own even more. "I don't think anyone has ever dared speak to me like that."

"Come near me again and it won't be the last time it happens." Sam spun on her heel and knelt down to unhook the bottom corner of the curtain that hung in the doorway.

"This is not over," Alma told her as she straightened up.

She gave him one last scathing, hate-filled glare and said, "Yes, it is."

Sam stepped inside her home, but Alma didn't try to detain her. He had somehow ruined everything. Alma stood there for some time before he finally turned to walk back to his own home. With each step he became more resolute, his thoughts fixed on ideas on how to win Sam over. He would marry her. King Noah had once remarked that when Alma set himself to any task, the king had no worries that it would be accomplished. Alma always pursued his goal relentlessly. He would not let anything, or anyone, turn him from his course.

Not even Sam.

CHAPTER TWO

Sam had a harder time than usual waking up that morning. She had come home so late, through no fault of her own. She had been on her way to fetch the evening water for their last meal of the day when the king's soldiers had kidnapped her and then forced her to stay for that awful party. Sam again whispered her gratitude to the Lord that the king had not taken a liking to her.

Shivering under her threadbare blanket, she wished she could light a fire. But she didn't want to wake her family. Wrapping her arms around herself, she resolved to get up soon. Sam wanted to rest for just a few more minutes.

She yawned, covering her mouth with her hand to soften the sound. She had not slept well the few hours she had been home. Although it was not something she would admit to anyone else, Sam knew why she had been so restless. Alma. That manipulative, sneaky, arrogant, vain, condescending, handsome—

Handsome? Sam's eyes flew open. Where had that come from? She had not been remotely attracted to him. Not one tiny bit.

She most certainly had not noticed that his hair was the exact same shade as newly ripened cacao beans. She had definitely not noticed how tall and strong he was. Or how he seemed to exude power and authority in a masculine sort of way that had made her feel a little giddy. No, she had not noticed any of those things. Alma had not affected her in the least.

Well, she supposed he had affected her some. He had made her want to run screaming into the wilderness just to get away from him. Sam still couldn't believe Alma had said he wanted to marry her. As if she would ever marry any high priest and become the latest wife in his collection.

Sam berated herself for not realizing that Alma was a high priest. How else could they have passed so easily by the guards? She was too shaken up to notice, wanting only to get home, where she had found her family in a state of panic. They knew all too well how last night could have ended.

Rolling to her side to get off her worn-out pallet, Sam tried to mentally list out the many tasks she had to accomplish that day. The distraction did not work, and Alma kept popping into her mind. She already hated morning water runs enough without thoughts of him plaguing her. "Stop that!" she finally whispered to herself in frustration.

One of her sisters snorted, and Sam clamped her lips together. They all had to work so hard. Her family deserved to sleep as long as they could before the day's labor began. Her sight adjusted to the dark, and Sam could make out the sleeping forms of her father and younger sisters. She stood and silently walked in between them toward the clay vases stored by the entrance.

Sam unhooked the bottom corners of the divider that hung in the entrance. She picked up two of the larger ceramic vases by their handles, hoping that she could make fewer trips today. Sam stepped out into the street and nearly tripped over a young boy that sat on the ground right in front of her home.

When the boy saw her, he got to his feet. "You Sam?"

"Yes," Sam said hesitantly. What was this about?

"Then that's for you," the boy said as he pointed toward a line of ten lidded vases.

"What are they?" Sam asked as she walked over to the containers. "What's in them?"

The boy followed behind her and said, "Water."

"Water?" Sam repeated. "Why would *you* bring me water?"

The boy grinned at her. "Because I was paid to."

"Who paid you?" she asked in an indignant tone. But Sam already knew who had paid the boy, who would do something so underhanded. So Alma thought he could buy her agreement to marriage? She might have underestimated his desire to wed her. Last night she thought her reaction to his offer was enough to repel him permanently. Obviously, she had been very wrong.

"Not supposed to tell who paid me," the boy said, looking as if he enjoyed keeping his not-so-very-secret secret. "But you'll never have to get your own water again. Just be sure to leave the empty vases outside, and I'll fill them. Want me to take these inside?"

"No, I can do it."

The boy left and Sam could hear him whistling a happy tune as he walked down the street. Sam wondered for a moment how much the boy had been paid. It only showed how little Alma understood her. She would have rather had the money than the water. She could have bought food, replaced Kelila's ragged tunic, purchased herbs and a healer for her father. She sighed. Even if Alma had offered her money, knowing herself the way that she did, she probably would have acted offended and thrown it back in his face.

Sam knew she was being unreasonable. If anyone else had done this for her, she might have found it sweet. Thoughtful. Romantic.

Reminding herself how much she hated all high priests, especially ones trying to lure her into marriage, Sam lashed out and kicked one of the containers over. She watched the water spill out into the dusty road, creating a thin layer of mud before she stalked back inside her home. Just because Alma had arranged for the water to be brought to her didn't mean she had to accept it.

A few minutes later Sam went outside and picked up the first vase to take it into the hut. She might have been many things, but a complete fool was not one of them.

* * *

Alma knew he should pay attention to the documents that Helam read to him, the reports on the king's latest extravagant building and decorating projects financed through the taxes collected from the people. Normally Alma would have been keeping a tally of costs and possible completion dates in his mind. But today his thoughts were elsewhere.

After Sam's rejection, Alma hadn't been able to sleep. He began to think of schemes to win her affection. He did not expect love. Not right away. He knew it might take years for her to feel about him the way he felt about her. And while not usually a patient man, Alma could wait. Until then, he seized upon a plan for his first gesture.

He had arranged for Sam's least favorite chore to be taken away from her. Through a referral from an extremely sleepy Helam, Alma had found a young boy with a business acumen that made Alma chuckle. Deciding Sam was worth the expense, Alma had paid an unseemly amount to have his wishes carried out.

Not able to stay behind and wonder what her reaction would be, Alma had gone to that mess she called her home and hid. He watched her appear in the dawn's first light, and his breath caught in his throat. She was even more beautiful than he remembered.

He watched her confusion, her comprehension of the situation, and then her anger. He smiled at her rejection of his gift and spirited retreat into the hut and then laughed out loud when she returned to get the water.

Sam would not be won over as easily as he had hoped. But Alma could work around that. It was a challenge he knew he would win.

After he knew that Sam would accept his gift, Alma went home. He fell asleep as soon as he lay down. He did not sleep well. Sam haunted his dreams. She always stood several feet away from him, a teasing smile lighting up her features. When he got close to her, she would turn into wisps of smoke and disappear. No matter how hard he tried to take hold of her, she was always just beyond his grasp.

Alma awoke out of frustration and decided to report to the palace early to begin work. Early, of course, meaning early by the court's standards. No one conducted any business before noon as King Noah did not rise until then.

So it surprised him when King Noah came into the throne room not long after Alma had arrived. Everyone in the room stood at the king's entrance. Alma saw the king whisper something to one of his attendants.

The attendant crossed the room toward where Alma and Helam stood, and said, "The king wishes to speak to you, Alma. Alone." The attendant fixed his gaze on Helam.

"We can finish this later," Alma told Helam before following the attendant back to King Noah.

Alma knelt to bow in front of his king and then stood back up at the king's command. "How can I serve you, my king?"

King Noah had grown rather large over the last few years. His eyes had a perpetual redness to them, as did the bulb of his nose, from his extensive wine imbibing. He was not a man who could physically lead them into battle if the Lamanites struck again. Alma speculated on how long he would be tolerated as king if such an attack happened. Another disloyal thought. Alma furrowed his brows at the recent recurrence of these sort of judgments against the king. King Noah had specially selected him to serve in one of the highest offices in the land. The king had given him prosperity and power. Alma knew he should be the king's man through and through.

The king arranged himself against some luxurious cushions. "Sit," he invited, pointing to an unused cushion. Alma didn't care for the command, feeling a bit like the king's black and white hunting dogs that sat at his feet. But Alma obeyed.

Despite the lateness of the hour, the king was being served breakfast. The king insisted on having *atole,* a cornmeal gruel taken with chili peppers. He had told Alma once that it gave King Noah a paternal happiness to eat the same thing as all of his "children" in the kingdom. Somehow he had arrived at the conclusion that deigning to share in their lowness made him more suited to rule them. Alma wondered if the king ever saw the inherently flawed logic of his reasoning since King Noah followed the *atole* with a dizzying array of meats and vegetable and fruit dishes that no commoner could afford.

"I am told that you left here with a woman last night."

Alma knew not to show his shock at King Noah's announcement. Alma's standing within the palace had something to do with his ability to always say what the king wanted to hear and to conceal his true reactions and emotions. He should not have been surprised in the first place. The king had eyes and ears everywhere. He should have known that his activities last night would not have gone unnoticed. "I did."

"Who was she? I've never known you to select a woman from one of my gatherings the way the other priests do."

"Sam," Alma said, not able to keep his eyes from lighting up. "Her name is Sam."

"And you desired her." King Noah's poison tester tried the *atole* and when he didn't die, the king took the hollowed-out gourd and began to drink the mixture. The king had an irrational fear that someone was going to kill him. He took extraordinary precautions to protect himself, like employing tasters to check his food for hidden poison, and having a group of soldiers to guard him at all hours. It was why he kept such close watch on people he thought might be threats to his throne. Even men like Alma, whom the king claimed to trust and love. Alma understood that King Noah had to try to make sense of Alma behaving oddly for his own peace of mind.

Alma's feelings for Sam were more than mere desire. He had a connection with Sam unlike anything else he had ever experienced. "It's more than that."

"More?"

"I think I love her."

"Excellent." The king put his empty gourd down. He gave Alma a conspiratory smile. "I find falling in love every few days is good for your health."

Alma bristled at the king equating what he felt for his concubines with what Alma felt for Sam. Defensiveness welled up inside him, and he found again that Sam meddled with his ability to think clearly. He didn't mean to say, "I want her to be my wife."

The king leaned over to clap Alma on the shoulder. "Even better! When will the marriage take place?"

"There are no plans for—" Alma coughed to clear his throat, "That is, I mean to say—"

King Noah roared with laughter. "Don't tell me she said no!"

The embarrassment on Alma's face answered the statement and the king lay back, shaking with mirth. When he finally calmed down, he said, "Your Sam—she was the one in the corner with the black hair? The one who looked like she hated the world?"

"Yes."

"Ah," the king said, as if gaining some sort of insight about the situation. "You know, I considered her for a moment but could see she had too much fire in her. I prefer more willing companions. Of course, when I was your age I might have enjoyed breaking her spirit."

But Alma didn't want to break Sam's spirit. He wanted to savor it.

"Such a beauty should be tamed," the king said, signaling for his next course to be brought out.

Alma had heard enough. He never liked laughter at his expense and liked it even less coming from the king. Alma felt ridiculous. He wanted to get away. Flattery might be the quickest route to escape.

"I know you're right," Alma said with his best fake sincere voice. "You always are. I am fortunate to have someone like you to guide me in such things. But if you will excuse me, I have much to do."

Fortunately the ruse had worked, and King Noah dismissed Alma. Alma fled for the sanctuary of the chambers he kept at the palace. He had no desire to stay in the throne room for another moment.

After Alma left, the king gestured for a nearby attendant to approach. When the attendant came close enough, the king leaned toward him with a self-satisfied expression. "Find the guard that followed Alma last night. Have him brought to me. We are going to arrange a little surprise."

* * *

Amulon had spent his time since the previous night plotting Alma's downfall. While he had merely been bothered that Alma had interfered with his plans for the girl at the party, he had been terrified at Alma's threat. It was not a feeling he wished to experience again, and it galled him to know that Alma could bring that terror back with only a few words. He had to discover Alma's weakness to protect himself and everything that belonged to him. He would never, ever go back to his old life. He worried Alma had the power to make that happen.

He had to outmaneuver Alma, had to find something Alma feared. Or something Alma wanted. Something to give him leverage. Amulon had total confidence that he would eventually discover some fact about Alma that would give him the upper hand. His grandmother attributed his success in these sorts of matters as the result of Amulon being born under a lucky star. Opportunities seemed to have a way of just falling into his lap. His grandmother didn't realize that Amulon made his own luck.

Like now, where he hovered out of sight of the king and Alma. It was not luck that put him in this corner to overhear the discussion between Alma and the king.

So Alma had fallen in love? Amulon had to stop himself from laughing along with the king. Men befuddled with love were the easiest kind to manipulate. If he truly wanted to remove Alma as a threat, all he had to do was strike Alma where it would hurt the most.

Amulon would marry Sam. It would destroy Alma.

And Amulon would be safe.

* * *

The old man stepped out of the cave that had been his home for the past two years. Twilight softened his surroundings and the twittering, howling, and buzzing noises from the jungle soothed him like a lullaby. The delicate scent of nighttime orchids just beginning to blossom tickled his nose. Everything here had become familiar. He felt at one with it, with all of creation.

He climbed up the side of the hill that housed his cave. At its apex the hill smoothed out into a flat surface. This was where he meditated, where he prayed, where he listened.

This was where he had found out that he had to go back. Where he had been told that this would be his last mission. He would never again return to his haven here.

He would obey. He knew what the outcome of his obedience would be but knew that he had to do what was right. Even if he could not convince them, the message still had to be delivered.

Tomorrow he would gather water and provisions. Then he would make the long journey to the land of Lehi-Nephi.

Where he would die.

CHAPTER THREE

"I seek an audience, my king."

Amulon waited until Alma left and then approached King Noah. The king barely glanced up from his salted fish. "What do you want?"

Trying not to recoil from the harshness in the king's voice, Amulon wistfully remembered when the king used to joke with him, when all of Amulon's wishes had been granted. Now that the king had Alma, Amulon had been forgotten. King Noah seemed capable of only caring about one of his high priests at a time.

"I would like to make a request."

That got the king's attention as he glared at Amulon. Amulon knew King Noah didn't like to grant favors to others. The king preferred that people do things for him.

"And that request would be . . . ?" King Noah sounded impatient. Amulon had to hurry.

"There is a woman. She was here at the palace yesterday. I would like to take her as a wife."

"What do I care if you take a wife?"

"Then I have your permission?" Amulon said. "You will give me leave to marry her?"

King Noah waved his hand as if to shoo Amulon away. It looked like an acquiescence to Amulon. Suppressing a grin, Amulon bowed and thanked the king. With the king's backing, no one would be able to stop him. Especially not Alma. Eager to carry out his plans, Amulon had nearly reached the doorway on the west side of the room when the king called out, "Wait. What is her name?"

Amulon heard the distrust in King Noah's voice. Despite his usual lack of awareness, somehow the king had become suspicious of Amulon. Amulon considered lying. Unfortunately, there were at least twenty people in the throne room listening to this conversation. If Amulon had been alone with the king, he could have easily lied and then later fooled the king into thinking he had misheard Amulon. But with all these witnesses, Amulon would not be able to carry out his deception. The king didn't mind the high priests being dishonest with the people, but he did not tolerate lies told to him.

"I believe it was Sam, my lord."

King Noah narrowed his eyes at Amulon. "I know of only one woman at the party last night named Sam. And she is promised to another."

"I would like an opportunity to vie for her hand," Amulon said, ignoring the beads of sweat that covered his entire back. He risked the king's total disfavor. Such a thing could exile him to the outer powerless circles of the court.

The king lay back against his cushions in a blue tunic trimmed with gold ribbons, and Amulon had the thought that he looked like a beached whale. An ostentatious beached whale.

"Very well," the king announced, sounding highly amused. It made Amulon wary. "You may accompany my messenger and present your offer to the girl's father. We will let him decide which man Sam will marry."

"Thank you. You are too gracious to your loyal subjects," Amulon said, leaving before the king could change his mind.

At least King Noah had given him a chance. Amulon would have to make it count.

* * *

Sam blamed her total exhaustion on Alma, whom she held personally responsible for causing her inability to sleep. She was normally tired after working the fields, but not like this. She had filled only one wooden crib with corn. She should have filled at least two. One way or another, the fields had to be cleared in time to start the new planting before the rainy season began. For a moment, Sam envied the women of the city who only had to care for their homes. Her father had no sons, and their kin had their own fields to worry over. With her father being ill, Sam was the only person who could bring in the harvest. At least she didn't have to try to bring the heavy wood crib back with her. King Noah insisted that all the cribs be left in the fields so that he could extract his one-fifth tax. He didn't want to be cheated by starving families who needed the food more than he did.

Sam had to stop and sit down to rest. Her limbs felt numb. She didn't know how she would make it all the way back to the city. Finding a large acacia tree, Sam sank down to the ground, resting her back against the trunk.

At least her day had finished. She saw that while she rested, men still worked in the king's vineyards. Spiky agave plants stretched all the way to the horizon on prime farming land that had been confiscated by the king.

She watched while the men near her cleared the dirt away from one of the plants. The long leaves were attached to a short stem, which in turn was attached to a large fleshy base. Instead of allowing the base to flower, the men cut a large hole in the top, removing the heart of the plant.

Sam knew that shortly the agave plant would fill in the hole with a sweet sap that would be scooped out and then left to ferment. This resulting wine would be strong enough for most people, but the king insisted on adding bark of the acacia tree, like the one she sat against, to his wine to make it even more intoxicating.

Sam shifted her weight to the left, and a long thorn growing out of the tree's base brushed against her shoulder. Not just any thorn. A thorn on an acacia tree. Sam suddenly realized what that meant. Stinging bites on her bare arms confirmed her fear. Acacias were fiercely guarded by ants that attacked anyone who dared touch their tree. Sam scraped the ants off her upper arm, but her skin started to throb from all the red bumps.

"Can this day get any worse?" Sam yelled.

The men in the vineyards stopped their labors to stare at Sam as she hollered and swung her arms around. Anger invigorating her, Sam stomped back to the city, muttering the whole way.

At least she had dinner to look forward to. Even if dinner meant a watery stew made by her sisters and composed solely of vegetables and roots. Wealthier families could afford to add meat to their stew. Sam couldn't remember what meat tasted like.

She entered the hut to see her father propped up on his pallet, staring at her intently. Sam's relief at being home was cut short because of the expression on her father's face. She had never seen him so serious. "Father?"

"Kelila, Lael, go and fetch water." Despite his illness, her father retained his authoritative voice.

"But we don't need to get any water," Kelila protested. "There's plenty of—"

"Now," her father said over Kelila. Another man might have shouted, but he spoke in a calm, soft, but resolute voice that tolerated no argument.

Lael pulled Kelila to her feet and dragged her out to the street despite Kelila's protestations. Sam knew Kelila always wanted to understand everything, to know why things happened. In that moment Sam felt the same way. Her father's behavior was so strange. He looked afraid.

Sam studied him to see if she could make sense of his trepidation. The lines on his face ran deep like furrows in the fields, framed by his shock of white hair that fell down to his shoulders. He had told her once that when he was younger he'd had hair blacker than her own. But Sam couldn't remember his hair being anything but white.

"Sit, my child." Sam did as her father asked and sat on the floor next to his pallet. Her heart started a low, heavy thudding in her chest.

"Father, you're scaring me. What is it?"

Her father sighed, and his exhaled breath sounded like parchment being torn. "You are to be married."

"Married?" Sam could barely repeat the word. "To whom?"

A coughing fit racked Sam's father, and he couldn't answer. Sam fetched a cup of water and rag for him. He managed to get the water down. He coughed several more times into the rag, and when he pulled it away, Sam thought she saw blood on it. He lay down, taking several ragged breaths before looking back at Sam.

"You have two choices. You are to marry either Alma or Amulon."

"This must be some sort of jest," Sam said in disbelief.

"It is no jest," her father said. "You will go to the palace tomorrow before sundown with your decision."

"Or else?"

"There is no 'or else.' You will choose which man you will marry, and then you will marry him." Sam saw that her father couldn't quite meet her gaze. She sensed that there was something more that he wasn't telling her.

Her heart actually stopped. Sam felt all the air in the room leave, and she could barely breathe.

"I can't choose. It's like asking me to choose which way I prefer to die. How could anyone make that kind of decision?"

"You will make it, or I will have to make it for you." His words sounded harsh, and from a different man, they might have been. Some fathers saw daughters as drains on their resources until they married and brought home sons-in-law to help in the fields. Not her father. He never made her feel less for having been a girl instead of a boy. He had never done anything but love her. But he asked the impossible.

"I can't."

Now her father looked angry. "Don't say you can't. You can and you will. You are my daughter. Your duty is to listen and obey."

Sam didn't know what to say. She wanted to protest, to tell her father she could never marry either man. She wanted to rage at the unfairness of it all. But she had too much respect for her father to rail against him. Sam might have utterly refused to do as her father bid her had it not been for the tears she saw welled up in his eyes. Her father took her hand in his crippled one and held it against his chest. "I wish that I could . . . I would not . . . I cannot tell you why . . ." Her father tripped over his own words. Taking a calming breath, he said, "You must do this."

"Will you tell me why?"

She felt a slight pressure on her hand, as if her father was trying to comfort her. "I cannot."

So she had been right. Her father was keeping something from her. Something he would not tell her. Sam knew better than to press him. He would never tell her unless he wanted to. But whatever the secret was, it was bad enough that he put her in this position. Sam saw no hope, no way to escape. She would have to marry.

"You know that Amulon is out of the question," she finally said.

"I know. In Alma's favor, the emissary who visited today presented a rather glowing picture of the young high priest." Her father pressed her hand again. "And I should tell you that Amulon also came to present himself."

Sam sucked in a sharp breath. "Amulon was here?"

Letting out a short cough, her father said, "Yes, he was here and he threatened me. Said we hadn't fulfilled our obligations to him, that we owed him, and he wanted you as recompense."

"But Amulon is already married."

"It makes no difference to such a man."

A dark fury filled Sam's entire body. She wished for a moment that she were a man so she could physically keep Amulon away from herself and her family. He was like a plague that sickened and destroyed everything that he touched. Pushing her shoulders back, Sam decided she would not let Amulon destroy her.

As if reading her thoughts, her father added, "All we know of Alma is that he has the king to recommend him, but I will try not to hold it against him." Sam managed a small smile at her father's teasing remark. The seriousness returned to his voice. "Anything has to be better than Amulon. And this way, at least," her father paused and this time really looked at her. "At least you have some say in your fate."

"I understand," Sam said. To a certain extent she understood that this was the only choice and her life had been forever altered. She didn't like it. But she knew she couldn't fight her way out of it. "I'm going to go check on Lael and Kelila."

Using her sisters as an excuse, Sam fled from her home, willing herself not to cry. She would not ever shed a tear over either man.

Alma or Amulon. Amulon or Alma. Sam leaned against a tall stone building for support. The wall felt cool against her forehead. It wouldn't be a difficult decision. It wasn't much of a decision at all. Alma seemed kind. Not that she believed such a thing was possible. How could any man who served the king be kind? She thought of the water. He had at least listened to her, remembered something seemingly insignificant that she had said. Although it could have all been a manipulative ploy to gain her trust.

She wondered if Alma knew about Amulon, knew what Amulon had done to her family. She wondered if this was all some elaborate ploy to trick her into marrying him. She wondered why Alma would force this on her. Why did he want to marry her so much? There must be a hundred women that would give anything to be Alma's wife. Well, not a hundred. Maybe dozens. Or a few. There definitely had to be at least one or two women who would want to marry him. Why not pick one of them? Why was he doing this to her? Why was Alma making her "choose" him when marriage to him was the last thing she wanted?

Sam supposed it didn't matter. Either way, come sundown tomorrow her life as she knew it would end. A thousand lifetimes had passed faster than she would have thought possible.

* * *

Alma was no closer to a plan today than he was yesterday. He knew another grand gesture was in order, but for it to mean something he needed to know Sam better. His mind buzzed like an overloaded beehive. Not only with the reports that he knew he needed to look over, the projects he needed to check on, but also with an ever present image of Sam that had burned itself into his brain. Perhaps it might be better to try and not think about anything for a while.

Holding to that idea, Alma headed to the king's library. He decided to again read and study copies of the books of Moses. When he entered the library, he inhaled the musty scent of old books and parchments. It made him smile.

Alma crossed over to the shelves where the words of Moses were kept. He lifted up books with bark and leather covers, again thinking he should do something to organize the library. But few people besides himself ever entered. Most of the high priests learned what they needed to learn and then never bothered with the library again.

A scraping noise to his left told Alma he was not alone. He glanced up and saw Limhi, one of King Noah's many sons. He sat on a stone bench that extended from the wall and seemed deeply engrossed in his creased papyrus. Limhi had always struck Alma as very different than the rest of his family. While the king's other sons joined in their father's reveling, Limhi never did. He seemed more serious, more studious. He did not seem to enjoy the king's lifestyle.

Alma cleared his throat to alert Limhi to his presence. Limhi seemed startled and blinked several times. "Interesting reading?" Alma asked.

"Oh, er, just the journal of my grandfather Zeniff." Limhi looked self-conscious and uncomfortable.

That intrigued Alma. He hadn't realized that Zeniff had kept a journal. He would have liked to read it, but Limhi had put his body between Alma and the parchment. Limhi's message was clear. Perhaps another time. Alma had expected to stay in the library to read, but with the prince's behavior, he thought it better to retire to his own chambers.

"I'm sorry to have interrupted you. I have what I came for. I hope you enjoy the journal."

Alma went to his rooms and had just settled into cushions in one corner when he heard a heavy panting sound outside of his door.

One edge of his mouth curled up in a half-smile. Where could he hide this time? Someplace new.

A rug had recently been hung on one of the walls in the room and Alma darted behind it, holding completely still.

There was a tapping sound of something hard hitting the stone floor and Alma tried not to laugh when the sound came straight at him. Hunter stuck his head underneath the corner of the rug and looked up at Alma expectantly.

"Knew right where I was, didn't you?" Alma said, coming out from underneath the rug.

The dog settled onto the floor in front of him. His tongue lolled out of his mouth and his tail wagged back and forth. Hide and seek was the dog's favorite game, and Alma always obliged him.

Maybe that was the reason he was Hunter's favorite person. Hunter loved Alma to the king's great consternation. He was from a highly anticipated litter of the king's prized hunting dogs. The king expected the litter to adore him above all others, but Hunter wouldn't have anything to do with King Noah. Hunter had been given some sort of royal, formal name at his birth, but Alma didn't know what it was. Not that the dog ever responded to anything besides Hunter, which had been the name Alma had given him.

Alma opened a satchel he kept in his room and took out several thick pieces of hardened tapir leather. He tossed them to Hunter, who wagged his tail even faster as he gnawed on them. The animal seemed obsessed with chewing on things. Alma had heard that the dog had destroyed several pairs of one of the queen's expensive shoes. But because the king loved his dogs more than almost anything—or anyone—else, Hunter could chew his way through every scrap of leather in the palace and no one would touch him. Alma thought of him as an out-of-control, overgrown puppy but was entertained by his company.

Besides being amusing, the dog sometimes proved useful. Like now when Hunter stopped chewing on his strip, looked to the door, and barked. A few seconds later Teomner, a fellow high priest, entered the room. He wore a strange expression that Alma couldn't decipher.

"The king has summoned you."

Alma knew he wouldn't get any further information from Teomner. He also knew that he had to respond quickly to the command or else risk incurring the king's wrath.

Following Teomner, Alma found the king waiting in a hallway. It surprised Alma. He had expected to go to the throne room or the king's chambers. He couldn't recall ever seeing the king loitering in this part of the palace.

"You sent for me?"

King Noah smiled broadly at Alma and clasped both of Alma's shoulders. "I did. I wanted to be the first to congratulate you."

Alma felt very confused. "Congratulate me? On what?"

"On your marriage. Come and say hello to your bride."

The king pushed aside the curtain behind him, and Alma almost fell over when he saw Sam waiting in the room.

CHAPTER FOUR

A wave of apprehension swept through Sam when she saw the curtain moved to one side. "Out," King Noah said to her father. Her father gave her one last sympathetic look and left. She wished her father had been allowed to stay with her. She didn't want to face Alma alone.

Her stomach churned with anxiety and fear when she saw Alma talking to the king. She heard Alma say, "She changed her mind?" and the king responded with, "She was persuaded to see reason."

Reason? Sam wanted to shriek that there was nothing logical or reasonable about this situation, but she liked her head being attached to her body. She didn't dare defy the king in his presence.

She would not be afraid. She would not let Alma see her weakness. The king said something quietly to Alma that she could not hear. Alma replied, also in a whisper. Alma then stepped into the room and the curtain fell down behind him. Sam swallowed hard, lifted her chin, and boldly met his gaze.

Alma stood across from her, not saying anything. She found his silence disconcerting. Turning her attention from him, Sam began to examine her surroundings. One of the guards had called this the king's sunroom. Several long slits in the limestone wall let the sunlight stream in. Sam walked to one of the windows to look out over the palace's fruit tree grove. Alma stepped into one of the rays of light and stared at Sam. His nearness made her stomach twist into knots. Sam noticed, not for the first time, the power and confidence Alma seemed to exude. But she decided not to notice his perfectly formed features or his dark eyes that seemed to keep secrets from her. *He is not handsome,* she told herself again. *Not handsome.*

"Your eyes," Alma said and the sudden sound startled Sam. She turned her head to look at him. "I wondered what color they were."

"They are just brown," Sam replied, not wanting him to keep looking at her that way but unable to tear her gaze away.

"No." Alma took a step toward her. She could feel the warmth that emanated from him and had to force herself not to back up. Alma studied her eyes and gave her a tender smile. "They're not 'just brown.' You have faint streaks of green and flecks of gold around your pupils. I don't know what color to call them, but they could never be 'just brown.'"

"Did you know about Miriam?" Sam blurted out. Her curiosity had gotten the better of her. She had to find out if Alma had manipulated her. She didn't understand why it felt so important to discover the truth, but it was. She could see from the puzzled look on Alma's face that he didn't know. She relaxed. Alma had not used Amulon against her.

"Miriam? Who is Miriam?"

Sam heard the bewilderment in Alma's voice. But that was not a part of herself she was willing to share with him. "It's not important."

They lapsed into an uncomfortable silence. Alma clasped his hands together in front of him. Then he let them fall to his sides. Then he put them behind his back and began to rock on his heels.

He broke the quiet by asking, "So, that was your grandfather?"

"No, my father. People often make that mistake."

"Oh." Alma sounded surprised. "He's older than I would have expected."

"He had a family before ours. They were killed in a Lamanite attack. He had no plans to marry again, but he met my mother, who had lost her husband in the same battle. She had a baby and my father married her to take care of them both. I think he loved my older sister before he loved my mother. He always treated my sister like his own."

Alma nodded while Sam spoke and then smiled at her. A ripple of shock cut through Sam. She couldn't believe what she had just said, how she had laid her family's history out for Alma to see. She didn't know why she told him about her father. She disliked Alma intensely yet had shared something very personal with him. Her mind tried to make sense of her loose tongue, and Sam realized that Alma was one of those people who seemed really interested in what one said. Who made one feel like he or she was the only person in the whole world, like everything he or she said mattered. It upset her how easily she had fallen into his trap.

"He sounds like a good man."

"He is."

Another awkward moment passed between them. Sam now felt even more uncomfortable. She didn't want to talk with Alma. She didn't even want to be civil with him. But their lives were about to be irrevocably joined, and this might be her only chance to find out anything about her impending future.

As if sensing her thoughts, Alma said, "Do you have anything you would like to ask me?"

"Will we . . . will we live with my family after we are . . ." Sam couldn't bring herself to say the word "married."

Alma looked slightly embarrassed. "I know that is customary, but I am head of my family. We will have to forgo the seven years of living with your family and will live in my home."

Head of his family? "Oh. How many wives and children do you have?"

"What?" Alma sputtered. "None. You will be the only one."

"The king has so many—I just assumed . . ." Sam stopped. She didn't want Alma to believe that she wasted any time thinking or assuming anything about him. Unfortunately, some part of her felt ridiculously pleased that Alma did not have other wives. Sam told that part to be quiet. It didn't matter to her at all that Alma had not followed in the king's footsteps as so many of the other high priests had done. Alma was her enemy. She had to remember that.

But it was difficult to remember it when she was so curious about him. She hated that she felt this way. She resolved to be strong, not to ask him anything else.

Sam wondered again if she could find a way out of this marriage. Perhaps she could scare him off. Looking at the high quality of his robes and tunic, Sam could see that money mattered to him. Maybe if he knew that he wouldn't gain anything by marrying her, he might be more interested in finding a wealthy wife.

"I have no dowry. I will bring no lands and no flocks from which you can increase your own wealth."

"That doesn't matter to me." Sam felt the hope that had gathered in her heart deflate and fall as Alma continued. "It might make you feel better to know that right before I came in here, the king offered a dowry in your father's stead, but I told him . . ."

"So then you *would* be getting a dowry from my father." Sam's eyes flashed with anger, her cheeks flushed a bright pink.

"What do you mean?"

"The king's money belongs to the people, he steals it from them, and now he wants to steal it again by giving it to you as a dowry."

Alma looked shocked. "He doesn't steal the money. He taxes the people to support the government."

"And I suppose that makes it right?" Sam let all the fury she felt over her current situation and over what the king did to her family and friends on a regular basis spill into her words.

"This is the way things have always been."

"That doesn't mean this is the way things should always be. Not all of us can get rich off the backs of others. Some of us are the backs."

Having finally had the chance to express some of her frustrations, Sam's explosive temper began to quickly subside. She'd been this way all of her life. She was quick to anger, but just as quick to calm down and even quicker to regret her outbursts. But as she looked at Alma, she saw that her anger worried him. He looked hesitant, as if he weren't certain what to do or say next. Sam again looked out the window.

Feeling an unexplainable urge to fill in the void between them with words, Sam asked, "The king arranged this?" She couldn't keep the sadness from her voice, the bleak despair that nothing she could say would make Alma call off their betrothal. She didn't understand why. She also didn't understand why the king would bother to force her into marriage. How did the king benefit from this? She couldn't imagine the king would do anything unless he stood to profit in some way. Why would he have arranged such a thing? Had Alma lied to her? Was this another manipulation on his part?

Sam saw from the corner of her eye that Alma reached out his hand toward her but then let his arm fall. "Yes, he did," Alma said. "It was as much a surprise to me as it was to you. A wonderful surprise, but still a surprise."

Sam could hear the smile in Alma's voice, could hear that he told the truth. She believed him that he had nothing to do with this, that it was all King Noah's doing. She didn't want to, but she believed him. That made her more uneasy than anything else.

Refusing to fidget, Sam stared down at her hands, willing them to stay still. Alma's gaze must have followed her own because he grabbed her hands. "What happened to them?" he asked. He sounded angry.

She had not considered how another might regard her hands and for a moment she felt embarrassed by their redness and calluses. Sam started to curl her fingers inward and stopped. She was not ashamed of what she had done to help her family stay alive. It was not beneath her to work in the fields. She jerked her hands away and crossed to a corner of the room.

The reality of her circumstances suddenly hit Sam. It felt like the earth opened up beneath her feet to swallow her whole. She would be married to a man she didn't respect, a man who didn't share her beliefs, a man who stood for everything she hated, a man who would take her away from her family and coerce her into being his wife. Feeling very sorry for herself, Sam blinked furiously. She bowed her head and let her hair fall around her face like a shield. She would not cry. Would not.

The tears fell anyway.

This time Alma did touch her. He reached out to brush the hair away from the side of her face. His fingers stilled when he touched moisture.

"You're crying. Please don't." His voice came out in a raspy, emotional tone. "Someone so beautiful should not be so sad." Alma sounded concerned. Like he cared. How could he care? He didn't even know her.

Now the tears came faster. "Beautiful," she spat out. "What has beauty brought me? Nothing but misery. The same thing it brought to . . ." She paused. She had almost done it again, revealed her deepest secret to Alma. To *Alma*. Trying to take deep breaths, Sam closed her eyes so she didn't have to look at him. In a shaky voice she continued, "If I could cut off my face I would."

She felt Alma take her by the shoulders and turn her toward him. "Open your eyes, Sam."

Sam reluctantly did so, but immediately felt burned by his gaze.

"Beauty may sometimes bring misery. But it can also bring great joy. It brings me great joy. And not just your appearance, but the beauty of the woman you are inside."

Sam gulped her tears down, refusing to shed any more of them, refusing to be touched by Alma's words. She turned her head and stepped back when Alma released her.

"And if nothing else, at least we'll make a handsome couple."

His vanity, his pure male arrogance, infuriated her. "I don't find you at all attractive." *Liar,* a voice whispered. For half a second Sam wondered which one of them she was trying to convince.

The remark had been designed to wound him. But Alma didn't seem crestfallen at her announcement. Instead he gave her a sly smile. "You'd be the first."

Sam gasped. She considered slapping Alma across the face for saying something so . . . so . . . for just saying it.

Before she could react, Alma had started to leave. He got as far as the curtain when he paused. "May I ask you one more question?"

Still feeling like she could breathe puffs of smoke, Sam gave a barely perceptible nod. What was one more question after all he had put her through?

"Why did you get the water every day if you hated it so much?"

"So no one else would have to."

Alma grinned. "That's what I thought. Thank you."

The curtain swung down behind Alma when he left. Sam started to pace the length of the room. How could she go through with this? How could she marry that man? How?

There had to be a way out of this. She would just have to find it.

* * *

Alma hid himself in an alcove in the hallway. He watched as the guards returned Sam's father to her. Sam and her father left immediately but made slow progress because of her father. Alma wondered what sort of affliction the man had. Alma heard her father's labored breathing and his shuffling gait. When Alma peered around the corner he saw that Sam's father leaned on her for support, and she carried most of his weight. Her compassion and strength made Alma love her even more. He put a hand over his heart and wondered how it had ever beat without Sam.

"There must be something else we can do," Sam said to her father. "You need me at home. Who will bring in the harvest when I am gone? Plant the new crops?"

"Lael and Kelila can help."

"They're too young!"

"They're older than you were when you started working with me," her father gently reminded Sam. "Besides, I will be better soon, and I won't need their help."

"I know you will, Father."

Alma thought he detected a sadness, a tone of unbelief, in Sam's voice. Perhaps it was only his imagination. Perhaps he was projecting his own thoughts on Sam because he doubted her father's health would improve. Her father looked and sounded very ill. Alma felt a pang of sympathy for Sam's trials. He would do his best to help her through them.

As Sam assisted her father out of the palace, Alma headed back toward his rooms. While Sam hadn't sounded happy, at least she had stopped crying. He had deliberately teased her into anger during their conversation, because he had wanted nothing more than to gather her in his arms again and stroke her dark hair until she was comforted. Sam's tears were his total undoing and made him feel completely helpless. He couldn't bear it. He also couldn't bear her rejection if she turned away as he tried to hold her. He preferred her anger to her tears, and it had been easy enough to provoke her. He just wanted her to stop crying.

But what Alma had really wanted to do during their talk was ask her why she agreed to marry him. He couldn't bring himself to do it. Some piece of him was actually scared to ask. For now, it was enough that she had said yes.

How quickly his whole life had changed. In one hour he had been a bachelor and in the next betrothed. Alma reached his chambers and sat back down in front of his books. Hunter trotted over and lay down next to Alma so that Alma could scratch his ears. Alma did so absentmindedly as he reveled in the alterations to his world. An indescribable joy had welled up inside him. Everything felt and looked different to him. The air seemed sweeter, the sun brighter, even Hunter's fur seemed softer. Alma laughed. He was looking at everything with new eyes.

Alma reached for the books of Moses. As he opened the first one to begin reading, Hunter stood up and walked over to the doorway. Hunter lay down on the ground, his head resting on his paws. Alma furrowed his eyebrows at the dog. What was he doing?

His confusion was cleared up when Helam entered the room and promptly tripped over Hunter. As Helam lay sprawled on the floor, Alma could swear that the dog actually smiled as he loped out of Alma's chambers.

It was not the first time the dog had tripped Helam. Helam usually didn't look where he was going, his nose always buried in some report. Alma went over to help Helam to his feet, trying to cover his amusement. "That dumb dog," Helam muttered under his breath.

As Helam stood his foot caught on the corner of one of his reports, ripping it in half. "Oh no," Helam wailed. "It will take me hours to recopy these figures."

"We can just hold them together, and I can still read it. You don't need to do it over." Alma held the pieces of parchment in his hand. Something about the way the paper had torn. It seemed familiar.

Going back over to the books of Moses, Alma passed through the pages and found several that were partially disintegrated. He had always assumed that the books were just old, that they had fallen apart with age. But now, on closer inspection, he saw that his recently torn report looked very similar to the pages in the books. "Do you see this?" Alma asked.

He handed the book to Helam. "I've never been allowed to see these records," Helam breathed, running his fingers lightly over the parchment's texture.

"Look here at the edges," Alma said, showing Helam one of the pages. "Now look at the edge of this report."

"It looks like this book was torn." Helam appeared as mystified as Alma felt.

Alma shook his head. "Who would tear ancient scripture?" Alma decided living in the king's court had made him entirely too suspicious. No one would deface scripture. Would they? Some of these books had never made sense to him because of missing passages. Alma hadn't considered it an issue before—some scriptures left in their entirety didn't make much sense either. Like the words of Isaiah. Perhaps if he had lived in Jerusalem, the land of their fathers, he would be able to understand it better. But Isaiah spoke of places, people, and things he had no knowledge of.

"Not only that, but look at this," Helam interrupted, handing the book back. "Someone's blurred the words together here and here."

"Are you sure?"

Helam raised one eyebrow at Alma. "You're asking me if I'm sure about something when it comes to writing?"

He had an excellent point. Few scribes were as gifted or as dedicated as Helam. Again, Alma had just assumed that the passing of time had caused the inscribing to bleed and the words to blend together. Helam insinuated that it was not natural, but deliberate.

Alma thought it merited further investigation. He was about to say so when Helam took the book out of his hand. "Before you get distracted, this report was for the tower being built in the east side of the city. They are behind schedule, and I thought this was something we should take care of before your wedding."

"My wedding?" Alma's mouth hung agape. "How have you heard of it already?"

"You know how things are in the palace. Nothing stays quiet for long." Helam gave Alma a knowing smile. "And since you will be very busy in the upcoming days, I thought we should go manage the project in person."

"Yes, let's go help." Alma put his arm around Helam's shoulders. Alma rushed the young scribe down the hall so fast that the much shorter man could barely keep up. Alma wanted to get all this work completed as quickly as possible. He had more important things now to focus on.

Alma had a marriage ceremony to plan.

* * *

"How much longer?"

The Lamanite king, Laman, son of Laman, grew tired of waiting. His captains gathered their armies. Supplies were being prepared. Weapons made. Sacrifices offered to their gods for victory in battle.

"Not much longer now," a nameless bureaucrat assured King Laman. "The harvest is nearly all collected."

Without the full harvest, the armies could not march. They had to have their provisions. The armies' families also had to have their storage in place before the rainy season began.

And King Laman had to have his revenge. He would teach the Nephites that they could not avoid paying their tribute. King Laman's spies told him of the massive buildings being erected, the precious metals being used. Noah thought to deprive him of his rightful tribute, after King Laman's own father had given the Nephites fertile land to live on.

King Laman would take it back.

It was King Laman's father who had made the treaty with the Nephites, who because of that treaty stood by while the Nephites slaughtered three thousand Lamanites. King Laman had not made the treaty. He was not bound by it. The blood of those fallen Lamanites cried out for vengeance. The blood price had to be satisfied in spilled Nephite blood.

So King Laman waited impatiently for the armies to be prepared and for his priests to tell him when the stars would align correctly to ensure their victory.

It would not be long until he waged war.

CHAPTER FIVE

"I have failed."

Amulon's grandmother made a soothing sound, running her withered and gnarled hands over his head. "You've only had a setback. It is not a failure."

It certainly felt like a failure to Amulon. The night before, the king had announced Alma's betrothal to Sam. Struggling to keep his true reaction from the court, Amulon could barely restrain his fury at his public humiliation. While no one would dare laugh in front of him, Amulon heard the whispers, saw the mocking stares. The other courtiers knew what Amulon had done, how he had presented his suit alongside Alma's. He had already been embarrassed at his reception in Sam's home, even more embarrassed that he had no representative to declare his intentions. Having to go himself had been entirely beneath him.

Now he knew he had suffered that indignity for nothing. He had lost. He hadn't thwarted Alma's desires. He couldn't stop the nuptials. The king's determination at seeing the marriage happen seemed to grow in direct proportion to Alma's happiness. There was no way to interfere. His schemes disintegrated into pieces around him.

His grandmother began to sing a song, telling the story of the little skunk and the jaguar. Amulon closed his eyes as he listened to the words. Her song comforted him, just as it always had in his childhood. His grandmother sat on a low stool and Amulon rested his head against her knees, feeling very much like that small boy again.

The musky, bittersweet scent of old age and guavas, the scent he always associated with his grandmother, seemed to emanate from her. It was a fragrance that Amulon loved and yet resented at the same time. Miriam had smelled of guavas. Besides her beauty, her intoxicating scent was what had drawn him to her. Guavas. How he hated guavas. They reminded him that once all he had to eat was the fruit they found in the wilderness.

But his grandmother continued to eat guavas daily. She had told him that she did it so she wouldn't forget. Amulon didn't need anything to help him remember. He still awoke from nightmares filled with severe hunger pains.

His grandmother was the only person he loved, the only part of his past he wanted to hold on to. In those awful years she had raised him. She had encouraged him. She had been the one to tell him that he could have anything if he planned and prepared for it. After his father had killed himself, his grandmother had taught him to be strong, not to be weak like his disgraced father. She was the only person who understood and appreciated him.

The last part of her song trailed off, and Amulon opened his eyes to look at her. "Am I the little skunk in the song? Too young and too inexperienced to be hunting on my own?"

She smiled down at him. "No, my child. You are the jaguar, claws sharpened and ready for the kill."

The kill. While the thought of Alma's death tempted him, a murder, no matter how natural or accidental it might appear, would turn all eyes to him. The entire court knew of Amulon's desire to marry Sam. King Noah already harbored suspicions about Amulon. If anything happened to Alma, he would be blamed for it.

But something had to be done. Alma's contentment would be dangerous to Amulon. Alma would be operating from an even greater position of power and confidence. Amulon had to put a stop to it somehow.

The image of a jaguar with its claws extended flashed through his mind, filling him with a strength he'd forgotten he possessed.

His grandmother was right. He was the jaguar. And if he couldn't kill his prey, he certainly knew how to cripple it.

"I know what has to be done," Amulon said.

His grandmother patted him on the head. "Of course you do."

* * *

Sam wished, as she often did, that her family lived in a compound on their fields as most of their relatives did. It would make her life so much easier to not have to go all the way back to the city every night. The walk seemed to tire her more than the actual field work.

But her father had never intended to be a farmer or to live in the fields. He had been a master craftsman and spent many nights describing to his daughters the kind of jewelry he used to make. His work necessitated that they live in the city. But then her father had been struck with a disease that had crippled his fingers so he could no longer do the intricate work. Their kin had granted their family a small field to cultivate to support themselves. Her father chose to remain in the city for his daughters' safety. Though he would never say it aloud, Sam knew he doubted his ability to protect them.

Tonight, it was not only her work or the walk back that exhausted her. Alma had sent word that he would visit her father tonight. Sam should have hurried back to receive him but instead found many other tasks that needed to be attended to. Like her sudden urge to gather firewood.

Ignoring the stack of wood already piled up outside their home, Sam put her bundle of long sticks against the outside wall under the eaves. She looked up and saw the special pots that hung from the rafters, the same pots they'd used for Jerusha's wedding. The pots she would use to prepare food for her own wedding. Suddenly feeling nauseated, Sam put the rest of the wood down and went inside.

At least she had time to prepare for her wedding and life with a husband. The arrangements, negotiations, and contracts for marriage could take months to accomplish. Things could drastically change over such a lengthy period. It was certainly enough time for Alma to turn his attentions to someone else. Sam chose not to examine that slight jealous twinge that accompanied her thought.

Once inside, Sam could tell from the sound of her father's even, steady breathing that he slept. Lael and Kelila knelt on reed mats on the west side of the fire to grind maize. Despite her fatigue, after washing the grime of the day off, Sam knelt next to them. She took the dough mixture her sisters had created. Sam patted the dough back and forth in her hands with a loud slapping sound until it reached the right consistency. Sam deliberately ignored her sisters' questioning glances as she put the now thin dough on a clay griddle next to the hearth. She didn't want to talk about Alma. But she would find no respite from him. While Lael looked thoughtful, Kelila looked ready to burst.

Sam stirred the vegetable stew cooking next to the fire, surprised at the different roots and meats she saw there. She put the mixture to her lips, blew on it, and took a sip. Salt. Someone had put salt in. And meat . . . Kelila explained that their kinsmen had brought over food for Alma's visit since Sam's family had nothing adequate to serve him. The kin group would not risk their family's honor by not having the proper food to offer a guest as important as Alma.

While they ate their unusually sumptuous dinner, Kelila's story bubbled out like a brook as she relayed the events of that evening. Sam tried to appear uninterested, but later that night after Kelila had gone to sleep, Sam made Lael tell her three times everything Alma had said. Lael recounted how Alma had formally asked their father for permission to marry Sam, how Alma had verified that Sam's family were not of the House of Nephi. Sam knew that those with common names and ancestors were not allowed to marry. She wished that her father could have been dishonest just this once, but knew it would have been easy enough for Alma to discover the truth of their origins.

"Then the matchmaker—"

Before Lael could finish her sentence Sam propped herself up on an elbow and asked, "The matchmaker? He brought the matchmaker already?"

Lael avoided her sister's demanding gaze. "Yes. They have made all the settlements. They set a day."

"When?" Sam's throat felt dry, as if she'd had nothing to drink in days.

"At the end of this week," Lael said, shedding the tears that Sam felt. Sam's stomach throbbed as if she had been stabbed.

Her sister had to be wrong. This was not the custom. This was not how marriages were arranged. Everything was happening too fast.

"How can it be so soon? That's not enough time for his mother to make our wedding clothes."

"His mother died last year," Lael said in between her sobs. "You will have to wear her wedding clothes because there is no one to make them for you."

Sam had an instant empathy for Alma that she didn't want to feel. She knew how it felt to lose a mother.

Her compassion didn't last long. Alma returned the next night with the matchmaker to go through the ritual of asking her father for her hand again. This time Sam came home on time so that she would be there when Alma arrived. When he came in, he didn't speak to her. He only smiled. Alma gave all his attention to her father and to presenting him with Sam's bride price. Alma brought jewelry, ribbons for her hair, bolts of cotton fabric, chocolate, and all sorts of food—gifts of such luxury and extravagance that Sam couldn't stop herself from staring at them. But she did swat Kelila's hand when her sister reached out to feel the soft linen.

Not caring that her manners were deliberately offensive, Sam refused to wait on Alma. The task fell to her sisters, who were properly demure. They kept their backs to him, served him with their eyes lowered. Sam had never been able to be proper and modest. Maybe it was because she had to do a man's work.

She had to bite her tongue when she saw her sisters respond to Alma's compliments and charming manner. Sam knew them well enough to see that they liked him. Lael would never be openly disloyal to her, but Kelila nearly flirted with the man. It made her ill.

Alma returned two more times to again formally petition for permission to marry Sam, to finalize the arrangements, and to continue paying Sam's bride price. Sam never saw the presents that her father gave to Alma. The exchange of gifts was supposed to show others the similarity in wealth and stature between the families. Sam felt mortified that her family could not return gifts of equal value. She could only imagine how her father felt.

And while Alma seemed to enjoy talking to her sisters and spoke at length with her father, he never tried to talk to Sam. For some reason it annoyed her. He just met her glares with smiles.

Until the fourth night.

The contracts had been completed, all the financial obligations met and their marriage set to take place in two days. Sam's father had asked Alma about the food needed for the wedding feast that normally took weeks to prepare. Alma had explained that the king wished for their marriage to take place at the palace. The king's servants would see to the celebration feast. Alma asked her father's forgiveness for not having the wedding here at their home as was typical, but Sam's father said he understood that the king's desires must be fulfilled.

Frustrated that her life was being ruined because of men's desires, Sam had to leave the house. She went around back to her family's small garden. They had a few fruit trees, some vegetables that barely grew. No one had time to attend to it. Her anger flared when she realized that now she would never have the time to fix it. Leaning against a tree, Sam crossed her arms.

That was how Alma found her. She sensed him before she saw him. He approached cautiously, the way a hunter might walk toward a wild deer.

"I don't want to disturb you."

It's too late for that, she thought. He disturbed her in more ways than she could list. When Sam didn't respond to his statement, Alma walked until he stood in front of her. He held out two wrapped bundles, one large, one small. "I would like to give these to you."

Her curiosity was stronger than her anger, and Sam took the large bundle first. She pushed the cloth aside and found a wedding dress made of the most expensive linen she had ever felt. She ran her fingers over the material. In the dark Sam could just make out the elaborate stitching. Then her fingers clenched against the dress as she realized its implications. Before she could speak, Alma handed her the smaller bundle.

Sam laid it on top of the dress and opened it. Turning her hand so that she could see what she held, she gasped when the moonlight hit the package. Alma had given her a pair of earrings and bracelets, delicate coral inlaid with silver.

"They were my mother's. I thought they would suit you."

She picked up one of the bracelets, lifting it to better look at it. "Alma, I . . ." Her words trailed off because when she looked up to thank him, she saw that he had already gone.

* * *

The day of Sam's wedding came quickly. That morning she went to the lake to do the ritual cleansing and then dressed in Alma's mother's clothes. Her feet wiggled into the untanned deer hide sandals that wrapped around her toes and ankles with hemp cords. Unaccustomed to wearing shoes, she felt uncomfortable in them.

Her sisters had accompanied her and helped her dress. Kelila insisted on putting white blossoms from a ceiba tree in Sam's hair. Sam returned to her home to find the streets lined with flowers in every color. Her extended family had started to gather to accompany her on her walk to the palace. Sam didn't know what made her duck inside to put on the jewelry Alma had given her.

Sam's family sang songs, blew conch shells and flutes, and beat drums as Sam walked toward the center of the city to the palace. Red, blue, yellow, white, pink, and purple flowers were arranged all around her. Sam felt smothered by the floral scent.

The day began to fly by in a sort of dreamy haze. She saw Alma, who, she tried to convince herself, most certainly did not look extremely attractive in his wedding tunic. He led her to an altar where an elderly high priest officiated. Alma stood on the right, Sam on the left. Swarmed with flowers, the altar had a burning candle on each corner with one candle unlit in the center. Sam and Alma's friends and family formed a circle around them. The priest lectured them on what they should expect from married life, how they should embrace their roles of husband and wife.

While the priest droned on, Sam briefly considered what would happen if she jumped up and ran away screaming. Someone would undoubtedly catch her, and she'd probably have to endure the rest of her wedding tied up. Her shoulders sagged as she knew she could never embarrass her kinsmen in that way. They might never recover from such a humiliation.

The priest stopped talking and asked Alma to light the candle in the center of the altar. Alma then turned to Sam and presented her with maize and cacao seeds. Someone nudged Sam, and she picked up her return gifts: cooked maize and pressed cacao powder. Alma was symbolically showing that he would provide Sam with the necessities of life. Her gifts showed that she would take such raw materials and make them useful.

Alma then took a gulp of a frothy, spicy chocolate drink. He passed the cup to Sam. She hesitated and then drank from it as well. When she pulled the cup away from her lips, the crowd surrounding them burst into cheers.

People began to congratulate Sam, and it seemed like the entire city had turned out for the wedding. Sam received congratulations and well wishes from the highest nobleman down to the lowliest servant.

The celebratory feast began but Sam had no chance to eat. Music played and Sam went through one dance after another. Not that she could have tasted the food. She went through the motions in a state of numbness.

As the sun began to set, a group of her male relatives came and placed Sam on a litter, on which she would be transported to Alma's house. Since Alma didn't live far from the palace, the journey was a short one. Alma arrived at his home first and led Sam inside.

In the front foyer a maize dish had been left, which Alma offered to Sam. Feeling a thousand eyes on her, Sam took a bite. By entering his home and eating the food Alma gave her, their marriage had become official. She was now truly his wife. Another cheer broke out from the crowd.

"One last gift," Alma said, turning his back toward the open doorway. Sam's hands shook as she took the cloth from Alma. Inside she found a light pink jade pendant, held in place with a delicate silver chain.

"This is beautiful. Was it your mother's?"

"No. It was your mother's."

"My mother's?" Sam said. She had no memory of her mother wearing anything so fine.

"Your father sent it to me as a gift for you. He said he wanted you and your sisters to have something of your mother's when you married. It's a piece that he created himself when he was younger."

Sam had never seen anything her father had made. She lifted the necklace by its chain and let the pendant dangle down. Alma didn't have to give the necklace to her. It would have been his right to keep it and pass it on to their son or daughter. From the light in Alma's eyes, she saw that somehow he had known what this would mean to her. It was why he had given it to her. How could he already understand her so well? She wanted to ask him but found that she couldn't speak. Sam locked eyes with him, again finding herself unable to look away.

Some of Sam's married female cousins burst into the room, their high-pitched chatter breaking the moment between Alma and Sam. They herded her toward the back of the house and Sam found herself in what had to be Alma's bedchamber.

Instead of laying out their wedding gifts for all the city's residents to see, Alma had them stored here in the room he obviously expected to share with her. Bowls, vases, baskets—everything a new couple would need to start a life together—covered the floor.

After preparing Sam, her cousins left, giggling to themselves. Sam walked over to the wooden platform bed, covered with a new reed mattress and thick, luxurious blankets. Sam sat down on the edge, wearied after the long day. Her eyes rested on a small clay statue. Sam reached for it, and her eyes widened as she realized what she held. An idol. Someone had given them an idol as a wedding gift. Her knuckles turned white as she gripped the idol tightly. It reminded her that she had just married someone who did not share her beliefs.

It was quite possibly the worst day of her life.

CHAPTER SIX

It was quite possibly the best day of his life.

Not able to hold back a large grin, Alma kept saying his pointed good-nights to the large body of people gathered outside his home. Wedding guests continued their congratulations and teasing but began to drift away. Alma heard the ribald and drunken jokes made at his expense, but the laughter and voices finally faded.

Alma hooked the curtain up over the doorway, shutting the continuing celebration out. Time to find his wife. His wife. Alma repeated the words over and over. Sam was his wife. It felt like a dream, like it was happening to someone else. He didn't know such happiness was possible. How had he been so fortunate?

A strange nervousness filled him. Alma laughed at himself, shrugging off his desire to find a piece of chicle to chew until the sensation passed. He calmed himself with the thought that Sam probably felt the same way.

Alma found her in their room. Twilight had turned into evening, and in the candlelight Sam looked like the Lamanite moon goddess in her pale gown, the white flowers in her black hair like stars twinkling in the night sky.

Words failed him.

They did not, however, fail Sam.

"Do you know what this is?" she hissed at him, holding something in her hand. "An idol. Someone gave us this as a wedding present."

The small clay statue exploded into fragments when Sam threw it against the wall next to him.

"Sam!" he yelped, as he barely managed to duck when Sam heaved a large, red ceramic bowl at his head.

"What is wrong with you?" Alma asked before he jumped to his left to avoid the next projectile.

"What is wrong with me?" Sam repeated while picking up a vase to throw at him. "*You* are what's wrong with me!"

The vase shattered. "Can't we talk about this?"

"I can't believe I'm married to you. You! A false high priest!" Sam punctuated each of her exclamations by throwing something else at Alma. He twisted and turned to get out of the way.

"And now you think you can just come in here and that I'll just . . . just . . ." Sam repeated the word as she looked for something new to toss at him.

"Sam, stop!" Alma hadn't meant to yell at her, and she looked as shocked as he felt. He put his hands out in a placating gesture. "Please, calm down. We can discuss this rationally." He took a step toward her but held still when Sam backed herself into a corner.

"Don't touch me," she said through gritted teeth, her eyes shining bright with tears. "I'd rather die than let you touch me."

Alma dropped his hands to his sides. A confusing mixture of emotions coursed through him. He loved her so much, and he felt such misery at her obvious pain, even greater misery that he seemed to be the cause of it. He hated that she hurt and that he could do nothing to ease it. The worst feeling of all was the realization that he was the last person she would seek comfort from.

"What happened to that woman I met the first night?"

Sam let out a choked, desperate laugh. "You mean the terrorized, trapped, crying woman? You have her already."

The venom in her words clawed at his heart. He couldn't keep his anguish out of his reply. "No, the woman that spoke so sweetly to me, that allowed herself to smile at me, the one who was so vulnerable and trusting."

"Someone forced her to marry a man she hated."

Her statement sucked all the air out of the room. Something inside of Alma broke. He knew that Sam didn't feel the same love that he did. But he had such a strong connection to her that on some level he had convinced himself his feelings could not be one sided. But Sam stood there trembling, looking terrified and indignant all at once. He realized that she feared him. He wanted only to care for her, to protect her. And she hated him.

"I see."

He didn't really see. He didn't understand. But he knew nothing would be solved this night. Not trusting himself to speak further, Alma left. He faltered outside when he heard Sam's tortured sobs, and it took all his strength not to rush back in and hold her. She didn't want that. She didn't want him.

Alma went into his old room, the one he had grown up in. Sinking onto his bed, Alma thought of how his enemies would laugh at him if they saw him now. He had been utterly defeated, brought to his knees, by a mere woman. A woman who held his soul captive.

A woman who hated him.

He wished for dawn. In the light of day he would find a way to change Sam's mind. He would see the path to take. The darkness weighed him down with his own wretchedness, his suffering increasing every moment with the sound of Sam's crying.

The morning could not come quickly enough.

* * *

Somehow just before dawn Alma managed to finally fall asleep, and when he awoke, the sun had nearly reached its apex in the sky. In that first few seconds of wakefulness, Alma felt peaceful and contented. Then he remembered, and the crushing weight returned. It took great effort to even move. Alma didn't want to go to the palace, but he didn't want to stay home either.

He called for a manservant to bring him a change of clothing. Reflecting on last night, he found it was Sam's accusations that troubled him the most. He hadn't forced her to marry him. Why would she say he did? The king's representative had made Alma's offer, and Sam had accepted. He didn't understand her anger. He would never force her to do anything.

Alma got ready for his day quickly. It took little time to reach the palace. As Alma walked through one of the courtyards engrossed in his thoughts, he glanced to his left and saw Helam. Confused, Alma walked toward him. His young scribe seemed to be going through scrolls in Amulon's chambers. "Helam?"

Helam looked at him with a startled then guilty expression.

"What are you doing in Amulon's rooms?"

"Oh, I'm in Amulon's rooms? My mistake. I thought I was in your rooms, and speaking of you—" Helam said in a rushed breath as he joined Alma in the courtyard, "What are you doing here today?"

Wondering why Helam shifted the focus from his actions to Alma, he made a mental note to interrogate Helam about it further. For now he wanted to know why his scribe had asked such an impertinent question. "Why wouldn't I be here?"

Helam squirmed, looking very uncomfortable. "Oh, uh, no reason. We should probably be on our way."

Helam took a few steps away from Alma. Alma glared at him with his arms crossed. "Tell me."

"Everyone knows. About last night."

Wonderful. Now he had horrific humiliation to add to his suffering. He knew he had been a source of great amusement for his fellow priests this last week. It was undignified for a man to seek out his own wife the way Alma had. Alma knew it and didn't care about their snide remarks and gossip. But this was different. Now they had become privy to details of his personal life that he wouldn't have shared with anyone. The damage to his standing at court might be irreparable. "How do they know?"

"Teomner's scribe thinks that Amulon bribed one of your servants."

"There's the new husband!" Alma looked to see King Noah walking toward him, followed by an entourage of servants and priests, including Amulon. "But this is not the look of a young man in love. Having a bit of trouble, I hear. Would you like my advice?"

Alma had a good idea of what the king's advice would entail, and it turned his stomach. "Thank you, my king, but I think I can resolve this on my own."

"It doesn't matter if you can't," the king said with a wave of his hand. "I would guess that your next wife will be more willing."

"My next wife?" Alma choked on the words.

King Noah narrowed his eyes at Alma. "You know that you will have to make a proper and true marriage with a woman befitting your station and noble line. Your current wife is beneath you in status, class, and wealth."

Alma vaguely recalled those things mattering to him in the past, and it surprised him to find they no longer had a hold on him. He had never even considered them when it came to Sam. She was who she was, and it hadn't occurred to him to feel superior to her upbringing or her family's lack of wealth.

Apparently angry over Alma's slowness to agree with his dictate, the king walked over to Alma and poked Alma in the shoulder with his index finger. "You wanted her as a wife, and since it pleased me to give her to you, you got a wife. If you'd asked for her as a concubine, I would have arranged it. But you will make a real marriage with a woman of my choosing, and I will hear no more about this."

The thought of taking another wife made Alma feel sick, and he feared that it showed on his face. He tried to relax his expression. He couldn't afford to upset the king any further. He should say something to smooth this problem out. But Alma couldn't find the words to flatter or cajole the king. He had lost his taste for it.

But he had to answer. "Of course, my king."

Satisfied with Alma's response, the king turned to walk away from Alma with a dramatic flap of his cloak. His retainers followed behind him except for Amulon. With a sardonic smile he said, "I wonder if your wife will be there when you go home."

Tired of operating from a position of weakness, Alma fought the urge to run home to make sure that Sam hadn't left him. Lifting his head higher, he decided to stay. He would not grovel before his wife and beg her to love him. He had more pride, more dignity, than that.

He just had to treat the Sam problem the same way he dealt with any crisis. Hard work, determination, and charisma had overcome every insurmountable obstacle he had ever faced. They would have to overcome this obstacle as well.

*　*　*

Sam had waited hours for Alma to leave. She wondered what kind of cold and unfeeling man could have slept so long and so easily when she could find no rest.

After making certain that Alma left, Sam ran toward her home. Out of breath when she finally arrived, Sam let herself in. Kelila and Lael were gone, as she had known they would be. Her father slept in his corner. Sam considered waiting for him to wake up but couldn't. She didn't know how much time she had.

"Father?" Sam said, leaning down to shake his shoulder.

Her father grumbled but opened his eyes. After blinking a few times, he said with a gruff voice, "Sam, what are you doing here?"

After the tears she had shed last night, Sam thought she had no more tears left to cry. But her vision blurred as she knelt down next to her father. "Father, I can't be married to Alma. I can't. Please let me stay here. Don't make me go back to him. Please." Tears streaked down her face, and Sam inhaled large gulps of breath while she spoke.

She felt her father's crooked thumb wiping the tears from her face. "I would give anything to take away your pain. But we never had a choice in this situation. This is your fate. You must learn to accept it."

Sam shook her head. "I can't. There has to be something we can do." Her eyes lit up as she considered a possibility that had never occurred to her before. "We could leave. We could try to find Zarahemla. That's where Jerusha and her husband went. We could join them."

"We don't know where it is. We don't even know if Zarahemla still stands. We have received no word, no messages. It might have been destroyed. But if it does exist, with the wilderness between here and there, the journey would be too dangerous. We don't know if your sister's group made it."

"Don't talk that way." Sam wiped the tears away with the back of her hand. "I'm sure they found it. Maybe they will tell the people in Zarahemla where we are. Perhaps they will send help."

Her father gave her a sad smile. "Perhaps. But until then we have to live here. Hemmed in by wild animals, Lamanites, and the king's men."

Sam lowered her head in despair. She had thought her father would help her. She wanted him to fix her life, to make everything better the way he had when she was little. But he couldn't. She had no hope, nothing to look forward to but a lifetime of being tied to Alma.

"I think you're not being fair to your husband."

Sam snapped her head back up. "What?"

"I spent this week getting to know him. I watched him with your sisters. I watched him watch you. He seems to care for you. He seems like a good man. A little misguided, but you might be able to be an example for him. You might influence how he thinks."

It wasn't her job to be an example to Alma. She would have to speak to him to be an example, and since she didn't plan on ever being in the same room with him again, talking to him would be difficult.

A coughing fit struck her father, interrupting her thoughts. Sam worried that the coughing seemed to be getting worse. Her father turned on his side for relief. After the fit had ended, he said, "Alma is as innocent in all this as you are."

"He forced me to marry him, and you call him innocent?" Each word Sam spoke rose in volume. But one sharp look from her father made her apologize for yelling at him.

"My understanding is that this was all the king's doing."

Sam lifted her hand up to her mouth. "Just like with Miriam." Her horror at their circumstances was followed by a twinge of guilt. What if her father was right? What if Alma was not to blame? Had she treated him unfairly?

"If I had refused, the king said he would collect on the tax debt I owe him. He would have imprisoned me and then you and your sisters would have been alone."

Any sympathy she might have mustered in those moments left. The king threatened her father to make this marriage happen? Alma might not have been directly responsible, but had it not been for Alma wanting to have her, none of it would have happened. "There shouldn't be a tax debt." She touched the pendant around her neck. Her father's eyes followed the movement and they widened at what he saw.

He smiled. "You're wearing your mother's necklace."

"Why didn't you tell me about the jewelry?"

"You know why."

"Because I would have made you sell them so that we could have the money." It seemed like a sensible solution to Sam. They could have paid the debt, and then she wouldn't be married.

In a raspy tone her father said, "Our family gave up everything to join with the Nephites here. When you walk out into the fields surrounding this city, you do not see lands that have been harvested by your ancestors for centuries. You do not live in the home that your own father was born in. You have nothing of your past, of your history, to hold onto. But this," her father reached up and tapped the pendant with his finger, "this you can look at and see your heritage. You can see your mother in this necklace. You can see me in it. You will look at it and you will always remember us. That has no price. It is worth more than all the wealth in the world. Everyone needs something they belong to."

Sam understood what her father was saying, the words he said without speaking them. This was a farewell gift. She no longer belonged here. She certainly didn't belong with Alma. She didn't belong anywhere.

He broke the sad silence between them. "I agreed to the marriage because I was afraid the king would do to you what he did to Miriam. Even if we had paid the debt, you know as well as I do that the king could have imprisoned me for no cause."

"But the law—"

Her father shook his head. "The king is the law."

Sam wondered why the king seemed to take such pleasure from personally torturing her family. "I know we can't, but I wish we could get away from King Noah, that we could leave this place, just run away from everything."

Giving her a fierce look, her father said, "You are not a quitter. My daughter is not someone who runs away. She stays. She fights. Like her father."

Some of her fire returned at her father's words. He was right. She did not quit. She did not give in. She would stay. And she would most definitely fight.

"You need to go home and make your husband his evening meal."

"He has servants," Sam said in a sulky voice. She didn't want to do anything for Alma.

Her father gave her a look that let her know she had pushed him to the edge with her disobedience. "No, now he has a wife. It is your duty. Your mother did not raise you to act this way."

Feeling thoroughly chastened, Sam said good-bye to her father. She waited until he couldn't hear her to start grumbling about Alma. She walked toward Alma's house until an idea occurred to her. She veered off to the marketplace. "I'll make him dinner. I'll make him a dinner he'll never forget."

CHAPTER SEVEN

Alma arrived home with a thick knot in his stomach, not knowing what to expect. He left the scrolls he had brought with him to work on near the front entrance. The savory aroma of dinner reached him, and he decided to eat before doing anything else.

He seated himself in the southeast corner at the head of his long, low dining table. Alma heard footsteps behind him, and the scent of vanilla surrounded him. Bowls of water for rinsing his mouth and hands before the meal were placed on the table. Alma looked up to thank the servant, but the words died in his mouth when he saw Sam.

"You're here," he finally managed.

"Where else would I be?" Sam snapped as she practically threw the gourd filled with tortillas onto the table.

Not wanting to tell her his fears, Alma fell silent. Sam brought over black beans, salt, stew, and a plate laden with tamales. When he saw the cornhusk-wrapped food, his spirits were lifted. He asked, "Are we celebrating something?" He knew tamales took a great deal of work to make, so they were usually only served on special occasions or holidays. Why had she gone to this effort? He didn't dare hope that she did it for him.

When Sam didn't respond to his question, Alma tried to engage her again. "It smells delicious. Did you prepare it yourself?"

He saw her hesitate, and then Sam said, "Yes."

It was something. She had spoken to him without throwing anything. That had to be a good sign. "Thank you for preparing it."

Sam gave a nod of acknowledgment to his gratitude. Alma realized that she was leaving, and as she walked by him he reached out and grabbed her wrist. "Wait. Please, stay and eat with me."

Sam gave him a puzzled look, and Alma understood her confusion. Men and women did not eat together. Most women he knew spent their days snacking on the food they prepared, and any formal meals they had were held after the men had eaten. But Alma wanted Sam to stay. Right now it was enough just to be near her.

He saw her swallow, nod, and then she extricated herself from his grasp. She moved to the other end of the table and sat down on a mat. "Whatever you wish, my master."

Alma had picked up a tamale to eat and stopped with it midair, his mouth open. "Master? I am your husband, not your master. Please call me Alma." Alma suddenly realized that he had never heard Sam say his name. He was struck with a strange longing to hear her say it. He wondered what it would sound like coming from her lips.

Sam glared at him. "I am here against my will. I am a slave, not a wife."

"You are not a slave," Alma said as he put the food back down. "You can come and go as you please. This house is yours. Make any changes or improvements you want to make, buy anything from the marketplace that you choose. I want you to feel at home here. And if there is anything I can do to make you happier, you have only to ask."

Sam seemed to be considering his words. With her head lowered, she said in a voice so soft that Alma nearly missed her saying, "I wish my family could be here."

"I wanted to invite your father to move in with us, but I thought it would offend him."

"You're probably right," Sam sighed.

"Well, there's something I never thought I'd hear you say."

Alma saw a smile play on Sam's lips, and his heart leapt at the sight, at the beauty her smile brought to her face. The smile faded as quickly as it had come. But she had smiled. He saw it. Alma felt delighted at the major accomplishment.

He sprinkled the salt onto his beans and chose not to remark about Sam's lack of appetite. Alma didn't want to press her too much. Today she sat at the table; perhaps soon she would actually eat.

Knowing their marriage had to be addressed somehow, Alma scooped the beans up with a tortilla and after he finished swallowing said, "You have a very large family. I was surprised at the wedding yesterday how many kinsmen you have."

She didn't run, and she didn't toss her mat at his face despite his mentioning the wedding. Yes, definite progress.

Pushing her a bit further, he repeated, "I don't know anyone with as many cousins as you seem to have."

Sam sighed, but to Alma's satisfaction she did explain. "My family stayed behind in Nephi when King Mosiah and his subjects left. They were wealthy and didn't want to leave their homes and lands. But then the other Nephites started to ally themselves with the Lamanites. Now a Lamanite king sits on the throne of the City of Nephi. When that began to happen, King Zeniff and his people arrived. My family thought it would be better to give up everything and join the people of Zeniff than to live under the Lamanites."

Alma felt thrilled that they were having a real conversation. "I didn't know that. I thought your family had come up from Zarahemla with King Zeniff."

Sam shook her head. Her movement caused the scent of vanilla to come wafting through the air to him.

"You smell like vanilla."

"Yes. Does it bother you?"

"No," Alma said. "I like it. It smells . . ." She smelled intoxicating, but not wanting to frighten her, he lamely finished with, "Nice."

Her cheeks colored pink, and Sam looked down at her hands. "Your servants scented my bath water."

"They used to do the same thing for my mother. She loved orchids."

"When did she die?" Sam's question surprised Alma, but he liked that she had finally asked something about him. He set down his bowl of stew.

"It was a year ago. She was in another room and was talking to me, and then she suddenly just went silent. I called out to her, and when I went to check on her, she was dead. It was so sudden. Was your mother's death sudden?"

"No." Sam raised her gaze to look at Alma and then looked back down at her hands. "It happened after my oldest sister died. My mother became full of grief. She wouldn't get up in the morning, wouldn't talk to us. She cried all the time. She wouldn't eat, wouldn't drink. My father said my mother's heart had broken and she didn't want to live."

"I'm sorry for your loss."

"Thank you."

Alma finished his stew and his beans, then stifled a yawn. He apologized for his rudeness, telling Sam it was not the company. "I didn't sleep well last night."

"Neither did I."

"Yes, well, about that." Alma was loathe to break the fragile peace they had achieved, but they had to come to an understanding. "While I don't pretend to understand your reasons, you made your feelings about me and our marriage clear last night. And I hope that eventually you'll trust me enough to tell me why you tried to break all of our new pottery over my head."

That elicited another tiny smile from Sam, and Alma again felt triumphant. "I also hope that in time your feelings toward me will change. I want you to know that I'm willing to wait for as long as it takes." The smile on Sam's face disappeared.

"Be prepared to wait forever."

Alma gave Sam a crooked grin. "I can do that. I've already waited a thousand lifetimes." Sam again flushed at his words. He picked his tamale up. "You never know. You might learn to love me. I'm quite charming."

"Wait. Don't eat that." Sam suddenly looked panicked.

He paused. "Why?"

"I'm . . . I'm not a very good cook. Just don't eat it."

"I'm sure it tastes wonderful." To prove his point Alma took a large mouthful. Seconds later his entire head felt like it was on fire.

She must have put a habanero pepper in there, some still-functioning part of his mind realized. Alma started taking big gasps and half-expected flames to shoot out of his mouth. Instinctively he picked up his bowl of rinsing water and drank it. Although he should have realized what would happen from taking a drink, it was too late. The water made his mouth feel even hotter. Large beads of sweat broke out on his forehead, and every breath he took made it worse. Alma put his hands to his cheeks. Even his skin felt hot.

"Don't touch your eyes!"

Alma could only give her a withering look. He wasn't *that* stupid.

Feeling dizzy, he lay back on the floor, finding it difficult to sit up. Alma concentrated on getting a burning breath out and dragging another one back in. His tongue and lips had gone completely numb. He could hear Sam jumping up and running to him. She leaned over him.

"Are you all right?"

He tried to say, "Do I look like I'm all right?" but it came out a garbled, mumbled mess.

Sam started to back away from him. "I'm so sorry. I didn't know that you'd be . . . I thought that you would . . . I shouldn't have . . . I'm so sorry."

She fled the room, leaving Alma to wonder if anyone had ever died from eating a pepper.

* * *

Sam had never felt so guilty. She spent the night trembling in her room, sure that Alma would punish her for her childish antic. He had every right to beat her after what she had done. She certainly deserved it.

Unable to sleep, Sam kept running the evening's events over and over in her mind. Although it had happened hours earlier, she found that her wrist, where Alma had touched her, still tingled. When he asked her to stay, encircling her wrist with his strong hand, her stomach had done a funny flip while her heart slammed against her chest. At the time she told herself that she stayed because she wanted to see his face when he ate the pepper. Now she wondered if there had been another reason.

She cursed her weakness. It had all started with that bath, her first hot bath ever. It was a luxury she had reveled in despite her determination not to. When she'd mentioned to one of the maidservants that she loved the scent of vanilla, she never imagined that they could put the essence into her bath. That pampering had definitely weakened her resolve.

Then at dinner Sam had expected a tyrant. She waited for a man who would lecture her and demand his husbandly rights. But no such man ever appeared. Alma had been inquisitive and interested in the things she said. He had appreciated her perfume and thanked her for cooking dinner. He had teased her and nearly made her laugh out loud. He had been patient. Understanding. He had been kind. A little arrogant and vain, but still kind. She wanted to see it as a manipulative trick, but she knew it wasn't.

In one night Alma proved that he wasn't the man Sam believed him to be. And it worried her.

Why did the defensive wall she built around herself start to crash down with only a smile from him? She had felt perfectly justified in her actions. She had rationalized that she was fighting a horrible monster. But now Sam hated what she had done, hated that she hadn't been truthful with him when he asked why he shouldn't eat the tamale. Sam didn't like to lie. But she didn't want him to know how immature she had been.

And it grieved her that she had caused Alma pain. She had imagined she would feel smug or victorious. When she saw his face and what she had done, she only felt horrible.

Just before dawn crept over the horizon, Sam promised herself that she would never stoop to another trick like that one. She also wanted to find a way to make things better with Alma. She would accept whatever punishment he decided on.

She got up and prepared him breakfast, but Alma never appeared. Not that she could blame him.

Needing to escape her own thoughts and guilt, Sam began to work on cleaning Alma's house. The cleaning would take a long time to complete. His home was not palatial, but her entire home could have fit in one corner of Alma's smallest storage room. Sam felt grateful for the hard work, the penance she had given herself. She waved away the servants who came and asked to help. She would do it alone.

She lost track of time, and it surprised her when a servant reminded her about dinner. Sam hadn't even realized that the sun had set. The same servant delivered a message that Alma would not be home for the evening meal. He had gone to get his sister, Hannah.

A sister? Alma had never mentioned that he had a sister. Sam wondered how close they were and if Alma would tell Hannah how awful Sam had been. The gnawing worry increased. Sam knew she would have to go to him and apologize, but she didn't know how she would ever face him again.

She had also expected any message from Alma to be full of stinging words. But there had been no retribution, no words of rebuke for her behavior. It made her feel even worse.

After Sam finished scrubbing the walls in what must be Alma's study, a room filled with scrolls and writing utensils, she decided to explore her surroundings. She walked along the gallery, past an open courtyard. A high wall ran along the south side of the courtyard that made Sam curious to see what lay beyond it. She found herself under the night sky in an ornamental garden. Beautiful, fragrant trees supported lianas covered in blooming nighttime orchids. It was totally ridiculous. Gardens were meant to provide food. But despite its impracticality, the garden beckoned to her. Sam found a stone bench and, sinking down onto it, enjoyed her view. She lay down on the bench, resting her head on her arms. She let her eyes drift shut. She would rest for just a few minutes.

She awoke with a start when a maidservant gently shook her shoulders. "How long have I been asleep?" Sam asked.

The servant indicated she didn't know. Looking up at the stars, Sam realized she had been asleep for hours.

Feeling foolish that she had been woken up just to prepare for bed, Sam went back into the main house and this time walked through the gallery on the west side. She went past a series of guest rooms used to house family members during celebrations. She stopped when she heard a female voice shriek, "Ow!"

Looking to her right, she saw a young woman sitting in front of a rounded off, polished iron pyrite mirror in one of the guest rooms. The girl looked like a feminine version of Alma. She had to be Hannah. Hannah tried to drag a turtle shell comb through her long brown hair, but Sam saw that it snagged. Hannah cried out in pain again.

"Can I help? I have four sisters. I'm well versed in the art of hair tangles."

Hannah turned to look at Sam and just stared.

Feeling stupid at her failed attempt at humor, Sam realized she hadn't introduced herself. "I'm Sam. I'm . . ." She didn't know how to finish. *I'm your sister-in-law? Alma's wife? The evil brat who tortured your brother?*

But Hannah suddenly grinned at her, and it made Sam's heart twist. Hannah's smile reminded her of Alma's. "I know who you are. I'm Hannah, Alma's sister. We actually met at your wedding, but you had five other people talking to you at the same time. And yes, I could use your help." Hannah said the words in one big excited rush and held her comb out to Sam.

Putting down the rags and lime solution she had used to clean, Sam went into Hannah's room and took the comb. Hannah turned back toward the mirror, and Sam started to brush through Hannah's hair. She saw that Hannah bit her lip and closed her eyes when Sam started in on a knot. "How did you get so many snarls?"

Hannah opened her eyes to look at Sam. "My mother used to brush my hair. Every night. I've tried to brush it myself, but when I hit a tangle, it hurts too much for me to keep going, so it doesn't happen often. I haven't let anyone else touch my hair since she died."

Sam's hand stilled. "Why are you letting me?"

Hannah looked at her with such trust that Sam almost flinched. "You're my family now."

Sam ducked her head down and went back to working out the knot. Several minutes passed before Hannah said, "I have a confession to make. I've been intimidated about talking to you."

"Why?" Sam asked with a mixture of a laugh and disbelief. Her smile faded when she realized that Alma might have given Hannah a very good reason to fear her. Shame washed through her. "Did he . . . did he mention . . ."

Oblivious to Sam's discomfort, Hannah went on. "My brother thinks you are perfection itself. Why wouldn't I be intimidated?"

This time Sam did laugh. "Perfect? Me? Not exactly."

"Not according to Alma."

"I have lots of flaws," Sam said, loosening the rest of the knot from Hannah's hair.

"Like what?" Hannah had that awkward mix of a girl no longer a child, but not yet a woman. Her trust and naïveté made Sam even more uncomfortable. Alma had not told Hannah about the tamale.

"Like I have a horrible temper. I'm impossibly impulsive and then always immediately regret what I've done."

That made Hannah grin at her again. "I'm glad you're human after all." The duo entered into an easy conversation and chatted as if they had always known each other. Hannah asked her endless questions about her family. Sam found herself being very open with Hannah. She even told Hannah about her worry for her father surviving the next rainy season without adequate shelter. She had never even told her own sisters that. What was it about this family that made her volunteer such information?

"There. Very pretty," Sam said when she finished. Hannah's shiny hair was now tangle free. "Better?"

"Much better. Thank you." Hannah took her comb back from Sam. Hannah then preened in front of the mirror. "Maybe now Alma will finally concede that I'm the more attractive sibling. What do you think?"

"What?" How had the conversation turned this way? Sam didn't want to risk alienating Hannah by insulting Alma and took the only safe answer she could think of. "I think you're both very attractive." Wanting to leave before their talk got any more dangerous, Sam bid Hannah a good night.

"Sam, wait. There's something else I want to tell you." Hannah twisted the edge of her tunic back and forth in a nervous manner. "I know it isn't my place, but I think there's something you should know about Alma. My brother doesn't do anything in half measures. He does everything wholehearted. He never tries—he either does something or he doesn't. He either believes something or he doesn't." Hannah paused, making sure she had Sam's full attention and said her next words with deliberation. "He either loves someone or he doesn't. It is all or nothing for him. I just thought you should know that."

* * *

Before Hannah could go on any further, Alma cleared his throat.

He hadn't meant to eavesdrop on their conversation. He was not the sort of man to skulk about in the shadows. But until now he hadn't wanted to interrupt them.

Alma found it difficult to stay angry at Sam. Especially at the sight of the two women he loved most in the world talking and laughing together. Truthfully, his anger had left him as soon as the after effects of the pepper had.

He had deliberately stayed away all day but found himself missing Sam, despite what she had done. He retrieved Hannah, and they had returned to a home that practically sparkled. After questioning some of the servants, he discovered that Sam had done it by herself. Although he wanted to believe the best of her, Alma wondered whether Sam was setting some new trap for him.

When he went to find Hannah for her lessons, he had found them together and he couldn't help but listen. Alma had never heard

Sam laugh before, and his heart leapt at the sound. Then, though he thought it possible his ears might be deceiving him, he heard Sam say she thought he was attractive. It made him grin.

Both of the women went still when Alma made his presence known. Putting on a solemn face, he said, "Hannah, I'd like to speak to Sam alone. Would you please wait in my study?"

Hannah nodded and left. Sam looked petrified as Alma entered Hannah's room. He kept silent, letting her fidget under his gaze. She looked at her feet, at Hannah's bed, anywhere but at him. "You cleaned the house," he finally said.

"Yes."

"Why? Should I expect to find snakes in my bed tonight? Spiders in my bowls?"

"No," Sam whispered. "You have every right to think that, but no. I promise you I will never do anything like that again. My actions were childish and foolish. I'm so sorry."

"Yes, I think you mentioned how sorry you were last night."

At hearing the amusement he could no longer suppress in his voice, Sam finally looked up at him. "Why are you smiling like that?" she asked.

"You said I was attractive."

"I don't recall that," Sam said in a haughty tone.

"You did."

"Where has Hannah been?"

Amused even further at Sam's unsubtle attempt to change the course of their conversation, Alma had to compress his lips to keep from laughing out loud. After swallowing his laughter down he said, "She stayed with friends of my family so that we could have some privacy. Since that's not necessary, I brought her back home."

Sam flushed three different shades of red at his words. Alma crossed his arms and leaned against the wall behind him.

"I thought you were angry with her."

"Why would I be angry with Hannah?"

"I don't know," Sam said. "Why did you send her to your study?"

"I'm teaching Hannah how to read scripture."

Sam's mouth opened and then shut, and then opened and shut again. "You teach her to read the ancient languages? No women are taught those."

"Most women aren't as intelligent as Hannah. Or as intelligent as you are. I could teach you if you wanted to learn."

"I could learn to read the words of the prophets?"

Alma nodded.

"When could we start?"

"It would have to be tomorrow. Tonight I have a great deal of work to finish after Hannah's lesson."

Alma had never seen Sam excited, but she almost glowed with a joy that he had caused. The thrill he had felt over making her smile was nothing compared to this sensation. He felt lighter, ecstatic, his chest swelling with pride that he had finally found something that would make Sam happy.

But then the light faded from her eyes, and she suddenly looked miserable again.

"What is it?" he asked.

"I don't deserve your kindness. I deserve whatever punishment you would give me."

In a low voice Alma told her, "I don't want to punish you. I don't want you to be unhappy. I do, however, want to teach you to read." It surprised him how much he wanted it. He looked forward to spending hours alone with his beautiful wife without any acts of violence being committed against him.

"Tomorrow night, then." Sam bit her lower lip before letting a smile break out on her face. She went to pick up some rags and a bowl before Alma stopped her. He walked over to her, putting his hand on her shoulder. She jumped, but she didn't pull away.

"I don't have to be your enemy, Sam. I think we could be friends."

Her eyes slanted down. She nodded.

"And the next time you want to kill me, do you think you could find a less painful way of doing it?"

Although he was obviously teasing, Sam looked at him seriously. "I don't want to kill you."

Reluctantly, Alma pulled his hand away. "That's a start."

Sam couldn't escape quickly enough, and this time Alma did let himself laugh. The dinner escapade notwithstanding, there was obviously room for civility between him and Sam and then maybe someday, somehow, something more.

CHAPTER EIGHT

Sam took Alma's words to heart. She would make his home her own.
She would use the wealth given to him by the king to help others.

Early the next morning she went to the market. There she hired
servants and sent them to Alma's home. She also found her cousin
Gideon after sending him a message requesting that he meet her in
the labor quarter. Sam asked him to discover who among their
extended family owed tax debts to the king. It amused her to think
that she would use the king's money to pay the king. After Gideon
told her which families he already knew of that were in need of debt
relief, Sam said good-bye to him and went to the food section of the
market. She bought a little bit of everything, hiring young boys to
follow her back to her father's home.

Feeling like a conquering queen, Sam had the boys stay outside
while she went in by herself.

The entire inside of her family's hut was covered in large storage
vases. "What is this?" asked Sam.

Kelila poked her head around one of the vases. "Alma."

"Why aren't you in the fields?"

Lael appeared from behind another vase. "Alma hired men to
clear the crops for us. He also had all this food delivered, and each of
the merchants were told to refill whatever we use at no cost to us."

Her sisters wore identical guilty expressions. Sam could tell they
were thrilled but guessed they didn't want to show their excitement to
her. They knew how she felt about Alma. It made her question herself

again. A man who would do something like this was not a man she needed to fear or hate.

"What does Father say?" she finally asked. Sam didn't want her father to be insulted.

"You know that Alma forgave the bridegroom price we should have paid to Alma's father to compensate for the loss of his son, since Alma did not live with us," Lael said. "And because Alma is not living here and helping, he sent this as payment for the services he would have given. What could Father say to that?"

Sam had heard of other situations similar to her own, where the son-in-law could not come and live with his wife's family. She'd heard of small gifts being offered instead of services. But she had never heard of this kind of overwhelming gesture.

"Alma sent a messenger to tell you that?" Sam's words came out in a strangled whisper.

"He came himself."

Sam's mind buzzed with confusion. "Why would he do this?"

Kelila looked at her sister like Sam was stupid. "Why else? Even I know why. He did this for you."

* * *

King Noah had his arm around Alma, and the two men laughed as they walked. Amulon hung back at the fringes of the king's entourage, seething.

Despite his anger, Amulon had to admit a grudging respect for Alma's ability to please the king through words alone. Few could flatter or admire the way Alma could. Few possessed his natural charisma.

And no one worked as hard as Alma did. Amulon personally abhorred physical effort of any kind, as did most of his fellow priests. There were far too many pleasures to be had to spend any time laboring. That's what lesser men were for. But King Noah often commented on how Alma practically ran the land by himself, and the king appreciated that Alma made his life easier.

The priests usually came into this calling the way Alma had—full of fire and energy. King Noah liked that naïve, conquer-the-world attitude, and Amulon suspected that's why the king always selected his youngest high priest as his favorite. It was why Amulon had been the favorite for many years before Alma had been selected.

It was why Alma had to be eliminated.

Alma's misery in his home life should have been enough for Amulon, but he wanted to utterly annihilate Alma. So if he couldn't kill Alma, he would destroy his influence. Since Amulon had grown up in disgrace, he knew exactly how to do it.

Of course, timing would be everything. He had to set things up in such a way that no blame would ever fall back on him. Engrossed in his plotting, Amulon only half-listened to the conversation between the king and Alma until King Noah said, "Then you will take management of the trade runs to Nephi." The king patted Alma on the back as he spoke.

"If that is your desire."

Amulon stopped. There it was. Like always, he had only to wait, to observe, and fate handed him a golden opportunity.

Detaching himself from the group, Amulon rushed through the palace. He needed to find someone gullible, someone greedy and grasping.

He found not one but two men to suit his purposes. Amulon slowed down as he entered the room where Orihah and Lib, two high priests, lounged about with members of the king's harem. The king didn't seem to mind if his priests dallied with the concubines he had tired of. Amulon had often wondered how many of the royal children were actually the king's offspring.

If Alma represented the beginning of a priest's rise to power, all noble and full of good intentions, then the two men in front of Amulon represented the priest at the height of that climb—idolatrous, lazy, and pleasure seeking. Amulon knew that greed was a powerful lure and that there was no such thing as too much wealth.

The great wealth came first, the desire for even more came second.

Then the desire to revel in the fruits of that wealth came third. Amulon remembered that feeling of invincibility, that you could have anything for the asking. There seemed to be no limits to their power or their possessions. When a priest realized that he didn't have to work and had only to indulge himself in whatever whim he fancied, the journey was nearly complete. The high priests were then told the truth about their position, about the things they taught the people. And not one of them ever cared.

Amulon cared least of all.

A dark-eyed beauty fed Lib pieces of melon while he lay against pillows. "Enjoy that while you can." When Amulon spoke, everyone in the room ceased what they were doing to look at him. Settling himself onto the cushions near Lib, he waited. He knew it would not take long.

It did not. "What do you mean by that?" Orihah asked.

Still Amulon held his tongue. He raised one shoulder and looked away. It had the desired effect. The other two high priests sent the women away and came over to Amulon.

"You have information," Lib said with a worried look.

Studying his fingernails Amulon said, "I may have overheard something."

"You must tell us," Orihah demanded.

"The king is putting Alma in charge of trading with the Lamanites."

Both men looked outraged, as Amulon knew they would. The other high priests already resented Alma and his industriousness. They interpreted his zealousness as an attempt to make the rest of them look bad. This would be too much for them. The high priests routinely skimmed money from the taxes and the profits from the trade runs. King Noah paid no attention to their activities as long as his own coffers were full. Amulon knew that, like himself, the other priests would do anything to protect their wealth and would fight against anyone who threatened it.

"I have also heard that Alma will be taking over more ceremonial responsibilities." Amulon couldn't help but add that and had to hold in his glee over the fury that seized the men in front of him. The priests used religious ceremonies as a way to collect tribute and offerings. If Alma took that as well . . .

"He is plotting against us!" Lib declared, knocking over his cup of wine in an angry fit. "He would take our wealth from us! How can anyone be so selfish?"

"He must be stopped," Orihah said in a huff.

Amulon couldn't agree more. He sat quietly as Lib and Orihah made plans of their own on how Alma's authority and responsibilities could be limited.

Neither man possessed his own skills and talents in this sort of thing, but Amulon kept silent. It was enough that these two high priests thought stopping Alma their idea. They would take the fall if things went badly. But Amulon had confidence that he had set the right events in motion. It would be only a matter of time now. Fate would provide him with more opportunities, more ways to obliterate Alma into nothingness.

More than these courtly intrigues, the best way to destroy Alma was through his new wife. Amulon had considered trying to lure Sam away from Alma, but Sam's hatred of Amulon doomed the endeavor. That didn't mean, however, that he lacked other ways to hurt her. And by hurting Sam he would hurt Alma.

Which made Amulon happier than he had been in a very long time.

* * *

Alma came home later that night than he expected because of the new responsibility that the king had assigned to him. Helam had been almost giddy with the thought of all the new reports and lists he would get to make.

Alma walked up the steps of the platform that his home had been built on. Seeing a lot of movement in his mother's garden, Alma strode toward it. Instead of one gardener pruning the night flowers, he saw four men working.

Puzzled, Alma went into the house, and his confusion only grew when he passed a group of women carrying water inside. Knowing the hour to be late, Alma decided to look for Sam and Hannah for an explanation and to postpone their lessons. He hoped they would understand.

He heard Sam speaking and followed her voice, figuring she must be with Hannah. He didn't know why it made him so glad that Sam and Hannah seemed to get along so well. Or why he suddenly envied his little sister so much.

"Do you know that we have four gardeners now?" Alma asked before he went into Sam's room, and his mouth stopped working when he saw Sam on her knees. Praying.

"Sam?"

Sam finished her prayer and then got to her feet slowly. She wrapped her arms around herself as if she were cold. "I hired more servants today. You said I could make changes to the home. There are people who need work, and I gave it to them."

"Were you praying?"

Sam said nothing.

"Were you praying?" Alma repeated. But he didn't need to ask the question, didn't need Sam to confirm it.

"You're a believer." Alma could hardly comprehend that he had uttered those words to his wife. He had heard rumblings and whispers about the believers, a group of people who thought the king's religion to be false and had one of their own. He knew there had been an incident two years ago when a man had preached some religious nonsense, trying to stir the people up to rebellion. The man had been exiled.

The king feared the believers, convinced that they were out to destroy him. Some seemed to think the believers' influence had even infiltrated the upper levels of the palace. While Alma didn't understand everything they believed, what little he did know felt strange and foreign to him.

Like his wife praying on her own.

"Perhaps you should have tried to learn some things about me before you married me."

What would he do? The king had ruled baptisms to be a foolish tradition of their fathers, and the kind of prayer Sam was doing was nothing short of treason. It was forbidden.

"The priests are supposed to pray on your behalf. In the temple on the designated days," Alma said, trying to make sense of this situation.

Sam drew her shoulders back and tilted her head up at Alma. "I have a God who loves me, and I pray to Him in my own way. I don't need someone else to speak for me."

Letting out a short moan, Alma sat down on a stool, burying his face in his hands.

"Are you going to tell the king?" Sam asked quietly.

He put his hands down to look at her. "No. Never." He would turn himself in before he would report Sam. King Noah would kill her.

"Then what are you going to do?"

"I don't know." It was the only honest answer he could give her. "I have to go."

Alma's mind spun as he sought the refuge of his room. His wife had been seriously led astray. In addition to trying to win her over, he now had to keep her beliefs a secret from anyone in the palace and to try to convince her to see the error of her ways.

Usually confronting things face first, Alma couldn't do it this time. If he acknowledged what Sam was doing, he would have to deal with it in a way he didn't want to. If he spent time thinking about it, words might accidentally slip from him in front of the wrong people. The thought that he could put her life in danger made his flesh feel cold.

Then again, if he ignored it, pretended it never happened, he wouldn't have to worry about making that kind of mistake. He could keep Sam safe. Yes, that was what he would do. He would carry on as if he had never walked into that room.

And he would hope his wife had enough sense to keep them both out of danger.

* * *

Sam didn't know what she expected Alma's reaction to be after their confrontation, but it certainly wasn't his acting like nothing had ever occurred.

Alma invited Sam to start her lessons, never once mentioning her praying. Sam knew she probably should have talked to him about it, but selfishly she didn't want him to retract his offer to teach her to read the languages of their ancestors.

Unfortunately, the more she was around him, the more she had to admit that Alma had been right. They could be friends. Though she wouldn't have confessed the truth to anyone else, Sam enjoyed the time she and Alma spent together.

Part of that came from Sam realizing that anger exhausted her. Such furious passion was difficult to maintain. She didn't want to be mad all the time.

But letting go of her anger meant that she relaxed around Alma. Laughed at his jokes, told him stories of her childhood, and listened to the stories he told her. It was complicating everything. Things were much easier when she had assigned Alma a role to play and could keep him there in her mind. But Alma kept insisting on being totally different from what she imagined him to be.

Sam shifted the basket filled with herbal remedies for her father from her right arm to her left. A healer came by every day to check on her father's health. Earlier that morning the healer gave Sam a list of ingredients to bring to him today at her father's house. Sam had just finished collecting them from the marketplace and now went to bring them to the healer.

Her steps faltered as she walked down the path to the house. She had the herbs but had somehow lost her father's home.

The hut had been demolished. Long pieces of wood and the thick grasses that had made up the roof lay all over the ground. She saw two men pulling up the three hearthstones used for their cooking fire from where the house had once stood. Behind the ruins she saw a new, much larger house being constructed.

She spotted Kelila and waved her over. "What's happening?"

Jumping up and down, Kelila grabbed Sam's hands, nearly disrupting the contents of Sam's basket. "We're getting a new house!"

"Alma?" Not that she needed Kelila to answer. Who else would hire men to build her family a new home?

"Alma," Kelila confirmed. From a way off, Sam saw Lael struggling with a large water vase. Lael called out to Kelila, who skipped away to help.

Several men worked up in the rafters, lashing the joists with thick vines. They had stripped to the waist due to the hard work and hot sun overhead.

The man nearest Sam caught her eye. She admired his strong back, the way his muscles flexed as he tightened a vine. Sam immediately berated herself. She should not be looking at another man. She was a married woman now. She should not be looking at . . . her *husband?*

Sam gasped, immediately putting her hand over her mouth to stifle the sound. She wasn't quick enough, and Alma heard. "Sam!" He lowered himself down off the roof, jumping the rest of the way to the ground.

She willed her heart to return to a normal beat as he walked toward her. Sam suddenly noticed the sky had a particularly beautiful shade of blue today. And that the dirt underneath her foot seemed very . . . filled with pebbles. She looked at everything and everyone except for him.

"I didn't expect to see you here today," she heard him say.

Well, that definitely made two of them.

"What do you think?" Alma said with a sweep of his hand toward the new house.

Sam opened her mouth, and while she wanted words to come out, that initially didn't happen. Finally she managed, "I think I had no idea that you knew how to build a house."

Alma gave her one of his lopsided grins. "There's probably a lot of things I can do that would surprise you." Alma took her basket from her, setting it on the ground. "I like to help with the construction work when the men are behind their building schedules. Helam helps sometimes too, but he's worried about his scribe hands being ruined." Alma wiggled his fingers, making Sam smile. That certainly sounded like Helam. She had come to know him a little bit on the several occasions when he'd been to their home for dinner on nights he worked late with Alma.

"I do love it when you smile," Alma said, and his tone made Sam forget the rest of the world existed.

The moment ended when Helam groaned from the roof, "I think I just got a splinter!"

Alma chuckled. "That's Helam's way of saying he's done." Alma walked toward the building frame, and Sam followed. "This is only temporary. I plan on building them something more permanent but I wanted your family to have something sturdy and watertight before the next rainy season."

"Why do you do these things?" Sam asked in a low voice, her heart thudding with a feeling she couldn't name. "Do you expect favors in return? Some type of reward?"

Alma's smile faltered for a moment before it returned. "No, I don't expect anything from you. Doing things for you makes me happy. That's reward enough."

She did it again—automatically assumed the worst about Alma when he had not intended to make her feel guilty or manipulate her. Sam thought she should apologize. Or she should at least thank him. She must seem like an ungrateful child. While she was trying to think of the right thing to say, Alma suddenly spoke.

"You need to get these herbs to your father." Alma picked up the basket, handing it back to Sam. "And I want to get this work finished before nightfall."

Sam took the basket from Alma. "All right. Then I'll meet you at home later?"

Alma nodded, and Sam had taken six steps before she realized what she had just said. When had she started to think of Alma's house as her home?

CHAPTER NINE

Alma hurried along the darkened street. Almost home.

The sound of heavy breathing made Alma stop. Something emerged from the shadows onto the path in front of him.

"How did you find me?"

Hunter sat down on his haunches, his tail thumping on the ground. It never ceased to amaze Alma that the dog somehow always knew how to track him down, no matter where he was.

"The king wouldn't like this, you know. You're supposed to stay in the palace."

The dog yawned in response.

"I can't leave you out here. Come on."

Hunter fell into step alongside Alma. When he reached his home, Alma called out for Sam. She emerged from the dining room, wiping her hands on a cloth. The dog bounded over to her and did something Alma had never seen him do before. He rolled over onto his back, exposing his stomach for Sam to scratch. She knelt down, cooing at the dog. "Aren't you adorable?" She rubbed his belly and planted a kiss on the top of Hunter's front paw.

Alma had never wanted to be a dog so badly in his life.

The sight of Sam on her knees gave Alma an uncomfortable reminder of the last time he had seen her that way, while she was praying. The things she had said to him that night about prayer, about what she believed—they had stayed with him despite his not wanting them to. He tried to forget them. She was obviously wrong.

But it bothered Alma, and he didn't know why. He didn't understand the tiny pricks of something that felt like guilt that seemed to poke at him. He chose to ignore them.

Apparently taking advantage of the fact that he had a new audience, Hunter leapt up and began to run in circles, chasing his tail. His path grew wider and wider until he slammed into Alma, knocking Alma down. His cloak flew up, covering his head when he fell. Sam let out great peals of infectious laughter that echoed throughout the room.

"I'm sorry, I know women should never laugh at men," Sam said in between her gasps for air. "It was just . . . the expression on your face . . ."

Pushing his cloak off his head, Alma propped himself up on his elbows to laugh along with Sam. The sound of her laughter somehow managed to thrill and calm him at the same time. It was music his soul rejoiced in. Even if it came at his expense.

Sam walked over, extending her hand to help him to his feet. Once he stood, Sam withdrew her hand quickly and stepped back. He flexed his fingers as if to relieve them of the burning, tingling sensation that had engulfed his entire hand from Sam's touch.

"Have you eaten?" Sam asked in a breathy voice that made Alma wonder if she had been affected the same way he had.

This was pure torture. Knowing Sam, being this close to her all the time, loving her this desperately, and not even being able to hold her or stroke her hair or kiss her or tell her how crazy she made him.

He hadn't eaten, but he needed to get away from her so that he could collect himself. "I'm not hungry."

Alma retired to his study and noticed the household accounts lying on the table. Seizing on the opportunity to busy himself with work, to get away from his thoughts, Alma picked them up. They were Sam's responsibility, but Alma liked being meticulous and thorough in all aspects of his life.

As he reviewed the accounting, he noticed something peculiar. Sam had not purchased any trinkets. No baubles, no jewels, not even material to make clothing. She still wore the same sort of drab outfits she had worn before their marriage. While Alma was not embarrassed by what she wore, he wanted to see her in an indigo blue. A sunshine yellow. He wondered what a forest green would do for her eyes.

Later that night when Sam came in for her language lesson, Alma broached the subject with her. "I was thinking of ordering some fabric. I thought your sisters and Hannah might like some new clothes."

He knew Sam couldn't refuse. If he had offered her the gift for herself alone, she might have said no. But she wouldn't deny her sisters.

"I think they would love that," Sam said.

Alma looked down at the book they were reading from. "And perhaps you could make something for yourself as well."

"Perhaps."

He tried to hide his smile. Such progress always made him happy. Maybe he should have Helam draw up something to keep track of it. She had laughed out loud at his joke on Tuesday. Didn't flinch when he held her hand in his to show her the right brush-stroke on Thursday. Had confided in him on Saturday. And she hadn't thrown anything at him in two weeks, two days, and three hours.

Hunter burst into the room, frantically yapping and barking as he zigzagged back and forth. Then he dove underneath a bench. He lay there, shaking.

"What is wrong with that dog?" Sam asked in a bewildered tone.

"He's not the brightest of creatures."

Alma heard the sound of distant rumbling thunder. "A storm this time of year?" Both he and Sam got up to walk over to the window to investigate the source of the noise.

The ground underneath them began to tremble. Not a thunderstorm. An earthquake.

The earth rocked and roiled all around them. Sam lost her footing and pitched forward. Alma grabbed her and braced himself against the wall.

The main part of the earthquake lasted for a few more seconds and then faded away. Alma knew there would be several smaller quakes later on, but the worst of it seemed to be over. With the loud sound gone, Alma noticed that Sam's breathing sounded harsh and erratic.

"It's all right," Alma murmured against her hair. "It was just a little one. It's all right." He continued to soothe her until her breathing eased.

Holding her so tightly, however, seemed to have stopped his own ability to breathe.

"I'm sorry," Alma said.

Sam tilted her face up to him. With wide eyes, all innocence and trust, she asked, "For what?"

"For this."

His lips covered hers with a hunger Alma couldn't disguise. He kissed her with all the pent-up frustration, passion, and love he possessed. He felt like a starving man being given his first taste of food. It was utter bliss.

He finally broke the kiss off when he could bear no more.

"Alma?"

Now neither one of them could breathe properly. Alma had to push himself away from her. "I was afraid if I didn't do that, I might go mad."

Sam stood there, looking beautiful and unattainable, her eyes full of wonder. She put her fingers to her lips, and all Alma wanted to do was kiss her again. He commanded his feet not to move, but he swayed toward her. Before Alma could do anything else, Sam bolted from the room.

His back to the wall, Alma slid down to the floor. He had hoped that if he just kissed her, it might make him crave her less.

All the kiss had done was turn his small fire of need into a raging inferno.

And he wanted to be consumed.

* * *

The next morning, Alma couldn't escape early enough. As he walked through the front foyer, he saw Hunter lying on the floor next to the doorway.

Alma gave him a low whistle. "Let's go."

The dog lifted his head off his paws, blinked at Alma, and then put his head back down.

"Staying, I see." Alma scratched the top of Hunter's head in between his ears. "You like her better than me, do you? I understand. I like her better too. Take care of my girls for me."

Not knowing how he would explain the dog's absence if the king questioned him, Alma decided to stay away from the throne room and King Noah. He certainly had enough to keep him occupied in his chambers for the rest of the day.

Last night, before Alma had taken leave of his senses, Sam had asked him why he worked so hard. Since Sam had no problem constantly expressing her negative, treasonous opinions about the government, Alma knew exactly what her reaction would be if he told her about the level of corruption that existed. The total deceit and dishonesty, the way the other priests stole money from the king. Their laziness made it so that, were it left to them, nothing would get accomplished. The running of the government fell on Alma's shoulders. As the youngest high priest, he shouldn't be responsible for all that, but he often suspected that if he did not take care of things, the entire system might fall apart. Besides, Alma couldn't help it when there was something that needed to be done. He had to complete every task he started.

Thinking of Sam and her particularly descriptive phrases to describe the high priests, Alma had to push down the hollow feeling in his stomach. Now going in to fulfill his duties was like playing in a pit of vipers, like sallying into the jaguar's den. He had always enjoyed using his cleverness to gain his own desires, to curry the king's favor above all others. But now it felt like drudgery, like something he had to wade through in an attempt to survive.

Immersing himself in his responsibilities had the same effect it always did—he thought of nothing but the parchment in front of him, of the things that had to be done. His concentration was interrupted several hours later when Hunter trotted into the room. He settled at Alma's feet, looking up at Alma expectantly. "So you've returned, you traitorous dog. What, nothing to chew on in my house?"

Alma tossed the dog some tapir leather. Now that he had been distracted, his thoughts, as they usually did, turned to Sam. Since Hunter did not like to be alone, he wondered if Sam had gone out. He wondered what she was doing right then.

He wondered if she ever wondered about him.

* * *

Fabric merchants had arrived at the home that morning with bolts of heavy cotton cloth in every texture and color. Hannah selected the linen and cotton she wanted while Sam hung back.

"Aren't you going to pick out things for your sisters?" Hannah asked.

The merchants clamored around her, each asking her to feel how fine their material was. Overwhelmed, Sam couldn't choose anything. Fortunately Hannah stepped in. "She'll take one of each."

Such extravagance felt strange to Sam, but Hannah acted as if Sam's concerns over the cost were humorous. "Don't worry. My brother can afford it."

Running a piece of fine-twined yellow linen against her cheek, Sam felt her reluctance fade. Though accustomed to them, Sam knew her own clothes were coarse and itchy. She had never felt anything so soft. A sudden, desperate urge struck her. She had to have a dress of this material. She pondered for a moment whether that made her vain and shallow.

"One outfit wouldn't hurt," Sam murmured.

Hannah helped Sam make a dress for herself. Sam chose the yellow linen to make an under tunic. Sam and Hannah talked as they worked, fingers flying with bone needles to stitch up the edges of the tunic. When they finished, Sam took a length of bright blue, cutting out a hole in the middle to slip it over her head. She tied the outer garment with a belt to hold it in place.

Hannah clapped appreciatively and insisted they go to the market to find a necklace to match. Sam protested, but Hannah would not be denied.

That was how Sam found herself wandering through the animal section of the marketplace. She quickly became bored with Hannah's quest to find the perfect beads to make a necklace and promised to meet Hannah in an hour or so. Surely Hannah would be finished by then.

She heard loud yelling to her left and saw a merchant with a hand full of dust. A counterfeiter had tried to pass off dried clay cacao bean imitations as the real thing, and the merchant called for the guard to take the counterfeiter prisoner. The rest of the animal section was in a similar uproar. All around her, men inspected animals, looking at their teeth and tongues. Turkeys with bright iridescent wings gobbled loudly, fat peccaries grunted and squealed, playful coatis chittered in their cages. One man trying to bring a tapir under control ended up rolling around with it in the mud as spectators cheered him on.

As she turned a corner, Sam came upon a bird vendor. Some birds were in cages while others had thin ropes tied to their feet. One green parrot cocked his head to eye her. Sam whistled to the bird, and it whistled in reply. Delighted, Sam asked the merchant if the bird could speak.

"He speaks all right."

Puffing up the feathers on its chest, the parrot chose that moment to display his special talent and shouted out a profanity that left Sam unable to decide whether to gasp or to giggle.

"But he only says the one word."

The merchant offered to make Sam a good deal on the bird, but she gave him a firm no. The merchant kept lowering his price every time Sam refused.

"Look. Both you and that bird are wearing such pretty colors today."

Sam knew that voice. She didn't even bother to turn to look at him before she walked away. "Get away from me."

But Amulon followed closely behind. "Did Alma buy all his other women dresses in that color as well?"

That made Sam stop. "Other women? What are you talking about?" An overpowering wave of nausea coursed through her as she understood Amulon's implication. "I am Alma's only wife."

"Yes, you are the only one he bothered to actually marry. You must be very special for him to have finally given in. Some of his concubines have been trying to become his wife during the past year."

Amulon's predatory gaze, combined with the vile things he spewed out of his mouth, made Sam put her hand against a wall to steady herself. Mentally berating her weakness, she decided she would not show him fear. She didn't want to let what he said affect her.

But she couldn't help herself from asking, "Concubines?" Sam could barely get the word out. She made herself stop. This was Amulon talking. He and the truth were not well acquainted. "Alma does not have concubines," she said with more confidence than she felt.

Amulon gave her what on another person might have looked like a sympathetic smile but on him just looked evil and twisted. "Oh, I assure you he does. More than several of the other priests put together."

"Why are you telling me this?"

Amulon reached out and placed a hand on her shoulder. "I feel it's my duty. We were family at one time."

Sam jerked away from his touch, pushing at his arm. "We were not."

"I don't remember Miriam being this much of a harridan," Amulon said as he narrowed his eyes at her.

"Don't you dare say her name to me," Sam said through clenched teeth, willing her angry tears not to fall. "And don't you dare come anywhere near me and mine again."

Amulon made a tsk-ing sound. "Poor, poor Sam. Look at how upset you are. Did you really believe you mattered to him? That you were anything more than just a passing fancy? That he would never take another wife?"

"Alma would never—" Sam tried to say, but Amulon cut her words off.

"Oh, Alma certainly would. Why else would Alma tell King Noah that he planned to marry again?"

"I don't believe you."

Amulon smiled. "You don't have to believe me. Ask your husband."

Not able to respond, Sam left. She heard Amulon laughing as she pushed her way through the crowd, her tears blinding her.

How could Alma do this? How could he be so kind to her, hold her and kiss her the way he had last night, when he spent the rest of his time frequenting concubines? How could he act like he cared so much when in truth he cared so little?

And when had she become so jealous? Sam hated that she was jealous. She hated this proprietary feeling for Alma that she had no right to feel. He didn't belong to her, and despite what he might think, she certainly didn't belong to him. He didn't respect her. He didn't respect the vows he had made.

She had been right about Alma all along, and it broke her heart.

* * *

Alma didn't know what had changed.

But when he entered the dining room, he could tell from Sam's face that something had happened. The way she looked at him—she hadn't looked at him that way since their wedding day. A flash of fear gripped him.

"What is it?"

Sam said nothing, just staring at him with a mutinous expression.

"Whatever it is, you can tell me. We can work through it together."

"Together?" Sam exploded. "There is nothing we can do together. I want nothing to do with you. Nothing! Go back to your concubines."

"My what?" Alma's voice caught.

"You heard me. You're just like all the others. It makes me sick to think of you with a different woman every night, and then you want to come back here and kiss me and—"

Alma cut her off. "Who told you that?"

"Amulon."

"And you believed him?" he asked in an incredulous tone. Sam didn't respond. How could Sam believe Amulon? All he ever heard was how much she loathed Amulon, and yet she took Amulon's word over his own? This was the opinion she had of him. Despite all his efforts, all his sincerity, all his vulnerability to her, this was what she thought of him.

"Did you tell the king that you would marry again?"

Alma sensed the trap that Amulon had laid for him. He hoped Sam would let him explain. "Yes, but it isn't what you think. I had no choice."

"Just as you had no choice in keeping concubines?"

Something inside of Alma snapped. His arms reached out, grabbing her shoulders and pulling her tightly against him. In a harsh whisper he ground out, "There is no one else. I do not have any concubines. I have not touched any other woman. Every other woman in the world ceased to exist the moment I laid eyes on you."

CHAPTER TEN

Alma released her abruptly, causing Sam to almost lose her balance.

This time it was Alma who walked away, leaving Sam with the burning ferocity and truthfulness of his words. Sam immediately knew she had overreacted. She wrapped her arms around herself as she repeated what Alma said over and over in her mind.

There were no concubines. He had not been unfaithful to her. Alma had never lied to her. She knew he spoke the truth. She had been such a fool to listen to Amulon.

Seized with remorse over another one of her ill-timed outbursts, Sam couldn't let things be this way between them. She had to make amends. And not by cleaning or behaving better, but by apologizing.

She found Alma in his room. He hadn't lit any of his candles. In the dim light Sam could just make him out lying on his bed.

"Alma . . ."

"No more, Sam. No more accusations. There is no one else. And there never will be."

"Truly?"

"Truly."

Despite the weariness and defeated tone in Alma's voice, Sam felt an inexplicable happiness that seemed to make even her toes dance for joy. She decided that the only reason she was glad was because it meant she wasn't a poor judge of character. There was no other reason that this statement could possibly make her happy. None at all.

Not even managing to convince herself this time, Sam took a deep breath and walked further into his room.

"Do you believe me?" Alma asked quietly.

"Yes, I believe you. Please forgive me for my behavior earlier. It was inexcusable."

Alma's shadowy figure sat up, and he swung his legs over the edge of the bed. Sam felt rather than saw him looking at her. "Amulon can be persuasive when he wants to be. I'll make sure he doesn't bother you again."

Sam sat down on a stool next to Alma's washbasin. "Why does Amulon fear you?"

"Because I know something about him he doesn't want anyone else to know."

"What is that?"

"One night at a feast, Amulon got extremely drunk. Men have different reactions to being drunk. Some become louder, more boisterous. Some become more morose. Amulon apparently becomes talkative. He and I were alone, and he began to tell me about his past. When he was a young boy, Amulon's father did something that greatly displeased the king. His father was stripped of his lands, of his wealth. They lost everything. Disgraced, his father killed himself. Amulon somehow managed to claw his way back up to a position of respectability, but more than anything, Amulon fears a loss of power. He fears being poor. And since I know that, I think he views me as an enemy. I know how to hurt him."

"And you could do that? You have the ability to make his worst fears come true?"

Alma nodded. "I do."

"I wish you would." Sam said it and regretted it. She should be a better person. She should not wish for bad things to happen to Amulon. She knew it but sometimes couldn't help herself.

"Why do you hate Amulon so much?"

The darkness in which they sat wrapped around Sam like a comforting blanket. It gave her a feeling of anonymity, as if she could say anything and not worry about the consequences. She hadn't ever spoken of Miriam to anyone outside of her family. Her throat painfully closed in, and Sam had to swallow back a lump of emotion.

"My oldest sister, Miriam, was beautiful. More beautiful than I could ever hope to be."

"I very much doubt that."

That made Sam smile. That was just like Alma. To tease her away from an emotional collapse. To somehow manage with a simple phrase to give her the strength to go on.

"Men would stop in the streets to stare at her. Word of her beauty reached the palace, and the king demanded to see it for himself. Amulon was there. He was the king's favorite. He wanted Miriam. The king gave her to him."

She heard Alma's sharp intake of breath. "Like he did with you and me."

"With one major difference. Miriam was not a wife. She was Amulon's concubine. And she was happy about it." Sam had never spoken so disloyally about her eldest sister. Some part of her felt like she betrayed Miriam's memory, but it was the truth. It had bothered Sam then, and it bothered her now. "She loved the clothing, the food, the wealth, the attention from Amulon. And she loved him most of all."

Sam's voice faltered again, but she pressed on. "She loved him, and he couldn't be bothered with her. The things he would say to her, the way that he treated her, as if she were less than the dirt beneath his feet. She meant less than nothing to him. And Miriam lived for him."

She fell silent, the painful memories that had lain dormant for so long suddenly springing back to life.

"My sister . . . she became pregnant. I was with her when she went into labor. There was some sort of complication, but Miriam couldn't focus on anything but the fact that she wanted Amulon to be there. She called and called for him, begging us to bring him to her. But he was busy with . . . someone else. The midwife kept telling her to push. To struggle and fight, to bring her baby into this world. And Miriam wouldn't do it without him. She gave up. She died."

"And the child?"

Remembering Miriam's unborn child did make her eyes water, weakening her spirits to the point she feared not being able to continue. She didn't want to go on, but she felt like she owed it to Alma to finish the story.

"Never born. If it had been, I would have taken the baby and raised it myself."

"If it had been a son . . ." Alma's implication was clear. No man would allow a son to be taken from him.

"It would have made no difference to me," Sam said, finishing Alma's statement. "I would have kept him and run away to make sure that Amulon would have no hand in raising him, so that the baby wouldn't turn out to be like his father."

The anger she remembered feeling over Amulon's indifference flooded her veins as she recalled the way he repeatedly broke her sister's heart by taking concubine after concubine, how Miriam would have been rapturous with nothing more than a smile from him, wanting even the smallest acknowledgment that he noticed she existed, that she mattered to him. Taking a deep, shaky breath, Sam continued. "After Miriam died, all the life seemed to go out of my mother as well. As if Miriam couldn't bear to leave this world alone and had to take my mother with her."

"So Amulon caused the deaths of your sister and your mother."

No one had ever said that to Sam before. She believed no one in her family even thought it but her. They didn't blame Amulon for either death. Her father had repeatedly said that these things happened, death was a natural part of life. Many women died in childbirth. He said no one was at fault. But Sam was plagued by what-ifs. What if Amulon had come when Miriam needed him? Miriam would have lived. What if Miriam had lived? Her mother wouldn't have died. What if Amulon hadn't selfishly demanded Miriam as a concubine? Her mother and sister would be alive. For Sam, everything came back to the choices Amulon had made. His selfishness set off the chain of events that caused her to lose two of the most important people in her life.

"How . . . how did you do that?" she asked. "No one else has ever understood how I felt about this before."

Sam heard the wooden planks of the bed creak as Alma stood. He walked toward her, and every step he took made Sam's heart beat louder and faster. He reached down, taking Sam by the hands and pulled her to her feet. She felt his hands cupping her face, his thumb softly stroking her cheek.

"I understand because I love you."

Sam's knees threatened to give out in the same way they had the other night when he kissed her. "Love me? You don't even know me."

"I know you in ways that would surprise you. I know what makes you laugh, what makes you cry, what makes you hurl vases. I've seen your tenderness and kindness, your love for my sister and yours. I know you're too stubborn and strong willed for your own good. But I love your spirit and fire, I love your quick mind. I love your sweetness, your bitterness, your strengths, your weaknesses. There's no part of you that I don't love."

An entire flock of butterflies exploded into life in her stomach, and Sam feared she might actually faint. She held onto his arms to keep herself upright. "Alma . . ."

"Say it again," Alma whispered as he moved closer to Sam.

"What?"

"My name. Before tonight I don't think I've heard you say it."

In that moment Sam would have done anything he asked. She had lost all coherent thought. His nearness overwhelmed her. "Alma."

He was going to kiss her again. Sam knew it the way she knew that the sun would come up every morning. She didn't think to say no, to move, or protest. She wanted him to kiss her.

She thought she heard her own name being said, and the sound got closer and louder until she realized it was Lael. Lael was calling her name.

Lael burst into the room carrying a torch, followed by a clearly distressed Hannah.

Alma stepped away from her and asked, "What is it?"

"Sam," Lael said. Sam noticed the tearstains on her sister's face, and a dark dread filled her. Lael gulped before she said, "It's Father. You have to hurry."

* * *

Sam sent her sisters to stay with a cousin. She didn't want them to catch the illness that ravaged her poor father. She tried to send Alma away as well, but he refused.

Alma brought in a healer to listen to her father's blood. The healer put his fingers against her father's wrist on his right arm, then against his elbow. The healer did the same thing on the left side. He laid his head on her father's chest to check his heart and his breathing. He put a ground-up powder into a cup of water and gave it to Sam's father.

The healer then approached Alma. "He is too old and too ill. I have given him herbs to lessen his pain, but it will not be long."

"No." Sam stopped bathing her father's face in cool water to look at the other two men, her voice cracking. "No. He's going to be fine. He will get better. Tell us what to do to help him recover."

Ignoring Sam, the healer directed his instructions to Alma. "For pain take the roots, flowers, and leaves of the lobelia plant. They must be combined in a pot of boiling water. He will have to drink it at least twice a day for the next three days. For the fever you must give him a handful of leaves from a lace marigold that you boil in water. This he must also drink twice a day for three days. You can also let it cool and use the mixture to bathe his skin. In those three days you will know whether or not he will live. There is nothing else to be done but wait."

Sam heard Alma thank the healer. "You should go. You might get sick," she said once the healer left.

"I will go and get the plants your father needs. I will bring them back as fast as I can, even if I have to pick them myself. But you won't get rid of me. I'm staying with you."

When Alma returned with the supplies, he and Sam prepared the necessary medicines for her father. Sam administered them to her father per the healer's directions, but her father's pain and discomfort did not lessen. Sam sponged his skin with the marigold water, but it didn't make his fever fade. Her father alternated between moaning and total silence, his chest barely moving. Sam had to keep checking his pulse.

For two days Sam didn't eat, didn't sleep. She kept watch at her father's bedside, trying to get him to drink, silently praying for him to get better. Alma stayed there with her every moment. He did whatever he could to assist her, including helping Sam to hold down her father when he thrashed around.

"He's in so much pain," Sam said to Alma. Her exhaustion prevented her from spilling the tears she felt.

"He is." Alma reached over, taking Sam's hand in his own. "But I think he endures it for you and your sisters. He doesn't want to leave you."

Hours later when Alma had left to get more herbs, Sam prayed. At the beginning of her father's illness she had prayed for him to recover. But now she prayed for her father's pain to be stopped. A quiet, calming peace settled on her. If he was staying for her, she had to let him go. No one should have to suffer this way.

"Father," Sam said into his ear, hoping that he could still hear her. "I know Sams are fighters. I'm a fighter . . . you're a fighter. But you don't have to fight anymore. You don't have to stay. You can quit. You can run away to Mother. We will be all right."

Sam thought she saw the corners of her father's mouth rise up, almost into a smile. His breathing suddenly eased, his chest rising up and down in a smooth, fluid motion. He took deep, drawn-out breaths, pausing longer in between each new one until he finally paused and didn't breathe in again.

"Good-bye, Daddy."

* * *

When Alma returned, he found Sam crying hysterically while holding her father. Dropping the supplies he had brought with him, Alma pulled her arms free, tugging Sam to her feet.

"Alma, he's gone, he's gone," she wailed, and Alma hugged her tightly. The front of his tunic turned wet from her tears.

"We need to go home," he said. "You need to eat. To rest."

"But my father—I don't want him to be alone. It's so dark."

"I will have someone sit with him. He won't be alone."

She clung to the edges of his cloak as he guided her from her father's house. Sam stumbled while Alma supported her weight, keeping her upright.

"I can't believe he's gone."

"I know, I know," Alma said, wishing he had the right words that would convey how sorry he was, how he would do anything to make her feel better.

Sam stopped suddenly. "I have to tell my sisters. They don't know."

"You need to sleep. You haven't slept in almost three days. I'll tell your sisters."

"No, it should come from me." Sam swayed to the left, and Alma had to hold on tighter to her so she didn't fall. He turned her toward her, and he saw her eyes roll back into her head.

"Sam?" he asked. He repeated her name again. Frantically he yelled, "Sam!" He shook her, but there was no response. Her shoulders felt hot through her tunic. He put his hand against her forehead. She was burning up.

Alma put his arm under Sam's knees, swinging her up to carry her. While the thought of Sam catching the fever from her father had crossed his mind, he hadn't allowed himself to think of it as a possibility. Otherwise he might have physically prevented her from caring for her father. He knew how important it had been to her to be by her father's side. He would have felt the same way about his own father. But he couldn't lose her. She had to recover. Alma was almost overwhelmed with a sense of helplessness as he carried his unconscious wife. He could not make her better. No one could. As he raced through the streets and gardens in the city, all he could do was hope for a miracle.

CHAPTER ELEVEN

Alma paced the length of Sam's room. He hired more than a dozen different healers to come and administer to her. Strong cords of anxiety bound his heart, and Alma thought he might perish from it. This was too much. It was too hard to see Sam lying on her bed, her face pale and drawn, her skin clammy, the sweat matting her hair to her head.

But Alma couldn't tear himself away from her. The army of servants Sam had hired offered to care for their mistress in her illness, but Alma sent them all away. Sam was his wife. He didn't want to be anywhere else but by her side.

Sam moved restlessly from side to side, letting out low moans of pain. Alma whispered soothing words, pressing a rag soaked in herbal water to her forehead.

"Please take this from her. Let me have it in her stead. Let her be all right."

He didn't know whom he spoke to, only that his heart cried out the words, and Alma couldn't help but utter them. To his astonishment, he found himself routinely engaging in illegal prayers. The daykeeper priest had set the harvest festival for seven days from now. He could go to the temple then and pray for Sam. But it might be too late.

Alma had never been afraid of anything in his life. But now his fear consumed him, his terror that Sam might die making him unable to think about anything but her.

In the middle of the third night after Sam had fallen ill, Alma had an attack of panic when Sam suddenly became quiet. Rushing to her side, he saw that she finally slept peacefully. Her breathing sounded strong, and the color began to return to her face. When he laid his hand on her forehead, her skin felt cooler. With a sigh of relief, Alma knew Sam would live.

When Sam did wake up, Alma wondered how she would handle the news that he had buried her father during her illness. Surely she would understand that he couldn't wait, since the proper rituals had to be attended to.

After the funeral, Alma had begun to wonder where her father had gone. If Sam might join him there. He knew what the Lamanites thought of the next life, how the king thought little on it at all, how the scriptures the king had were silent on the subject. He supposed it made sense; the only way to truly understand the next life would be to die. But despite his lack of information, Alma was possessed with a burning desire to know what happened to a man's soul when he died.

A slight chill passed through Alma. His eyelids drooped, and he realized that he couldn't remember the last time he had eaten. Or slept. Sinking down onto the floor, he took one of the spare blankets at the foot of Sam's bed and wrapped it around himself. He lay down on the cold floor and felt himself passing from consciousness.

He was pulled from the netherworld of sleep by the sound of Hannah's voice saying his name.

"What?" he grumbled.

"You're sick. Let us help you to your room."

Alma tried to focus but found he couldn't. "I thought I sent you away and told you not to come back."

"And when was the last time I listened to you?"

"You always were a disobedient thing." Alma felt several hands helping him to his feet. A crush of people propelled him to his room, and Alma sank gratefully onto the bed. "I didn't want you to get ill."

"But it's all right for you to get sick?" Hannah asked as she pulled a blanket over Alma.

"Hannah, I had to be with her," Alma murmured.

"I know you did." Hannah kissed her older brother on his fore-head as he began to snore. "And I think Sam knows it too."

*　*　*

Sam awoke to find Hannah perched over her, staring down at her expectantly. "Feeling better?"

Sam's tongue felt fuzzy, like something had crawled into her mouth and died. She asked Hannah for some water, which Hannah gave her.

"Have you been here taking care of me the whole time?" Sam's voice sounded creaky and unused.

"No. Alma did that. He wouldn't let anyone else near you. He didn't want anyone getting sick."

"Where is he?"

"Sick," Hannah informed her with an exasperated tone. "But not as bad as you were. My brother is very strong. He wakes up, and he's still able to talk to us, which you couldn't do. I think he'll be over it soon."

"And what happened with my father?" Sam's voice only caught once. She missed her father desperately, but she knew what he would expect from her. After her mother's death, he had told them that while they would always miss her, their mother would want them to be happy. He took Sam aside and asked her to be an example for Lael and Kelila. At the time she had wondered if her father feared that the same sadness that overtook her mother might take them as well. Her father would want her to be strong. He would want her to endure. Even if she wanted to curl up in a ball and do nothing but cry. She could not let herself succumb to the sadness the way her mother had.

"Alma arranged the funeral and had your father buried here, near my mother's garden. Where our parents are buried."

"And my sisters? Are they still at my cousin's home?"

Hannah stood, holding a steaming bowl of water and several clean linen rags. "No, they're here. I went and got them, and we decided we were not going to let you and Alma make us stay away when you needed us. We're family, and family helps each other. You know, I always wanted sisters, and now I have three."

That made Sam smile. She did feel a twinge of concern, however, over the idea of Hannah and Kelila influencing each other. "Where are you going?"

"To give this to Alma."

"Let me." Sam sat up, pushing off her blankets. Her body still ached, but she wanted out of bed. "It's my turn to serve him."

Hannah tried to convince Sam to have a bath or to keep resting, but Sam got dressed, pulled a comb through her hair, and took Hannah's supplies.

Alma didn't look as sick as Sam feared he might. She knelt next to him, dipped the rag into the bowl, and dabbed the mixture on his face.

Alma opened his eyes and looked at her. "Am I dreaming?"

"No, you're not dreaming. It's the least I can do after the things you've done for me."

He smiled and closed his eyes until Sam asked him, "Why did you take in my sisters?"

"What sort of question is that?"

Sam put the rag back into the bowl and wrung out the excess. "We have kin that would have cared for them."

Alma reached up and took her by the wrist, stilling her movement. "You are my family. That makes them my family too." He released her hand. "I'm glad you're better. I was worried about you."

"I'm glad I'm better too. I can't imagine you trying to manage a house of the three silliest girls in Lehi-Nephi without me."

"I can't imagine anything without you."

Sam flushed a vivid red and put her rag back into the water to avoid looking at him. When she raised her head, she saw that Alma had fallen asleep again.

The rapid beating of her heart caused by being near him bothered her. She didn't want to be attracted to him. Or like him. Or care about him.

But even she had to admit that Alma was not Amulon. He had proven that time and again. It wasn't fair to treat him so coldly after all the wonderful things he had done for her. For her family. Their family.

The thought that Alma had become a part of her family, that he had become important to her, absolutely terrified her. She would not be Miriam. She could not let any man have that kind of control over her heart. But how could she stop how she felt?

* * *

Amulon dipped pieces of fruit into honey, being careful not to let any of it drip on his expensive clothing. He licked his fingers, wanting to enjoy every sweet drop.

King Noah was in a foul mood, one so dark he had even kicked his favorite hunting dog. Work on several building projects had ceased altogether with the disappearance of Alma. The trade supplies had not been collected properly. No one made sure that the king had all his favorite treats, and perhaps the gravest sin of all—the wine production had tapered off. Amulon had heard from the servant he bribed in Alma's household that both Alma and Sam had fallen sick. While disappointed that Alma had not managed to die on his own, Amulon did appreciate the havoc his involuntary absence created.

Finishing with his snack, Amulon slithered his way across the throne room until he sat at the king's feet. Although King Noah had not specifically mentioned Alma by name in his rants about everyone's ineptitude, they all knew who the king was angriest with.

"Where is Alma? He hasn't been to court in days. You need him, and he's not here to fulfill your wishes." His voice the very picture of innocence and concern, Amulon hoped it would fool the king. Although Amulon took a dangerous risk in posing his question, the gamble was worth it.

Amulon saw that his risk paid off when the king grunted, "His scribe said he was ill."

"That's convenient."

The king looked perplexed, as if he had never considered the possibility that Alma might not be sick. That Alma actually was ill made no difference to Amulon's plan. He only needed the king to believe that Alma might not be.

"If my king will forgive my boldness, I have had some concerns over Alma's changing feelings."

"What do you mean by that?"

Amulon knew he would have to be careful how he handled this. "I fear that Alma's affections have turned from you. He loves his wife more than he loves you," Amulon said with disgust in his voice that anyone would choose a mere woman over the king. "He is in your debt. If it were not for you, Alma wouldn't have even married that girl. And how does he show his gratitude? By neglecting you?"

King Noah seemed to be mulling Amulon's words over. "I cannot believe that Alma would do such a thing."

"I have it seen it myself. He is her lap dog. Alma cares for nothing but her whims."

Amulon had always possessed a gift for intuiting other people's feelings, reading their expressions, divining their thoughts. Now he sensed a great anger brewing within the king at Alma's apparent defection. The king wanted to be first in the people's hearts. And he especially expected total loyalty and devotion from his high priests.

Seeing that the time had come to retreat before the king kicked him too, Amulon gave an exaggerated sigh of concern. "I only fear that Alma will forget himself completely, that this distraction in his life will always be a stumbling block for him. I am afraid that when it matters, Alma will not choose you."

* * *

Sam awoke the morning of the harvest festival full of hope, and with an excitement that she would get to see Alma again that night. Although still weakened by his illness, Alma had to leave to participate in a fast before the celebration, to prepare for the religious rites he would see to and lead the people in. His preparation included his having to leave home to stay with the other high priests in a communal house near the temple. He had only been gone for two days, but Sam missed him.

With the help of her servants and her sisters, Sam finished all the necessary tasks to prepare their home for the festival. Hannah insisted that they all dress in their new, best clothes for the celebration. When Sam found herself wondering whether Alma would like her green tunic, she told herself to stop. She wore this for herself. Not for Alma. Besides, it didn't matter what Alma thought of her. That didn't prevent her from putting on his mother's earrings and bracelets, though.

The celebration began at twilight. Sam took the girls to the plaza between the temple and the palace, where her own marriage had taken place. The ceremonial dancing had already begun. A group of men performed the tale of their history, as a narrator explained the story aloud. The dancers told of their ancestors returning to the land, of their people taking back the lands of their forebears. The tale was necessary for those couldn't read, so that they would all remember. It puzzled Sam, though, that there was no mention of King Zeniff or of God. Why would anyone excise those important pieces from the story?

Before she could voice her question, her sisters tugged her toward the food merchants to sample their wares. They were engulfed in the crowd, surrounded by the mouthwatering smells of the feast being prepared, the sounds of music and laughter, the bright lights of fires burning all around them.

His duties apparently done, Alma joined them next to a spit where a large green iguana roasted. Hannah had made a comment about the striking resemblance between the man turning the spit and the iguana that made Sam laugh. She immediately covered her mouth. Her father had just died. She shouldn't be laughing.

Alma came up next to her and whispered, "You will always miss your father. You should mourn him. But life is for the living. You shouldn't be afraid to be happy again."

How did Alma do that? How did he know her feelings, the words in her mind? Sam felt exposed, worried that Alma could read all of her thoughts. Closing her mind off, she turned to face him. Her breath caught when she realized just how much she had missed him.

"Sam, listen! They're playing a dance for us!" Kelila grabbed Sam's arm and pulled her into the dance that only women performed, asking for another season of fertility for their crops and for themselves. Sam couldn't help but look over her shoulder to see Alma staring after her, his dark eyes unreadable.

When the dance ended, the musicians ceased playing to allow people a chance to rest. Out of breath, Sam sat down. She didn't feel completely recovered from her sickness. Sam caught a glimpse of the king, strutting about like a multicolored turkey. He had put on a special headdress that held a wooden framework shaped in the face of a jaguar. Quetzal feathers and jade carvings decorated the outer edges of the framework. Sam had the urge to giggle at how desperately King Noah tried to copy the style of the Lamanites.

Sam used Lael's newly purchased feather fan to cool herself off. The music started again, the drums thudding lowly, the bone and gourd rattles shaking to the beat, the clay and wood flutes playing a merry melody. Sam recognized the tune as one of the few dances that men and women could dance together. Alma appeared, pulling Sam to her feet and into the dance despite her laughing protests that she was too tired.

Hundreds of dancers twisted and turned, the women whirling in skirts all the colors of the rainbow. They all moved in one accord, not one person missing a step. Alma grabbed her hands to twirl her around, and Sam threw her head back to laugh, reveling in this perfect moment.

When the dance ended and both she and Alma were out of breath, he said to her, "You seem to be enjoying yourself."

"I am. I could stay here all night." The sound of someone vomiting behind her made her turn to see Hannah emptying the contents of her stomach onto the stone plaza. "Or until Hannah throws up."

"I'm fine," Hannah protested as Alma decided they should go home. "I'm not sick. I don't have your fever. I just wanted to try a little bit of everything, and I had too much to eat. I'm fine now. We should stay."

Sam noticed how tired Kelila and Lael appeared, and she seconded Alma's decision to leave the festival.

As they walked back to their home, Sam noticed a large group gathering on the south edge of the plaza, near the temple. She wondered for a moment what was going on before Alma's laughter returned her attention to Kelila's recounting of all the things Hannah had eaten that night.

* * *

The old man disguised himself before entering the city, putting his cloak over his head so that he wouldn't be recognized. He came at night, into the center of the city where the fallen people gathered in a celebration of the harvest, neglecting to thank their God for their bounty.

He saw King Noah sitting on a makeshift throne at the foot of the temple, saw how the people called out his praises. He knew how they supported the king in his wickedness, how they had turned their hearts from their God.

He had come among them once before to tell them of their need to repent. His exile had been their answer. Now he came to offer them a last chance, one he already knew they would not accept.

His message was not for the people. It was for their king, their priests, those personally responsible for leading the people to sin.

He had no hope of securing an audience before the king by going to the palace himself. The guards would cut him down before he got close enough. King Noah had told him that if he returned, his punishment would be death.

But he did not fear the king, nor did he fear death. He only needed to deliver the Lord's message.

Climbing the steps to the plaza, the old man threw off his blanket and began to cry repentance to them. He revealed his mission to them, his purpose in being there. He deliberately revealed his identity and heard the gasps of shock and outrage. Perhaps because of their shock they allowed him to continue. He prophesied of the king's death. He prophesied of the afflictions—famine, pestilence, labor, hail—that would visit this people if they would not turn back to the true faith.

They did not listen. He knew they would not. People threw things at him, yelled curses at him, but he continued on. He felt no anger, no animosity for them. Only a deep pity. They had been horribly deceived.

The people pressed around him, taking him captive as he had hoped they would. They would safely deliver him to the king. They would demand his trial. He would get his chance to deliver his message.

Despite the man's age, the people who took him threw him on the stone ground before King Noah. When the old man stood, he saw anxiety in his former student's eyes. King Noah knew the iniquities he committed and did not like to be reminded of them.

The old man inclined his head at the king. "Noah."

Noah bared his teeth like a cornered wild animal. "Abinadi."

CHAPTER TWELVE

Alma took Sam and the girls home but then excused himself, explaining that there were still some ceremonial duties that he had to attend to back at the priests' communal house. He watched Sam's expression change from happy to furious after his announcement. He knew that Sam was bothered by his religious practices, but he couldn't deny the truth just to please her. He still had his responsibilities.

When he returned home later that night, he checked on Hannah to make sure she was feeling better, and his sister was sleeping soundly. As were Kelila and Lael, who, despite the fact that he had many rooms in his house, had chosen to share a room with Hannah.

Alma walked through the back courtyard to clear his mind, to think about how he should approach Sam about the differences in their beliefs. He had come far in his relationship with her. There had to be a way to convince her, a way to show her the right path. He didn't want this to come between them.

Having always found his mother's garden to be a place of refuge, Alma went there. He saw Sam sitting on his favorite stone bench, looking up at the garden. She ran her hands up and down her arms, shivering in the cool mountain air. Alma darted back to Hannah's room, retrieved a shawl from Hannah's chest, and brought it out to Sam.

When he wrapped the shawl around her, Sam looked up at him and gave him a half-smile. "This is just like you. Always thinking of me."

"I do always think of you. In fact, I find it hard to think of much else."

Sam looked away from him, pulling the shawl tightly across her arms. Alma sat on the bench next to her. "You had a good time tonight, didn't you?"

Still looking away Sam said, "I did."

"I'm not so terrible, am I?"

"No, you're not."

Since she was in such an agreeable mood, Alma pressed on. "And I'm devastatingly handsome, aren't I?"

That finally got her to turn to him and give him a real smile. "I suppose you're not horrible to look at."

"Then what is the problem between us?"

Sam stood, walking toward the garden and away from Alma. He stayed where he was, folding his hands in his lap.

He never knew what to expect from Sam, never knew what she might say or do. She continually surprised him and now was no different.

"Did you know the king threatened to put my father in prison for tax debt if I didn't marry you?"

Alma felt like someone had punched him. "I didn't know that."

"I know you didn't. But it made me angry with you when I thought you were a part of it. I thought you were like them. Like Amulon."

"I'm not like Amulon."

Sam didn't answer. Strands of her hair blew in the breeze, like the silk of corn ready to be harvested. Alma stood and walked over to where she rested against the trunk of an oak tree. Lianas wrapped themselves in the upper branches, covered in pale pink orchids. Alma picked one, tucking it in Sam's hair, above her ear. She moved away from his touch, giving an uneasy laugh.

"I never thought I would be mistress of a garden like this. Or a home like this. So much so that I feel like I'm living someone else's life. Like this is all pretend. As if none of it matters."

Alma stepped behind her so that they were almost touching. "Then let's pretend for one night. Pretend you are mistress of this home. Pretend you are happy here. Pretend . . ." Alma put his hands on Sam's shoulders to turn her around so that she faced him. "Pretend that you love me."

Then he kissed her again, but this time it was very different. Where their first kiss had been based on need and hunger, this one was filled with an indescribable softness, tenderness . . . love.

"No," Sam said, breaking off the kiss.

"Sam?"

She put the back of her hand to her mouth. "You're not like Amulon. You're worse."

"What?"

"Amulon only wanted me for one night. You have taken every night of the rest of my life."

Sam said the words without reproach, without emotion. Her words were cold and calm.

"I . . . I . . ." Alma sputtered, nearly unable to think, "I saved you from him."

"You didn't save me just to save me. You stopped Amulon because you wanted me for yourself."

The pain in his chest was so intense because what she said was true. Alma had no other explanation for his motivation that night. She was right.

"You were not being noble. You didn't want to save me from my horrible fate."

"But I did save you. That should at least count for something."

"How many other girls did you fail to save that night and every night since then?"

Sam left in a whisper of skirts and vanilla fragrance that left Alma reeling. Her anger he could have dealt with. That he understood.

But the indifference in her voice, the lack of any kind of emotion—that scared him more than anything else.

How could he feel so much and she so little? Why after everything he had done, the way he had opened his heart to her, professed his love, cared for her and her family—why did she still think of him as nothing more than her jailer?

Why did he suddenly feel like one?

* * *

"I'm not even going to ask."

Alma didn't slow down as he caught Helam in yet another place he shouldn't be. "I was looking for you!" his scribe protested.

"And you thought you'd find me in Lib's rooms?"

Helam ran to catch up with Alma's quick pace. "I really was looking for you. The king has summoned all the priests to a council."

"Why?" Alma turned a corner to enter the library and stopped short, causing Helam to bump into him.

The other eleven priests were in the library, talking to one another as they went through ancient texts. It surprised Alma to see them there doing something that actually looked like work. "Why are you all here?"

"Haven't you heard?" Teomner asked, putting his finger on the spot he had been reading. "There's going to be a trial of a man claiming to be a prophet. We are finding scriptures to refute his statements." Turning back to his fellow priests, Teomner asked, "Shouldn't we get the original . . ."

Orihah made a motion with his hand, and Teomner fell silent, returning to his reading.

"Get the original what?" Alma asked.

"It is none of your concern," one of the more senior high priests told him, causing the room to go completely silent.

Everywhere Alma looked he saw nothing but a sea of hostile glares. The other priests had been cold to him at the communal house where they fasted to prepare for the festival. Alma had assumed it was the lack of food that had made them all cranky. Now he saw that their anger continued and that it was directed specifically at him.

"What crimes does the man stand accused of?"

"He preaches treason and sedition," Teomner said, making Alma feel relieved that at least someone would still speak to him. "The people call out for his death. The king exiled the man two years ago for the same crimes and ordered his execution if he returned. He was foolish to return and even more foolish to reveal his name to the people. The king's command should be carried out easily enough. You know the penalty for false prophesying under the Law of Moses."

Alma did. The penalty was death.

One of the king's guards entered the room to tell the priests they were expected in the throne room.

Still talking amongst themselves and showing one another scriptures, the high priests filed out of the room. Amulon was the last to leave, and he gave Alma a smug, superior smile that made Alma worry. Amulon would not look like that unless he had done something horrible to someone else. Considering the shambles his own life was in, Alma wondered if he had been the unwitting target.

A servant entered the room, bowed to Alma, and then whispered something in Helam's ear. Helam looked stricken and said to Alma, "There is an emergency at home. I must go. I won't be able to take notes for you."

"Go home," Alma said, clasping his scribe on the shoulder. "I will take my own notes."

After Helam left, Alma fell into line behind Amulon and followed the other priests to the throne room. King Noah sat on his throne in his most expensive finery, his headdress adding another two feet to his height. The throne room was filled with courtiers, lawyers, some women from the king's harem, and those who clung to the palace life for their own support.

"There he is," Teomner said, pointing to a man across the room, sitting on the ground. "Abinadi."

Sitting upon his seat on the dais, Alma studied the false prophet. This Abinadi was much older than Alma would have expected, his heavy tan indicating that he was someone who spent most of his time outside. Alma had heard tales of this man's first visit to Lehi-Nephi, and he wondered what would make him come back to certain death. What intrigued Alma the most was that where another man might have been trembling or scared or begging for his life, Abinadi sat quietly, a certain kind of confidence radiating from him that one would not have expected considering his circumstances.

Abinadi turned and made eye contact with Alma, startling him. Alma's heart started to beat faster as Abinadi watched him. Alma felt exposed, as if this man could see every sin Alma had ever committed. He felt grateful when the man turned his gaze to someone else.

Amulon stood and called out to King Noah, "With your permission my king, we would ask that you bring him forward that we may question him."

The king commanded two of his guards to bring the prisoner to stand before the priests. The interrogation began, each of the priests asking Abinadi leading questions designed to catch him in a trap so that they could properly accuse him of having broken the law. Alma admired the way Abinadi boldly answered their questions, how he avoided each and every snare laid for him. Abinadi managed to confound even the most verbose of the priests.

Someone asked, "Do you deny that you proclaim yourself to be a prophet?"

"I do not deny it."

Orihah then stood and asked Abinadi the meaning of a passage from Isaiah, wherein Isaiah had proclaimed that true prophets brought forth peace and good tidings. Orihah's plan, of course, was that one such as Abinadi, who had prophesied of the king's and the people's destruction, could not be a prophet according to Isaiah's words.

An incredulous look took hold of Abinadi's features. "Are you priests, and pretend to teach this people, and to understand the spirit of prophesying, and yet desire to know of me what these things mean?"

Abinadi condemned the priests, saying they had perverted the ways of the Lord, that they did not apply their hearts to understanding, saying they had not been wise. Every word of Abinadi's attack felt personal, as if he spoke directly to Alma. Abinadi then asked, "What do you teach this people?"

"We teach the Law of Moses," Amulon snapped back.

Just as quickly, Abinadi replied, "If you teach the Law of Moses, why do you not keep it? Why do you set your hearts upon riches? Why do you commit whoredoms and spend your strength with harlots and cause this people to commit sin, that the Lord has cause to send me to prophesy against this people?"

How could Abinadi know that? He supposed the corruption, dishonesty, and carnal natures of the priests would be apparent to anyone who cared to look, but Abinadi spoke of their sins as if he knew them. As if the Lord he spoke of knew them. A strange sinking sensation filled Alma's stomach.

"You know I speak the truth, and you ought to tremble before God."

Alma did tremble. *He's talking about me,* Alma thought. He wondered if any of the other priests felt the same since no one spoke, and Abinadi was allowed to continue.

"You will be smitten for your iniquities, for you have said that you teach the Law of Moses. And what do you know concerning the Law of Moses? Does salvation come by the Law of Moses?"

"Of course it does," Teomner said.

Why would Abinadi ask such a thing? Unless . . . unless salvation didn't come from the Law of Moses. Alma gripped the breastwork in front of him tightly, leaning in to hear what Abinadi would say.

Abinadi instructed them that all of the commandments of God must be kept, along with the ones delivered to Moses on Mount Sinai. Abinadi quoted to them the first of the Ten Commandments saying, "Thou shalt have no other God before me. Thou shalt not make unto thee any graven image, or any likeness of any thing in heaven above, or things which are in the earth beneath." Having finished his recitation, Abinadi continued. "Have you done all this? No, you have not. And have you taught this people that they should do all these things? No, you have not."

King Noah suddenly stood, banging his fists on the arms of his throne. "Enough! Take him away and slay him. We will not listen to this anymore. He is mad!"

Several guards stepped forward to obey the king's command, but before they could reach the prisoner, Abinadi yelled with a voice of thunder, "Touch me not!"

The very walls seemed to shake from the power of his statement, the reverberation in his voice filling all of Alma's senses. "God will smite you if you lay your hands on me, for I have not delivered the message which the Lord sent me to deliver."

Alma looked at Abinadi and saw what had every person in the room cowering. Abinadi's face shone with a brightness and intensity that rendered Alma speechless. This man, this prophet—he did speak for God. Only someone with the power of God in them could appear so.

The guards sent to restrain him fled the room. Abinadi continued to speak and then said, "I perceive that it cuts you to your hearts because I tell you the truth concerning your iniquities." Abinadi turned to look at Alma. "My words fill you with wonder and amazement, and with anger."

Alma wanted to shrink away. He didn't want Abinadi to look at him. He felt like the prophet could scorch him with only a glance.

Abinadi delivered his message powerfully. No one dared to interrupt him, his face shining and lighting up even the dark corners in the room. Abinadi told them that what they chose to do to him would be a type and shadow of things to come. Before Alma could puzzle out what this statement meant, Abinadi recited all of the Ten Commandments to them. He said that the Law of Moses was not enough for salvation, that the law was given because the people needed a strict set of rules because of their iniquities. He told the priests they didn't understand the law because the only way a man could be saved was through the redemption of God.

Abinadi spoke of the Messiah, a term Alma had never heard before. Abinadi spoke of the words of the prophets, saying, "Have they not said that God himself should come down among the children of men, and take upon him the form of man, and go forth in mighty power upon the face of the earth?"

A collective gasp went through the throne room. It was total heresy to suggest that God would come and live among them, as a mortal. But Alma found that he believed Abinadi. It didn't make sense, it went against everything he had ever been taught, but this was truth. Alma knew it in a way that he could never have explained to anyone else. He knew it was true. He knew it.

Abinadi recited scripture from Isaiah from memory. He spoke of a Father and a Son. He spoke of redemption from sin, of listening to the words of the ancient prophets. He spoke of a Christ, a Savior, and Alma wanted to weep from the beauty of Abinadi's words.

"He was a high priest for King Zeniff," Teomner said next to him in a whisper Alma could barely hear.

"How do you know that?"

"How else could he quote scripture at us? The only scriptures are here in the palace. That man is no commoner."

But Abinadi spoke of scriptures, of prophecies that Alma had never heard of. Like the verse in the books of Moses said, Alma had not had a heart to perceive, eyes to see, ears to hear until this day. Alma felt mesmerized. He couldn't stop listening, taking all of Abinadi's words in until they seared themselves on his very soul. An earthquake could have tumbled down the walls around him and he would have been rooted to this spot, just listening.

Next to the joy Alma felt as Abinadi taught of this Christ, he also had crippling pain over his own sins, the mistakes he had made. But still, he wanted to learn more. He wanted Abinadi to talk forever.

"And now, ought you not to tremble and repent of your sins, and remember that only in and through Christ you can be saved? Therefore, if you teach the Law of Moses, also teach that it is a shadow of those things which are to come—Teach them that redemption comes through Christ the Lord, who is the very Eternal Father. Amen."

With that, Abinadi sealed his words against them. The light left Abinadi, and he collapsed to the floor.

King Noah, red faced and visibly shaking, ordered the priests to take Abinadi and put him to death.

Several priests stood to obey the king's command and Alma whispered, "No." It was inaudible in the noisy throne room where the people agreed with the king's decision. He watched as the priests put their hands on Abinadi, roughly pulling him up and out of the throne room.

Abinadi could not be killed. God would condemn them for putting a righteous, innocent man to death. His blood would be on their hands. On Alma's hands. He had to stop it.

"No!"

CHAPTER THIRTEEN

Amulon let his head loll back behind him, looking up at the ceiling. The entire proceeding made him immensely bored. Abinadi was no threat to them. The people themselves were the ones who brought him to the king. They obviously didn't believe him, and so had no plans of following him. He didn't understand why the king seemed to fear this Abinadi so much.

He started watching other people, tuning out Abinadi's lecture, which just seemed to go on and on. Amulon wanted to tell him to be quiet but figured it better to let the man hang himself with his words. Amulon watched the other priests and saw Alma's reaction to this madman. Why, Alma believed Abinadi! Amulon had to hold back a laugh at the pathetic look of trust and wonderment on Alma's face. How could he best use this to his advantage?

The answer again presented itself, as it always did for him, right after Abinadi finally tired of his own rhetoric and fell down. The king had some of the priests escort Abinadi from the room, and after they left, Alma stood up and yelled, "No!" Everyone went silent. Amulon grinned. At last.

Alma left the dais, hurrying over to the king's throne. Alma almost bumped into Prince Limhi and two royal guards, who had just entered the throne room. Stepping around the prince and the guards, Alma knelt at the king's feet. "Please, my king. This man has committed no crime. He does not deserve death. I beg you to show mercy, to spare his life. Please let him depart in peace. Return him to exile."

Amulon watched as a vein on the king's forehead popped out. Having been the recipient of the king's temper on more than one occasion, Amulon knew what was coming next.

The king did not disappoint. In a deadly voice laced with a simmering fury the king said, "After all that I've done for you, the favors I've granted you, the affection and gifts I showered on you, this is how you repay me? You question me? Defy me? Take up this traitor's cause?"

"I did not mean to—"

"Alma, you are hereby stripped of your lands, of your homes, your wealth, your title. You are sentenced to exile. Cast this betrayer out."

The guards still gone, several of the king's servants stepped forward to grab Alma by the arms and drag him from the throne room. Alma still called over his shoulder, begging the king not for a return of his material possessions as Amulon would have done had it been him, but for the release of Abinadi.

After Alma had been removed, Amulon made his way over to the still furious king. With an exaggerated sigh, he said, "It is as I feared."

"It is worse," the king retorted, gripping the arms of his throne.

"His disloyalty, his total ingratitude to you . . . how could Alma choose a lying, false prophet over his own king?"

King Noah gripped the arms of the throne even tighter. Amulon had to hide his smile.

"I hope you will forgive my impudence, but didn't we have evidence today of what happened the last time you exiled someone? Alma shouldn't be exiled. He should be put to death."

The king paused only for a moment before looking up at Amulon. "Make it so."

* * *

Alma walked away from the palace, his mind spinning with thoughts and darting back and forth between the two major problems he now faced. What would he tell Sam? How could he save Abinadi? What would they do with no income, no way to support themselves? How could he convince the king to change his mind about the prophet?

He went down the steps of the center plaza and stopped when he heard a shout behind him. Alma saw servants of the king running toward him. He quickly assessed his situation. They had already escorted him from the palace, reiterating the king's orders that he was to leave the city at once. Why would they be coming after him now? Unless the king had somehow altered his orders and Alma was not to be exiled. And the only thing worse than exile was . . .

Alma ran. His decision was made so quickly, Alma hardly understood it. He should go back to the palace. Surely the king would never put him to death. He had been too beloved for such an end. He should stay here and convince the king to let Abinadi go. Alma began to slow his escape, deciding to let himself be caught.

You have to run. Now. Abinadi will die and the king will kill you.

The voice sounded so sharp, so clear that Alma looked around him to see who had spoken. The words rocked him to his core, pushed him forward, and Alma ran on. He heard the servants behind him yelling at him to stop, yelling at the startled citizens to grab him. No one did.

Fortunately the servants did not have the same physical stamina that the king's guards did, and Alma quickly outpaced them. He headed toward the back wall of the city. *What if the king did plan on killing me?* Abinadi's words would be lost. No one would ever hear them. He couldn't let that happen.

Seized with an overwhelming desire to live, to record all of Abinadi's words, Alma raced along even faster.

He thought of his family, of Sam. He thought of what the king might do to them, and Alma stopped. He couldn't let them be hurt.

The voice, the same one he had heard earlier spoke to him again. *They will be kept safe. Run!*

Alma didn't know why he believed the voice so entirely, but he absolutely knew his family would be safe. If he did go back, if the king's servants found him in his home, King Noah might think his family complicit in Alma's actions. But if he left the city, the king might focus all his efforts on finding Alma and leave them alone. His only hope to keep them safe was to stay away from them.

His heart pounded in his chest as he reached the back wall of the city, his breathing labored and heavy from running so far so fast. He would take the back pass out. He had to get clear of Lehi-Nephi, and then he would decide what to do next.

Alma flew along the nearly empty streets along the back side of the city. He could see the pass. Nearly there, just a bit further. *Oh no.*

His steps faltered when he saw Prince Limhi standing near the pass with one of the royal guard captains. A man named Gideon. Gideon was a large, powerful man. Alma could not escape. The two approached him. They both breathed heavily, as if they had run hard to get there first. Alma swallowed. This was it. He would die, and Abinadi's teachings would be lost.

Gideon withdrew his sword and Alma expected the captain to kill him. Alma braced himself for the blow. Instead, Gideon handed the sword to Alma along with a water skin and pack of food. "Once you get out of the city, there is a secret pass just east of here that will take you through the Land of Shilom. It will lead you into the wilderness. Using it will make it harder for the king to find you."

His mouth gaping open with shock, Alma finally asked, "Why are you doing this?"

"Because you are one of the most honest, hardworking men I know," Limhi said. "My father is wrong. You do not deserve to die because of his whims or because he is foolish enough to take the advice of evil men like Amulon."

"And I am doing it because we are family," Gideon told him, pushing him toward the pass. Family? Alma had worked alongside Gideon for almost two years and never knew of the connection. How could they be family unless . . . Sam. He had to be related to Sam. His thoughts were broken by Gideon adding, "It is also a delightful bonus that it will upset Amulon and the king so much to have you escape."

Limhi gave Gideon a warning look, which did not seem to subdue Gideon in the least. "Sam—" Alma started.

"I will find her and take her home with me. I will keep her safe for you," Gideon promised. "You don't have much time. The king will call the guards next and they will find you. You have to hide."

Still Alma hesitated. How could he leave? Everything that truly mattered to him lay within these city's walls.

At Gideon's urging Alma finally fled, feeling as though he left the best parts of himself behind.

* * *

Sam went through the motions of her daily activities like someone only partially awake. An all-encompassing numbness made her limbs feel heavy. Even walking a few feet took great effort.

She was so ashamed of the way she had treated Alma the previous night. Why couldn't she ever just say what she meant? What she felt?

It had begun because she had so thoroughly enjoyed herself at the festival. Even she had to admit that she had started to think of Alma differently. But she had let herself forget what Alma believed, what he taught the people. When Alma had mentioned his unfinished religious responsibilities, some fury inside her had roared to life.

She tried to clear her head by sitting in his mother's garden, but Alma had found her there. He was wonderful, as he always was. He made her smile, made her feel beautiful and amazing and a thousand other things. Then he had kissed her, a kiss so gentle and loving that Sam wanted to cry.

Sam realized that she could love Alma. That she might already be in love with him.

She stopped their kiss, unable to cope with her newly discovered feelings. She couldn't love him. Miriam had loved Amulon, and it had destroyed her. So Sam said things to Alma to hurt him, things to push him away. She knew her behavior didn't make any sense. She should have been honest with him, let him know her true feelings and how they had changed. Alma would have been ecstatic.

But instead she had lashed out at him, like a spoiled child breaking a toy before it could be taken from her. She didn't want to love him. If she gave herself over to it, she would be as lost as Miriam had been.

A sudden panic struck Sam, causing her to lean against the wall to stay upright. Her heart beat too quickly, her legs feeling too wobbly to stand. Something was wrong. Very, very wrong.

Something was wrong with Alma.

A sense of impending doom, of total dread and despair, made it so Sam couldn't breathe. Something was going to happen. She didn't know what, but she did know she had to get out of the house.

Pushing away from the wall Sam ran through the house, calling for her sisters and Hannah. Running through the back courtyard, Sam found the girls sitting together, giggling and weaving on back-strap looms.

"We have to leave. Right now. Get up." Sam started untying the strap on Hannah's waist.

"What are you talking about?" Kelila asked as Sam undid the tie on Kelila as well. Lael took her own strap off.

Sam pushed and pulled the girls to their feet, all of them asking her questions. She didn't have time for this. Ignoring their protests, Sam forced them toward the back of the house. They had just entered the rear garden when Sam heard a crash and raised voices in the front of the house. "We are here to arrest everyone in this house in the name of the king!" someone yelled.

"Run!" Sam whispered to the girls. The foursome got through the garden and burst out onto the street. Sam ran away from the center of the city, repeatedly checking over her shoulder to make sure they weren't being followed. They ran through gardens, along back streets and alleys, keeping away from any main streets. They entered the section of the city inhabited by their relatives, and Sam finally let them stop. Kelila collapsed to the ground, and Hannah fell down next to her, while Lael carefully knelt down. Sam couldn't rest, too anxious to hold still.

"Why are those men after us?" Hannah asked.

Sam shook her head. "I don't know."

"What do we do now?" Lael asked, her eyes brimming with tears.

"We have to find some place safe to go. Some place the king's men wouldn't think to look." Sam knew they couldn't go back to the home Alma had built for her father, and they obviously couldn't return to Alma's house. They would have to find one of their relatives to stay with, someone who wouldn't turn them over to the king. She knew of only one person she could trust completely when it came to defying the king.

"Gideon," Sam said. "Come on, get up. We'll go stay with Gideon."

"Who is Gideon?" Hannah asked as they stood up and followed Sam.

Sam peered around the corner of an alley to make certain they were alone before gesturing the girls out to the street. "He is our cousin."

"Why do you think we'll be safe with him?"

"Oh, Gideon completely hates the king," Kelila said before Lael nudged her.

"What? He does? Why?" Hannah asked. Hannah was getting as bad as Kelila with all her questions. They tried to walk down the street calmly, so as to not draw attention to themselves. But even Sam was having a hard time not shaking from fear.

"Gideon was betrothed to our oldest sister, Miriam. The king gave Miriam to one of his priests, Amulon, as a concubine. She died in childbirth." Sam found that talking helped her feel calmer. "Gideon always blamed Miriam's defection and death on the king."

"Talking about me?"

Hannah screamed when a man in a soldier's uniform came up behind them. Kelila put her hand over Hannah's mouth.

"Sorry," Kelila said. "I guess we forgot to mention Gideon is a captain in the king's royal guard."

"This way," Gideon said, taking the lead.

"He hates the king but serves in the guard?" Sam heard Hannah ask.

"He believes in keeping his enemies close," Kelila replied before Sam gave her a look, telling her to be quiet.

"How did you know we needed help?" Sam asked Gideon, feeling a bit more secure now that they were with him. He would keep them safe.

"Alma said—"

Sam cut him off. "You saw Alma? What happened?"

Gideon held his arm out, indicating he wanted the women to stop. He backed up and cut through a fruit orchard, leaving the street. "There was a trial for a man named Abinadi. I had been hunting with Prince Limhi. We arrived at the end of it to see Alma begging the king not to kill the man, and the king banished Alma. Amulon then convinced the king to kill Alma instead."

Her throat had gone so tight with fear that Sam felt like she was being strangled. She grabbed the front of Gideon's tunic, forcing him to stop. "Is Alma . . . is he . . ."

"As far as I know he's fine." Gideon pried Sam's fingers off and continued walking. "I helped him escape." Gideon then told Sam what he and Limhi had done for Alma.

"How did you know where to find him?"

Confusion flittered across Gideon's face. "I'm not sure how to explain it. I just knew where to go, and Alma was there."

They finally reached Gideon's humble hut, and Gideon hurried them all inside. Sam knew the king would never think to search the home of one of his captains. She wanted to feel relief, to relax the way the others were. But she couldn't. She could only think of Alma, out there all alone, running for his life.

"Please keep him safe," Sam pleaded with God over and over. "Please let me see him again. I promise I will tell him the truth. Please give me that chance."

* * *

Alma didn't know how many days he had been alone in the wilderness, two, maybe three. Time had lost all meaning as Alma replayed the words of Abinadi in his mind, committing each one to memory. Every time he remembered Abinadi's teachings, the more he believed them and the more he realized how wrong he had been. Other than that, he couldn't recall much. He seemed to remember eating some food from the pack Gideon had given him, finishing off the water skin and having to chew on some leaves to quench his thirst.

He also remembered that he still needed to return to the city. Alma had not gone there yet, because he knew the king would have his guards looking for him. Some of the land's finest trackers and hunters were part of the royal guard. He couldn't risk going close to Lehi-Nephi.

But he would have to go back soon. He needed supplies, things to write with. He needed to check on Sam and the girls to make sure they were safe.

A noise off to his left startled Alma. His head snapped up, his entire body holding still as he listened. Something was coming through the brush, something that didn't bother to hide the sound of its coming.

A harmless animal? A predator? A soldier?

Alma dived into a group of large ferns that completely covered him. It would be possible for a guard to walk right past and not even see him. It was what Alma hoped for.

The sound came closer and closer until it suddenly stopped. Whatever it was stood right outside Alma's clump of ferns. His heart beat so loudly Alma feared it would give him away. The entire forest seemed to go silent as Alma held his breath, waiting.

CHAPTER FOURTEEN

A black-nosed snout sniffed its way into Alma's hiding spot. Then Hunter shoved his entire head in and happily licked Alma's face. "What?" was the only thing Alma could think to say.

The dog barked once, and Alma heard someone running toward them. Knowing he could no longer hide, Alma pulled the drawstrings loose on the sheath that held his sword. Alma carefully took out the weapon. Grasping it tightly, Alma stood up, prepared to fight.

Nothing could have surprised him more than to see Helam crashing through the underbrush, nearly toppling over from the weight of the pack he carried on his back.

"Helam?" Alma wondered if he had gone without food and sleep for so long that he was hallucinating.

But Helam dispelled that when he reached out and clasped Alma's forearm, using his other hand to hold onto Alma to keep from falling. "I was afraid I wouldn't be able to find you. Well, I guess I didn't actually find you. This dog did."

"How?"

Helam removed the trumpline from his forehead, letting his burden roll off his back. "I suppose he tracked you."

Alma set down his sword and crouched to ruffle the dog's ears. While he had certainly used dogs to find deer or turkeys, he had never thought to use a dog to find a person before. "I suppose you're not so dumb after all." Looking back at Helam, Alma asked, "How did you know to follow him?"

"The story is a long one."

Holding his arms out wide, Alma said, "What else do I have but time?"

"I had already decided to try to find you. Right after I had heard what happened, I went into your chambers to make certain you didn't have any . . . um . . . incriminating evidence of your treasonous plot."

Alma tried not to glare. "I wasn't plotting treason."

"I know that. Now." Helam sat down on the ground next to Alma. "But while I was in there, this dog came in. He started following me everywhere. He even followed me home at night. He followed me as I searched for these."

Helam reached inside his pack and pulled out a bundle of books, all neatly folded and pressed. He handed them to Alma, who took them with a questioning look. "What are these?"

"Do you remember the day of your betrothal?"

Alma did. It felt like another lifetime.

"You showed me some scriptures that I told you had been tampered with. It made me curious. I wondered if, assuming those were copies, maybe the originals existed somewhere in the palace. I started searching storage rooms and the other high priests' chambers. I didn't find anything. After I had searched nearly every room in the palace, I realized I hadn't looked in the king's chambers."

"Tell me you didn't search the king's rooms." Helam had to be mad. If anyone had caught him . . .

"I did this morning. And I found them."

Alma opened the deerskin binding and folded out the white, lime-coated pages. He started to read. "These are an account of Father Lehi! I didn't know he kept a record."

Helam's eyes danced with pride. "When I heard about you and the prisoner, the way he talked about God and repentance, and that you defended him, I thought you had a greater need of them than the king."

Alma kept reading, his eyes devouring the parchment in front of him.

"I found them in a chest in the king's bedroom."

That made Alma stop. Helam, apparently proud of his accomplishment, obviously wanted Alma's full attention.

"I bumped into the chest accidentally, and it felt heavy. I saw King Zeniff's name on the chest, so I opened it and found these records. I realized what they were, but they didn't explain why the chest felt heavy. I started feeling around the inside wall and felt a bump. Inside the lining I found these. I don't know if King Noah even knew about them."

Helam removed a set of metal plates. Alma took them reverently, running his fingers over the smooth surface. He had heard once that his ancestors used to keep their records in this way. "I, Zeniff, having been taught in all the languages of the Nephites . . ." he read. "These are from King Zeniff. They should be returned to Limhi. I know he will want them."

"Won't Prince Limhi tell his father?"

Alma gave Helam back the plates. "No. The prince helped me escape. I believe we can trust him. He won't tell his father. But the king won't need Limhi to realize what you have done."

"The king won't think they're gone." Helam had a smug expression on his face. "When I figured out what they were, I went back to my own room and gave your stupid dog my records and lists to chew his way through. Then I put the chewed up parchment in the chest, knocked it over, and while I set everything up, I gave the dog some of the queen's sandals to gnaw on and left them there as well. The king will think the dog destroyed them."

Helam had to be a friend if he had let Hunter chew up his precious papers. "You took a terrible risk. You could have been discovered."

"You know I'm not one for risk taking. The palace was empty."

"Empty? Why?"

"Because they were planning to kill that man today. The one you defended."

"Abinadi? They're going to kill Abinadi?" Alma had hoped to figure out a way to free Abinadi, to learn more from him. Each of his plans to save the prophet seemed more foolish and nonsensical than the last, and now he was too late. "How?"

"I'm not certain. All I know is that after the king banished you, he had his guards take Abinadi and put him in prison. He had several councils with his priests, and they scheduled his execution for today."

Alma couldn't say anything. He put his face in his hands. Helam's words stunned and sickened Alma. That such a life should be taken, such knowledge extinguished, was almost more than Alma could bear. Alma realized that the king planned to kill Abinadi for the same reason he had hidden the records. By controlling the true scriptures, the knowledge and wisdom contained within them, the king controlled the people. He controlled the priests. Such information was power, and King Noah knew it. He stopped his people from understanding the truth, from making right choices, so that he could live the way he wanted.

For a moment Alma thought he should rebuke Helam for stealing something so precious. But as he looked at the words of Lehi, he knew that the people deserved to hear the truth. They deserved access to these histories. He knew that only by understanding where they had been could they understand where they needed to go. The king would obviously never share these. That left only Alma to do it.

"After I had finished getting the records, I decided to find you. I didn't know how I would do it, but today seemed like the perfect opportunity with everyone gone to the execution. I went to my room to gather some supplies for you. Once I got outside the city, your dog started to bark at me. He put his nose to the ground and barked at me again. He ran ahead and then stopped. When I caught up to him, he did it again. Strange as it sounds, I thought he wanted me to follow him. Then he led me here to you. I knew you wouldn't go far with your family still in the city."

"My family." Alma swallowed back the emotion that made his throat close up. "Has anything happened to them?"

Helam turned to his pack, pulling out more scriptures for Alma. "The king does not have them. They seem to be hiding as well."

Helam stopped to look at Alma. "You should know that Amulon has made the king determined to find you and kill you. They send out daily search parties."

Alma wondered how long he could stay here at this spot before he would be discovered. He would have to find a new place to hide.

Perhaps someplace that he could bring Sam and the girls to. Alma shook his head. He could never bring them out here. If Sam associated with him, lived here with him, the king might find them and kill her. He had already sat by her bedside terrified that she would die. How could he spend every moment worrying for her safety? He couldn't risk the king finding Sam and the girls with him. It was too dangerous. If Gideon would stay true to his promise, he could care for them and keep them safer than Alma ever could.

Helam placed a conch shell inkpot into Alma's hands, along with a container of ink, several brushes, and blank pressed fig bark paper. Amazed at how Helam could have so perfectly anticipated his needs, Alma felt a joy that he could now write down the words of Abinadi. "How did you know to bring me all this?"

In a serious voice, Helam said, "If I had to run away, I would want someone to bring me things to write with. But now I need to return to the city before I am missed. The king has called a new high priest, and I've been assigned as his scribe."

Alma knew it shouldn't have surprised him that the king would call another priest so quickly, but it did. It stung a little, his pride wounded that he had been so unimportant that he could be easily replaced.

Helam stood. "Alma, do you really think that Abinadi spoke the truth?"

"I know he did," Alma said with a fierceness that even caught himself off guard. He knew it, and he could never deny it.

"Then you will have to share his words with me another time. I really must go." Raising his hand in a farewell, Helam turned to leave.

"Wait," Alma said. "You said you gathered supplies. Did you bring any food? Any water? A blanket? It gets cold out here at night."

"Oh." Helam blinked two or three times. "I didn't think to bring you any of those things." Helam took off his own cloak and gave it to Alma. "I will return tomorrow with them, and perhaps then you can tell me more of what Abinadi said."

"I will be here."

Helam whistled for Hunter, but the dog walked in a circle three times and then lay down next to Alma. "I see your dog is staying."

Alma looked at the dog curled up in a ball next to him. It reminded Alma of when Hunter had done the same thing with Sam, and his heart lurched. He needed to know if she was safe. "Could you please find Gideon and see if my family is all right?"

"Gideon? Of the king's royal guard?"

Alma heard the astonishment in Helam's voice. "Yes."

"You certainly are keeping strange friends these days. But I will ask him, and I will return the plates to Limhi." Helam handed Alma the empty pack to keep the records in. "Did you want me to take a message to your family?"

Alma had already decided that the women in his life would be better off without him. They didn't deserve to be dragged into his problems. His only concern now was their security—something he couldn't give them.

"No," Alma's voice was strained. "No message."

* * *

Amulon wanted Abinadi to burn.

When the king counseled with the high priests for ideas on how to deal with Abinadi, Amulon, all false innocence and sincerity, put forth the idea that Abinadi should receive the death he predicted for the king. Abinadi should be consumed by a furnace of fire.

Having already given it a great deal of thought, but trying to make it seem as if it had only just occurred to him, Amulon then suggested that the death by fire should happen in the king's new ball court. The people needed to be reminded of what happened to those who would defy and question the king.

Amulon knew the public display would gratify the king's desire for drama, and Amulon wanted the entire kingdom to know what happened to Abinadi, what would happen to Alma and his family next.

If only Amulon could find them.

Despite having employed every tracker and hunter in the land, no one could manage to uncover the hiding places of Alma and his family.

Amulon's plan now consisted of eliminating Abinadi and turning all of the king's attention on Alma. He worried that after a few feasts the king might forget all about Alma. Amulon wouldn't let that happen.

Amulon didn't stop to examine his own irrational behavior. He knew his obsession with Alma didn't make sense—Alma certainly did not appear to be a threat to him now. But the fact that Alma still breathed made him an enemy that had to be finished off. He had learned early in life that he had to be aware of who his enemies were, and to hurt them before they could hurt him. Amulon's grandmother had told Amulon that his father had been pushed out of power by a man his father considered beneath his notice. So Amulon never underestimated anyone. Alma would have to be eliminated.

The king had raised some concerns over the burning. "I don't want Abinadi to become a martyr. It's what he wants."

"A martyr? Who would see him as a martyr? No one follows him or his cause. You know how devoted your subjects are to you." Amulon's silky words soothed the king, nudging him to agree with Amulon's point of view.

King Noah did as Amulon knew he would.

The king's new ball court that he had built in the Lamanite style was not yet complete, only one-half of the public stands being built. There were steep stone terraces to seat the spectators, and they were now filled to capacity.

A large, thick pole had been embedded deep into the ground, surrounded by a pile of dry wood that would light easily. As the king paraded onto the ball court, a large cheer went up from the gathered crowd. The king waved regally as the prisoner was brought out. Abinadi had been beaten, and his hands were tied behind his back. King Noah seated himself on his traveling throne, and Amulon took his place at the king's right hand.

The guards forced Abinadi to kneel in front of the king. King Noah held up his arm, and the crowd behind them went silent. Addressing the prisoner, the king said, "Abinadi . . ."

Before the king could go on, Abinadi interrupted. "Yes, Noah?"

"It is *King* Noah." The king furiously spat out the words.

"That is a title that must be earned, as your father earned it."

Roaring, King Noah stood and backhanded Abinadi, causing the old man's head to jerk backward. "Do not speak of my father to me! Your relationship with him is the only reason I was foolish enough to permit your exile. You have taken advantage of my generous nature."

As Abinadi slowly turned his head back toward King Noah, Amulon saw that the king had split Abinadi's lip. A trickle of blood trailed a path down his chin.

"And so now you will murder me."

The king reseated himself, pulling the edges of his cloak up so that they would not get caught underneath him. "It is not murder. I am putting a traitor to death. One who teaches false doctrine."

"You know that is not true." Abinadi shook his head. "You always were slow to remember and heed the words of the Lord."

"Perhaps I had a poor teacher."

Abinadi gave a small, sad smile. "Perhaps you did."

"That's all?" The king mocked Abinadi. "You have nothing else to say? You aren't going to say that you expected better from me? You certainly said it often enough in my youth."

"I had not expected better. I had hoped for it. But I did not expect it."

Amulon thought the king might hit Abinadi again. Instead in a loud voice King Noah announced, "Abinadi, we have found you guilty of blasphemy, and you are worthy of death. You have said that God Himself should come down among men. For this you will be put to death unless you will recall all the evil words which you have spoken concerning me and my people."

When the king said *unless* Amulon's head snapped up. Unless? What? Would the king actually let Abinadi go?

"I will not recall the words which I have said. They are true. I let myself fall into your hands so that you would also know they are true. I knew that you would put me to death, but I will not recall my words. They will stand as a testimony against you. If you kill me, you will shed innocent blood and this will also stand as a testimony against you at the last day."

Amulon rolled his eyes. The self-inflated grandiosity of it all made him want to laugh. Abinadi's words were meaningless and totally without merit. As if anyone would *allow* themselves to be caught when they *knew* that they would be killed. Abinadi spoke nonsense, claiming knowledge of things he could not have possibly known beforehand. How could anyone take such a statement seriously?

Suddenly noticing that King Noah had gone quiet, Amulon looked to his left to see the king. Great beads of sweat had broken out on the king's forehead, and he stared at Abinadi with an expression of total fear.

"All you have to do is recant," the king whispered. "I will let you go. I will return you to exile."

In sharp contrast to King Noah's reaction, and despite the fact that he was bruised, dirty, and bleeding, Abinadi appeared the picture of serene calm. "You know I will not do that."

Amulon bit the inside of his cheek to keep from snapping at King Noah. The fat fool sounded like an emotional drunk. Or like some scared little boy practically begging Abinadi to take back his words.

Bending over to speak in the king's ear, Amulon asked, "What are you doing?"

Amulon's disrespect didn't seem to register with King Noah, and he just shook his head, never taking his eyes off Abinadi. The king held still, as if some sort of unspeakable terror had immobilized him.

Stepping between the king and the prisoner, Amulon forced the king to look at him. "What are you afraid of?"

"Didn't you hear him? The judgments of God will come against me. I should let him go. Don't you think I should let him go?"

Amulon's lips compressed into a tight line. He needed Abinadi out of the way. He also needed King Noah to retain his position. If he showed himself as weak, the people might seek to remove him. Amulon's schemes only worked with King Noah in power. A new king might call all new high priests as King Noah did, and then where would Amulon be? Amulon needed King Noah to stop cringing and to act like a king.

"How can you let this man, this nobody, speak to you this way? Didn't God Himself appoint you as king? Who is this person to question that? You have a divine right to rule. Why would any judgments fall on you?"

The king seemed to come to himself, his eyes focusing on Amulon. "Listen to how he has reviled you. The King Noah I know would never let any man dare speak to him this way."

Amulon saw the faint outline of that vein in the king's forehead and knew he was close. He just needed one more push. Amulon bent at the waist so that his face was only inches away from the king's. "Everyone is listening, my king. Do you want to be seen as hesitant? As uncertain? You know what happens to kings the people perceive as being weak."

Playing on the king's irrational fear of death had been the right move. The vein popped to life, and the king ordered, "Carry out his sentence."

The gathered throng cheered again. They would be entertained by an execution today after all.

CHAPTER FIFTEEN

Then a calming peace settled on Abinadi. The air felt cool, the smoke seemed to dissipate. Abinadi recognized the presence of the Spirit.

"It was in vain, all of it. No one repented. I failed you."

An image flashed in his mind of the young high priest whom he had seen earlier in the throne room. Abinadi knew he hadn't failed. The young man had believed him.

Abinadi wanted to shout his happiness out loud, grateful for the knowledge that the Lord's work would continue. But then Abinadi became aware of tiny flames lapping at his feet, scorching his body. The flames began to press in all around him. Abinadi cried out in agony.

It would all be over soon, but first he had to finish his message.

* * *

Amulon watched impassively as the flames rose higher and higher. For a moment, it looked as if Abinadi spoke to someone. Amulon had stepped forward to see Abinadi more clearly.

The fire sprang to life, creating a wall that blocked Abinadi from view. Amulon put his hand in front of his face to protect himself from the heat and moved back.

"Got too close, did you?" King Noah's humor seemed to have returned along with his backbone.

The smile on the king's face died when Abinadi called out from the flames in a terrible voice, one that didn't sound human. Abinadi told them that their seed would put many to death by fire, that they would suffer as Abinadi suffered. Abinadi cursed them with diseases, saying that they would be scattered like flocks by wild beasts.

"And in that day you will be hunted, and you will be taken by the hand of your enemies, and then you will suffer, as I suffer, the pains of death by fire."

An involuntary shudder passed through Amulon at Abinadi's words. Amulon was not a superstitious or religious man, but Abinadi's statement sliced into him. It actually scared him. He was not the only person affected so. King Noah's face had gone pale. A man so frightened at the prospect of his own death, to hear it prophesied of so clearly, the manner of his death predicted, Amulon did not have to guess how the king felt. King Noah looked petrified.

The fire got even hotter, more intense. Amulon moved further back.

"O God, receive my soul."

Abinadi coughed loudly several times, and then slumped against his ropes as the fire engulfed him. Amulon shrugged off his fear. Abinadi was nothing more than a man, susceptible to death just as the rest of them were. His words were just that. Empty words. They had no power over Amulon.

Abinadi was dead. Finally dead.

Alma would be next.

* * *

Despite the temptation to pore over the scriptures that Helam had brought, Alma focused on writing down all the things Abinadi had said. He had rehearsed them so many times that the brush seemed to move of its own accord.

He remembered what it was like to sit in King Noah's throne room and how it felt to hear those words for the first time. The only thing he could think to compare it to was the first time he saw Sam. He felt like he recognized her, as if he had always known her. When Abinadi spoke, Alma didn't feel like he was learning the words for the first time so much as remembering them. He recognized them, the feeling a thousand times stronger than when he first saw his wife.

Alma deliberately turned his mind away from Sam, concentrating on recording Abinadi's teachings. Alma didn't know how many hours he wrote, each word indelibly burned into his heart. He wished Helam had stayed—the young scribe wrote much faster than Alma did.

His hand cramped up, his neck and shoulders ached from hovering over the parchment, but Alma finally finished. As soon as he did, he immediately picked up the lost scriptures. Alma read straight through the day and into the night. He said his thanks aloud that there was a full moon that enabled him to keep reading. He wouldn't have been able to make a fire for a reading light, as he was afraid the smoke would give away his location.

Alma read all through the night, sometimes tripping over the words, trying to read them as fast as possible. He learned for the first time the ordinances of the gospel of Jesus Christ. They were so simple. So true. Things that he had never considered before now seemed so vital to him. He read about all the workings of the gospel—faith, prayer, repentance, baptism, serving others, God's great eternal plan, that Christ would walk among them. He wept when he read how Christ would sacrifice himself, how he would take upon himself the sins of the world.

Christ would take upon himself the sins Alma had committed.

The more he read, the more Alma realized what he had done. As he sat alone in the stillness under the purple-black sky, Alma was brought to a perfect knowledge of his sins. He had to confront and deal with each one, with the excruciating and overwhelming physical and emotional pain of his wrongs. His body shook with the intensity of that knowledge.

Alma began to pray. He had been praying for his people, for his king's desires, when he had served as a high priest. But he had never experienced what he did now, this fire, this connection he felt. He knew someone listened to him and loved him. He wondered if this was how Sam felt.

He couldn't sleep when he thought of her and all the other things he had done, how contrary he had been to God's will. He divided his time among reading, praying, crying, and pouring out his sorrow to the Lord, asking the Lord to remove the pain that cut at his soul, begging for forgiveness.

He didn't know if he was worthy of being forgiven. He thought of all the wrong things he had taught the people. Alma had not only his own sins to repent for, but also the sins he caused others to commit.

Morning came and went. The day passed by quickly. Alma continued to call out, to repent of his multitude of sins. He promised the Lord that he would never commit any of them again. He promised to teach the people the truth, to bring them back to the Lord.

As twilight set in, Alma began to wonder if he should have gone to Abinadi, if he should have shared in the prophet's fate. While he logically knew that he never could have rescued Abinadi, that one man against the king's guards did not stand a chance, his heart wanted to fly to Abinadi's side, to die beside him for the truth that Alma now knew.

But Abinadi had finished his mission. Alma still had much to repent for, countless amends to make. He gave himself a mission to repair the damage he had done to the people in Lehi-Nephi.

Alma wanted to change. He no longer wanted to be the man he had been. He found himself on his knees again, asking the Lord if he could ever be forgiven, that if he labored all of his days to serve Him, could the Lord someday count him as a profitable servant?

He spent another night in torment, the pain exhausting him. Alma curled up in a ball on the ground, and his dog came over and lay against him, as if to offer him warmth. Alma's throat had gone hoarse, and he could no longer speak. So he thought the words in his mind, continuing to make promises to the Lord, apologizing over and over for the things he had done.

It was toward dawn as the sun began to creep over the mountains, as Alma lay in a heap unable to move, that a clear, small but piercing voice came to him on the wind.

Alma, your sins are forgiven. They are remembered no more.

Alma sat up, the words warming and comforting his soul. The strength returned to his limbs as he received the beautiful blessing of forgiveness. Alma began to cry. He did not deserve it.

Hunter came over and licked the tears off Alma's face, making Alma laugh. His spirit felt lighter than it had for several days. Could it be true? Could the Lord really have forgiven him?

Despite having read the scriptures and learning of the repentance process, despite having heard the Lord tell him that He would forget Alma's sins, Alma could not forget. He was aware now of the wickedness and darkness that had lived inside him for so long. He never wanted anyone else to feel of it, to know what he had done. Especially Sam. She was so pure, so good. She deserved someone better than him.

Alma thought back to the night of the festival, the night before the trial of Abinadi. He remembered the things Sam had said to him. She was right. He had selfishly forced her to marry him. He might have fooled himself into thinking he had noble motives, but the truth of the matter was that he wanted her and didn't care that she didn't want to marry him. He had horribly misused her. She had every right to be furious with him.

He had been underhanded and dishonest. With Sam and himself.

He should know better now. He should let them stay where they were safe, far away from him. But even now he wanted to continue to be selfish. Alma wanted to bring Sam, Hannah, and Sam's sisters out here with him. He missed Sam desperately, missed her musical laugh, her fiery temper, her kind heart, and her loyalty. He would even let her throw something at him if he could just see her again.

But their lives would be better and last longer if the women Alma loved stayed where they were. He had to be unselfish in at least this one thing. If he truly loved her, he would do whatever it took to keep her safe. Including denying himself the chance to be with her.

Something rustled in the underbrush to the south of them. Hunter perked his ears up, looking in that direction. There was a sound, like a man speaking. Alma realized that it was Helam calling Alma's name softly. He followed the sound of Helam's voice, and the scribe jumped when Alma came up behind him.

"I couldn't remember how to find you. I was worried I'd have to yell your name, and a search party would hear me. I'm glad I was close."

Helam unloaded his pack, giving Alma food, water, and blankets. "I know I said I'd come back yesterday, but I think Amulon's watching me. I had to wait until today to get away from the palace. I left while the king and his priests were having an archery contest."

"Then you will have to be careful. Amulon is dangerous." Alma bit into a slightly sour ball of cooked corn dough. Nothing had ever tasted better.

Helam gave Alma a funny look. "Alma, when did you eat or sleep last?"

Alma stopped eating. "I don't remember." Helam stayed quiet for several minutes, allowing Alma to eat and drink his fill. Alma then took several pieces of meat and gave them to the dog.

"I saw your family. They were very relieved to hear that you were all right."

"So they're safe." Alma felt a part of him relax and was glad to know that Gideon had kept his word.

"Yes. But they want to see you, to come out here and be with you."

"You know that's not possible. You can't ever bring them out here. I don't want them risking their lives."

Helam nodded with an expression that was all too familiar to Alma. It meant Helam would do as he asked but that Helam didn't agree with Alma's decision.

Altering the course of their conversation, Helam said, "You must tell me what you have learned."

At Helam's request, the words rushed out of Alma's mouth so quickly he could barely contain them. He spent hours recounting all that he had read, and as he talked, Alma knew what he had to do. Helam was not the only person Alma was meant to share this information with.

"I have to return to Lehi-Nephi."

Helam looked stunned. "The king will kill you."

"Only if he finds me."

* * *

Against Helam's protests, Alma returned to the city alone. He came at twilight and stood on the top of a rise that overlooked the whole valley. So many people to teach. So many wrongs to make right. As one kind of harvest ended, a new kind had begun.

Alma made his way down to the city, trying to ignore the erratic beating of his heart. His plan was to enter Lehi-Nephi along with the other day laborers and hunters that lived within the city walls. One man among many would be difficult to recognize.

He joined the mass of people moving toward the front entrance. Alma kept reminding himself that the men who stood guard would not notice him. He hunched his shoulders forward, trying to hide his height. As he entered the city, Alma watched the guards out of the corner of his eye. His skin felt hot and cold at the same time, and an almost suffocating sensation nearly overcame him.

But then he was safely inside Lehi-Nephi, and within minutes he had reached the prearranged meeting point with Helam. He had asked Helam to find a particular home, and his ever-efficient scribe had done just as Alma requested.

Helam told Alma on the way that he had spoken to Limhi, and the prince knew exactly where to find the man Alma sought.

They arrived at a long, rundown hut with a decrepit roof. A string with bells hung across the front entrance, which Helam shook several times. Alma hung back, cloaking himself within the shadows. A man who looked as worn out as his home came to the doorway. "Yes?"

Alma stepped forward. "Are you Ephraim?"

"I am. Who are you?"

"I'm Alma."

Ephraim let out a low laugh. "The former high priest? The one the king has offered such a bounty for?"

"I need to speak with you. You served as a high priest for King Zeniff?"

Ephraim's expression sobered. "I did."

"I think that we have much to discuss. Will you let us in?"

"You served King Noah. Why would I let someone like you into my home?"

"Because I have become a believer. I know the truth. And I need your help to find the others who want to learn it."

After a heart-stopping hesitation, Ephraim stepped aside and indicated that the two men could enter.

Alma nodded at Ephraim's family gathered inside. This is how it would begin. Like ripples in a pond. He would begin at the center, and the truth would spread itself, touching more and more people, bringing them to God's words. Alma threw his rock into the water and began.

* * *

Ephraim helped Alma find more families receptive to the message, and Alma spent every night teaching the people about the redemption that would come from Christ's power, sufferings, death, resurrection, and ascension into heaven.

Within a short time, there were so many wanted to hear Alma that he realized he would have to stop teaching within the city. He would have to find a new place for them to meet.

Helam accompanied Alma back into the wilderness one morning just before dawn. Alma told the scribe his concerns, and Helam agreed, pointing out that Alma would have to be more careful, because now Alma had not just himself to worry about, but his group of followers as well.

Alma suggested moving outside the kingdom's borders to the Land of Mormon, and Helam stopped walking to stare at him. "Are you serious? That place is far too dangerous for the people to come to you. You know the kind of wild beasts that live between here and there."

"Just the sort of thing to keep the king's guards out, isn't it? Don't worry, Helam. We are about the Lord's business. We will be kept safe."

With Helam voicing his vehement objections to Alma's decision, they headed back to the place where Alma had been living.

Hunter waited for them, his tail thumping against the moss-covered tree behind him. As Alma patted the dog's head, Hunter's entire demeanor suddenly changed. He went up all fours and pricked his ears up. He bristled the fur at his neck, growling lowly.

Someone was coming.

His suspicion was confirmed when a flock of bellbirds exploded from the canopy only a stone's throw away. Their loud "bonk" cries covered the sound of Alma grabbing his bags, as he told Helam to hurry as they ran through the waist-high leaves and bushes that covered the forest floor. The dog ran slightly ahead of Alma, so that when Alma found a dense strand of greenery to hide in he had to reach down and yank the dog inside.

Alma saw Helam's eyes go wide when the guards shouted to each other after finding Alma's recently abandoned living area. Alma feared that Hunter might attack or bark and so pulled the animal close to him, cradling the dog against his chest.

The guards were using long sticks to whack their way through the foliage, stabbing at possible hiding places in an attempt to find them. Alma heard the trilling of scampering quails that had been flushed out of their den.

One pole stabbed inside their hideout, the end coming down right in between Alma and Helam. Alma held his breath while the stick was retracted, clutching Hunter tighter when the stick landed again and just missed Alma's left foot.

Alma spent each second convinced that the guards would part the thick leaves and find them. But the pole was again withdrawn, and Alma heard the soldiers moving on. He and Helam sat in silence even as the sound of the guards faded away to be covered by the droning of insects and chirping of birds.

Helam turned to Alma. "So, the Land of Mormon is it? Sounds like an excellent idea."

CHAPTER SIXTEEN

Despite Helam's daily reassurances that Alma was fine, Sam couldn't help but worry. Where was he? What was he doing? Why hadn't he tried to come and see them?

Sam decided she'd had enough. If he wouldn't come to her, then she would go to him.

She told her sisters that she wanted to pick up some things in the marketplace and asked them to tell Gideon so he wouldn't be concerned, but instead Sam went to the center of the city. She waited outside the palace for Helam. She knew the jeopardy she placed herself in, but she had to see Alma.

As the sky began to darken, Helam finally emerged from the palace. Sam followed him down several streets until she felt safe enough to make her presence known.

When she called out his name, Helam had a momentary look of panic before he hissed at her, "What are you doing here? Do you know what will happen to you if the king or Amulon finds you? Why would you come so close to the palace?"

"I have to see Alma. I have to tell him that I . . . I have to see him. I need your help."

Helam grabbed her wrist and pulled her into an alley, out of sight. "I can't take you to him."

"Why not?"

"Because he asked me not to. I'm sorry."

Helam's words stung her. Why wouldn't Alma want to see her? Alma had once told her that he loved her. Had that changed? Both Gideon and Helam had explained to her what happened, what Alma had done in defending the prophet called Abinadi, how Alma now had the true records of their ancestors. The thought that such a change had occurred in Alma had made Sam feel exhilarated. Things could be so different between them now.

But Alma didn't want to see her. Why?

Too embarrassed to ask Helam the questions that burned inside her, Sam nodded mutely. Afraid that if she spoke she might start to cry, Sam turned to leave but stopped when Helam spoke.

"I wish I could take you to him. I wish that tomorrow, just before sunrise, you could follow me when I leave from the back pass in the back wall of the city to go listen to him preach. But I can't. I'm sure you understand."

Sam wanted to hug the serious young man but refrained. Suppressing her smile, she said. "I do understand. Thank you."

The next morning Helam didn't even so much as glance at her as he left the city with Sam dogging his steps. They took heavily used animal paths until the end of their journey, when Helam veered off the path and into the wilderness.

The thick canopy overhead made it impossible to see the sun's position to tell how long she had been walking. Sam wished she'd had the good sense to bring some water along.

Then they stepped out of the forest into a slight valley filled with the largest, most beautiful lake Sam had ever seen. Three high volcanoes and craggy mountains surrounded the sparkling water, casting their long shadows over the valley. "Where are we?"

"The Waters of Mormon," Helam said with a grin before he walked away. Sam walked toward the group of people gathered together and sat on the ground in the back. She watched as Helam walked toward the front of the congregation. She shielded her eyes against the sun to see Helam walk up to . . . Alma.

Her heart forgot to beat.

Sam wanted to run to him, to throw her arms around him and beg his forgiveness for her childishness. But Alma started to speak, and Sam couldn't move.

Alma preached about repentance, about redemption, about having faith in the Lord. There was something powerful in Alma's words. Sam wanted to sit and listen to him all day. Looking around her, she saw on other people's faces the same mixture of respect and joy that she felt.

It was Alma but not Alma. There was a humility, a sincerity, a spirituality to him that she had never experienced with him before. It was like he was a new person. She watched his animated excitement when he talked about Christ and Christ's mission in this world, how He would die to atone for their sins. It gave Sam a better and clearer understanding than what her own father had taught her. Her father's lessons had been based solely on his memory. He did not have the benefit of the words of the prophets as Alma now did. Sam wished her father could be here to listen to Alma.

Not that Sam was sure that she would have brought her father out here. The people gathered here put themselves in great danger. She, better than anyone else, appreciated what Alma's new beliefs meant. They had cost him everything—his position as high priest, his considerable fortune. It would cost him his life if the king found him. Everyone here would meet the same fate as Alma would just by listening to him.

Sam resolved that there was one thing Alma wouldn't lose. His family.

Alma concluded his sermon. Some members of the congregation went up to talk with Alma, while others went into the forest to return home to Lehi-Nephi. Sam saw that some people actually lived here in the valley with makeshift huts, that they had brought their flocks and animals to graze and water here.

Sam waited for the crowd around Alma to thin out. She studied her husband, a man who seemed more a stranger now than when she had first met him. He carried himself differently. There was still that confidence, that sense of power, but there were other things now too. His vanity and pride had always bothered her, but as she looked at his bedraggled appearance, it was obvious those were no longer character- istics that Alma possessed. She saw the smile on his face as he talked with those around him, how much he seemed to genuinely care for them.

Sam wondered if Alma still cared that much for her.

Finally Alma was alone. He gathered up his books, putting them into a large bag.

"Alma."

She saw him straighten up, keeping his back to her as he said with confusion, "Sam?"

Alma slowly turned around. Sam waited to see that light in his eyes, that warm expression he always seemed to have when he saw her. It wasn't there. He didn't look happy. He looked angry. Very angry.

Not able to help herself, Sam started to rush toward Alma to embrace him. Alma took a step back and averted his gaze. Sam felt as if she had just swallowed a sinking stone that threatened to drag her down. He didn't want her. He had changed so much that he no longer loved her.

"What do you think you're doing here?" His words were sharp.

"I belong here with you."

"You belong in Lehi-Nephi, where you're safe."

"I am your wife," Sam said, as if that alone could explain every- thing.

Alma's eyes flicked up at her before he again looked away. "In name only."

His words crippled her insides, twisting them into painful knots. Sam wrapped her arms around herself, trying to shield her heart from what he said. "Do you think the king and his priests know that? What do you think they will do to us if you leave us there? We will have no one."

Alma let out a hoarse laugh. "So now I am a step above no one."

"No, I didn't mean it like that." Sam was at a loss, unable to say what she really wanted to say with Alma being so cold and unresponsive.

"I can't believe you came out here today," Alma said as he turned away from her to slam a book into his bag. "It is too dangerous here for you. There are jaguars, ocelots, and all sorts of deadly snakes between here and the city."

"There are just as many predators living in the king's palace," Sam countered.

"It is me they want."

"Do you think that will stop them from hurting Hannah? Or me?"

Alma paused, holding a book in midair before putting it away. "You can't stay here. I am releasing you from our marriage contract."

The anguish she felt from his words was so intense that it became a physical pain. Sam put a hand to her stomach, willing herself not to become nauseated.

"You will go back to the city with Helam. I'm sure the king has ransacked the house, but have Gideon go there. In my—I mean—your room there is a loose stone on the east wall, three bricks up from the floor. I keep many valuable things hidden there. You can use those to support you and the others." Alma cleared his throat, still facing away from Sam. "I know it is probably too much to ask, but I need for Hannah to stay with you. She thinks of you as her sister."

"I love Hannah. Of course she will stay with me." She longed to hear Alma say that he loved Sam as well, that of course Sam would stay with him. But Alma only glanced at her over his shoulder and gave a slight nod. Then he picked up his bag and walked away.

Sam had done more than just miss him, more than just worry about him. She had learned to love him.

She loved him, and he had left her behind. Now she really was just like Miriam.

The tears that Sam refused to shed clouded her vision as she followed Helam back to the city. Her feet kept stumbling, and she nearly tripped a dozen times until Helam took her by the elbow to lead her through the foliage.

Alma's rejection had stunned her, and she punished herself with recriminations. She had so many should-haves. She should have told Alma the truth about how her feelings had changed. She should have refused to obey his commands. She should have stayed.

Sam's temper sprang to life. How could he say in one breath that he would release her from the marriage and then turn around in the next and order her about as if she were still his wife? Alma also had the full gospel, all of the scriptures. Did he actually think he could keep her from learning it? She had a right to it as much as anyone else.

She was through being ordered around. Sam decided to take her life into her own hands. If Alma didn't want her, well, that was too bad. He was stuck with her for the rest of his miserable life.

He had loved her once. He could learn to love her again.

After Helam had helped Sam sneak back inside the city, he insisted on escorting her back to Gideon's house. She told him it was unnecessary, and they went around and around until Helam finally gave in. Sam walked down a darkened street until she could no longer feel Helam's gaze on her. She turned around and saw that he had gone.

Going the opposite direction, Sam went to the house she had shared with Alma. The home was dark. It surprised Sam. She knew a new high priest had been called. She had assumed he would have been given the house.

Sam entered through the back garden, breathing in deeply the scent of the nighttime orchids that bloomed there. She looked around her, her eyes falling on her father's grave. It was the last time she would stand there. She said her final good-byes to him, to this place of refuge, and headed inside.

She found her way to the room easily even without any light. Sam counted the stones on the east wall until she found the loose one Alma had told her about. Digging her fingertips into the cracks in the plaster around the rock, Sam was able to work it free. How had she never noticed this before?

Sam reached inside and felt around. There were several cloth bundles. She pulled out all the bundles as quickly as she could, piling them into her shawl. She wanted to get back to her sisters. This place no longer had any warmth or life in it. It wasn't her home anymore.

But as she rushed back, Sam realized that Gideon's hut wasn't her home either.

Home was where Alma was. Whether he liked it or not.

Sam tried to placate a hysterical Lael, who had been convinced all day that Sam was in prison, and she deflected Kelila's and Hannah's countless questions of where she had been. After enduring Gideon's angry lecture on the importance of staying hidden and not taking needless risks, Sam knelt next to the cooking fire.

As Sam opened her shawl, she immediately noticed that two of the bundles had Kelila and Lael's names on them. When she opened them, she found necklaces, like the one her father had given Alma for her, in green and lavender jade. They were her sisters' only dowries now. She wrapped them back up and opened the other bundles. There were gems and jewelry inside each one. They had to have belonged to Alma's mother. She held an unbelievable fortune in her lap.

Sam set aside her sisters' necklaces. She took an expensive pearl and silver necklace, earrings and bracelet set for Hannah. Hannah should have a heritage to carry with her when they moved on from here.

There was another necklace that caught Sam's eye. Spondylus shell beads set off oval pieces of the palest green jade she had ever seen. It was gorgeous. This one she would keep. But not for herself. Although she would not say it aloud in order to retain some semblance of dignity, Sam wanted to keep it for the daughter she would have someday. A daughter with her father's dark eyes.

Gideon had gone to sleep, but Sam woke him up. She informed him of her decision to sell the jewelry, buy whatever supplies and animals they would need, and join Alma.

"Absolutely not." Gideon wiped the sleep from his eyes and sat up. "You and the girls will stay here and be safe. As I promised Alma."

"You don't have a say in what I do. I'm going, and you can either go with us and make sure that we're safe, like you promised, or you can stay here and wonder."

Gideon glared at her. "Your father didn't beat you nearly enough."

"He didn't beat me at all."

"I can tell." But even as he said it, Sam could see that Gideon struggled not to smile.

When Sam showed him the jewelry to be sold, Gideon told her she couldn't just walk into the marketplace and try to unload it all at once. It would cause too much of a stir, and it would be traced back to her. Gideon said he would sell it over the course of a few days to various vendors and get the necessary supplies slowly so as to not draw suspicion. Sam agreed to his plan.

Well, to almost all of his plan. Because Gideon's plan involved Sam staying hidden in the hut.

But early the next morning, Sam waited at the back wall for Helam to appear. He didn't. Sam had assumed that Helam journeyed out to Alma every day, but she realized that he still had his work as a scribe in the palace and probably went only when he could get away.

So the next day Sam hoped and waited at the wall again. This time to her delight, Helam did show up. He came to an abrupt halt when he saw her. He gave a sigh of disgust and shook his head. But Helam must have understood the look of determination Sam knew she wore. He walked past her, muttering about headstrong women who would get him into trouble. But he didn't try to stop her from following him.

Sam kept a long cloak wrapped around both of them as they walked. She had selected a very special outfit for when she saw Alma again, and she wanted to protect it from briars and pollen and anything else the forest might see fit to mar it with. She wore it in hopes that Alma would remember. Because Sam had no intention of ever letting him forget.

* * *

Alma climbed the mountain near the Waters of Mormon often to ponder and pray. From his vantage point he could see the whole valley, and now he watched the sun coming up, marveling at the way its rays beamed around the mountains to touch the lake below, turning the water into liquid amber.

He saw the people who lived in the valley feeding their flocks and herds and the others who made the long trip from Lehi-Nephi to their meeting place. Alma smiled. They had no idea yet how special this day would be.

As he walked down the gently sloping mountainside, he reflected on how far he had come. He had started to understand the promptings of the Spirit. He recognized the voice of the Lord when He spoke to him.

Last night he had been restless, unable to sleep. Much of that had been due to Sam's unexpected appearance. She had blinded his senses, his ability to reason. It was all he could do to steel himself against her, against his own instincts. Alma had to do what was best for her, no matter how much it made him die inside.

He had bundled himself up, left his hut, and climbed up the mountain. To force his mind from Sam, Alma instead recalled what he'd read earlier that day on the importance of baptism.

Just before dawn Alma had started to pray. Who had the authority to perform the baptisms? How should they be done? What would be said? Alma received answers to his questions and knew it was the Lord's desire that those who believed should be baptized in His name.

Alma greeted the other believers, had a word of prayer, and then began to teach them. Some were families of the previous high priests, some were like Sam and had been taught the true faith by their parents, and others were those who had grown up under the reign of the righteous King Zeniff. But without having had the words of the prophets taught to them on a continual basis, their beliefs and practices had been altered. They exulted at the opportunity to relearn the truth from Alma.

Today Alma asked them if they were desirous to come into the fold of God, to be called His people, if they were willing to bear one another's burdens, to comfort one another, and to stand as witnesses of God. Several people called back that they were. It was what Alma had hoped for.

Alma asked the congregation if they were willing to be baptized in the name of the Lord, to enter a covenant to serve the Lord and keep the commandments.

Cheers and expressions of joy erupted from the crowd. Alma knew that others here had sinned in the same ways he had and understood their excitement over the opportunity to have those sins washed away. An elderly man, walking with the help of a large cane, slowly lumbered his way up to Alma. He clasped Alma on the shoulder, gripping it tightly. Alma could see the unshed tears brimming in the frail man's eyes. "I think I speak for everyone when I say that this is the desire of our hearts."

Alma nodded in return, taking off his heavy cloak. He waded into the cold, pure water. "Helam?"

Helam had been furiously writing down all the words that Alma said but stopped when Alma spoke directly to him.

"Would you like to be baptized first?"

"Me?" Helam asked. "Why?"

Because Helam was his best friend. Because no one had supported him more through this ordeal than Helam. Because Helam served him now even though Alma had never asked him to. But all Alma said was, "Why not you?"

Helam threw his brush down, tore off his cloak, and raced into the water to stand alongside Alma. Alma prayed aloud that the Lord would give them His Spirit, that Alma could perform this task with holiness of heart.

Alma held his arm to the square and then said the words that impressed themselves on his mind. When he finished speaking, he guided Helam back into the water, and Alma went into the water with him.

They both emerged from the water laughing. Helam threw his arms around Alma, thumping Alma on the back. "This is the best day of my life!" Helam called out, and those who stood on the shoreline rejoiced along with them.

There was a steady stream of people after that, one right after the other. Alma did not lower himself in the water again, his baptism having been completed at the same time as Helam's. Alma said the baptismal words so many times, he knew he would never forget them.

After baptizing what felt like thousands, Alma stood with his hands on his hips looking at the lake. Over his shoulder he called to Helam, "How many so far?"

"Two hundred and three," Helam primly replied.

Alma grinned. He hadn't asked Helam to keep track, but if there was a list to be made, Helam couldn't help himself.

"And there is one more."

Alma turned to see Sam gliding across the water toward him. She wore her wedding clothes, and the fabric spread out around her on the lake's surface. Sam was so stunning that it actually hurt Alma to watch her. But Alma couldn't look away as she approached him like some sort of ethereal vision.

"I want to be baptized. I want you to baptize me," she said.

"No. I can't."

CHAPTER SEVENTEEN

The words had escaped Alma's lips before he could stop them. The despondent look on Sam's face made his chest feel tight. He couldn't make his lungs work. "I can't," Alma whispered. "I'm not fit to touch . . ." Alma found himself unable to form a thought, let alone finish a sentence. "I can't. It has to be someone else." He didn't deserve this privilege.

"There is no one else. There is only you."

Her words spoken so simply, so sweetly, made Alma feel even worse. "Sam, I'm sorry for everything I've done, for everything I put you through."

"I'm the one who should be apologizing. I should have taught you what I knew. I should have been an example. Instead I was horrible to you."

"Horrible to me?" Alma gave an incredulous laugh. "How? By running my home? By loving my sister? By taking care of me?"

"Alma, I don't want to argue," Sam said. "Please don't say no. I want to be baptized. I want to belong to this church. Please don't deny me this."

While Alma had managed to deny himself repeatedly where Sam was concerned, he had never been able to deny her anything. Especially not something this important.

"All right."

He hoped Sam didn't notice the way his hand shook as he held her, the way his voice wavered when he spoke.

When Alma pulled her out of the water, he didn't know it was possible to feel so much joy and guilt at the same time. Sam wore her dazzling smile, the one that seemed to rival the sun itself in brightness and warmth.

"I feel changed. It's like I'm starting over," she said.

Alma wished they could start over. But he knew it impossible. He would not put her life at risk. He knew he had to send her back.

With the baptisms completed, he and Sam walked back to the shore together.

Sam said, "I want you to know that I am packing up the family, and we're coming out here to live with you."

"No, you aren't."

"Yes, we are. Hannah, Lael, and Kelila should be taught the scriptures and should have the opportunity to be baptized if they want to be." Sam crossed her arms with that all too familiar defiant gleam in her eye. Alma thought she was a wonderful, delightful, dripping mess. He felt a pang for what could have been.

The pang passed because her words made Alma feel even guiltier. More than anything he wanted his family to understand the true principles of the gospel, to receive the blessings of baptism. But that would mean they'd have to come to Mormon. And what if the king found them? What if he couldn't protect them?

"I've already told you that it's not safe here."

"It's not safe in the city either. Eventually someone will discover us."

Alma had hopes that the king would find a new favored priest, gather a few more concubines, and that in time Alma would be nothing but a faded memory. When the king forgot, then Alma could go among the people and teach and baptize as he wished.

Alma opened his mouth to say as much, but Sam spoke before he could. "We will be here tomorrow evening. Gideon and some of his men will be accompanying us to ensure our safety." Sam picked up length of cloth to dry herself off with. She ran it over her hair and then tossed the wet cloth to Alma. "You will not release me from our marriage contract. I will live here, as will my sisters and Hannah. There is nothing you can say or do to stop me."

Sam turned on her heel and marched off.

He had always admired her spirit. But at times like these he wished she didn't have such an excess of it.

* * *

"I expected you to give me reasons why my building projects have slowed so significantly, not to make excuses."

The new high priest gulped several times before telling King Noah, "I can't pinpoint any other reason than we don't seem to have as many builders."

Amulon noticed that the new high priest's eyes bulged out, like a frog that had been stepped on. Amulon hadn't bothered to learn the priest's name. He probably had one, but Amulon didn't care.

"What else do the people have to do?" King Noah asked. "The harvest has been brought in. It is not yet time to plant the new crop. The men have nothing else to do but serve their king through working on my buildings."

Frog Eyes gulped again. "I don't have the answer, my king. The records we have from last season seem to have been misplaced somehow, but in speaking to the foremen, it is my understanding that not as many men have come to work."

"Where else would they be?"

Finally the king had asked an interesting question. Amulon wondered it himself. Where could the missing labor force have gone? There were penalties for not fulfilling their time obligations that the king had imposed. "Perhaps we should find out, my king."

The king grunted in agreement and waved the new high priest away. "He's no Alma."

Amulon couldn't have the king recalling only rosy memories of Alma. He needed him to remember the threat that Alma still presented. "Yes, I bet Frog Eyes over there won't be planning a rebellion against you anytime soon."

"You still think Alma is planning a rebellion? Do you think he would attack here?" Because Amulon had already planted this idea in

King Noah's mind, he made sure to reinforce it every chance he had. As a result, the king had pulled all of his guards from the surrounding lands as well as those who patrolled within the city and made them all return to the palace to keep him safe from Alma. There was one captain, the one who was friends with Limhi, who told the king he should not leave the people unprotected in this way. The king had not listened.

Amulon thought that King Noah should be worried. Amulon had seen Alma in the mock hand-to-hand fights arranged for the king's entertainment. Few could match Alma's skills. For all he knew, Alma really could be training an army in the wilderness.

"I'm not certain whether or not Alma will come here, but I think we should be ready if he does. I also think that if the men are not reporting to fulfill their duties, then we should discover where they are going. Perhaps we have been going about finding Alma the wrong way with blind searches. We should send spies to follow these missing men."

"Not the guards!" the king responded.

"No, we won't send the guards," Amulon said in a reassuring tone. Guards would be too conspicuous. They needed to send people who would blend in, who wouldn't be noticed. "Send your servants. Have them watch and wait outside the city's walls. If anyone goes into the wilderness, they should follow. And if they find Alma—"

"If they find Alma," the king interjected, "I will send the full strength of my army after him. I will kill every man, woman, and child with him. This rebellion will be stopped."

* * *

Amulon's plan worked faster than he had expected it to.

He stood outside in the late afternoon at the ceremonial center along with the other high priests overseeing the month's biggest market day. People came from outlying lands and hamlets for this market since it was ten times larger than the normal weekly market. They came to gossip, to sell their excess goods and grains, and to enjoy themselves.

Amulon's enjoyment came from watching as the taxes poured in. The king's personal scribes tallied up the taxes, and the priests' scribes made certain to skim off profits for their masters.

He noticed people running toward them. Amulon saw that they were the servants sent by the king to act as spies. Amulon had offered a large bribe to all the servants if they would bring any news to him first. Amulon wanted to be the one to tell the king, the one to take the glory.

They had found Alma.

The servants said that Alma had started some sort of colony just outside the kingdom's borders in the Land of Mormon. Grinning, Amulon went to the king. He asked for a private audience.

Once they were alone in the throne room, Amulon shared the information with King Noah.

"Are you certain?"

"Yes, my king. All you have to do now is gather your forces and wipe Alma out."

The king nodded. "Will you see that it is done? I want no survivors. I cannot tolerate this sort of rebellion against me."

"I will."

Amulon heard a soft scraping sound. His head snapped to his left, and he thought he saw a shadow move from the doorway.

"What is it?" King Noah asked, looking in the same direction.

Amulon took out his obsidian dagger from his belt. "I will find out."

He rushed to the door and saw a man running down the hall, along the gallery. Amulon called out for guards, for someone to stop him. But everyone was outside at the market celebration.

The man headed toward the central plaza, and Amulon guessed at once the man's intention. He planned on losing Amulon in the crowd.

Once outside, Amulon continued to call for help, but with all the loud singing, music, and talking no one could hear him. The man looked over his shoulder, and Amulon saw who he was. Helam. Amulon growled in frustration. He should have known Helam and Alma were still working together.

He had to stop Helam. Helam ran through a throng of dancers, and Amulon followed, closing the gap between them. Amulon elbowed and shoved dancers out of his way, stretching his arm to grab Helam. Helam remained just out of his reach.

Amulon thought of how his schemes would fall apart, what he would lose if Alma had warning of the king's army coming. This spurred him on faster. Helam twisted and turned his way through the crowd, but Amulon wouldn't let him escape.

Lunging forward, Amulon grabbed the end of Helam's cloak and yanked Helam to the ground. Helam tumbled down, rolling until he was front side up. Amulon pinned Helam's legs to the ground by sitting on them. Then he crouched over Helam with his dagger poised, ready to strike. Helam grabbed Amulon's right wrist with both hands, keeping the dagger from his body.

Amulon balled up his left hand into a fist and punched Helam's windpipe. Helam gasped for air, his hold weakening long enough for Amulon to bury his dagger in the scribe's stomach. Helam screamed from the pain, raising his torso off the ground to pull back and punch Amulon in the face, causing a sickening crunch. Blood spurted from his nose as Amulon fell backward from the force of Helam's blow.

Helam got unsteadily to his feet. Groaning, he pulled the dagger out of his stomach in one quick motion, letting it drop to the ground. Helam bunched up his fist and pressed it against the wound. He staggered back a few steps before turning to run into the crowd again.

Amulon lay on the ground, taking several deep breaths. He stood up slowly, using the edge of his cloak to stave off the bleeding from his nose. But Amulon didn't chase after Helam. He strode toward the palace, intent on getting the guards together. He didn't need to follow Helam because he knew exactly where Helam was going. The wound Amulon had given to him had been a lethal one that would eventually kill him. Helam wouldn't get far. Even if he did manage to make it all the way to Mormon to warn the people there, there was nothing Alma could do to defend himself.

The king's army was coming.

* * *

Alma had climbed halfway up his favorite mountain again, relishing the opportunity to have some time to himself. More and more people came to listen to his sermons, and so many decided to stay, to start over here, and not return to Lehi-Nephi. Alma spent much of his time functioning as a secular leader and instructing them on how to live together in God's church. He told the people to give of their substance to those who stood in need, so that everyone's temporal and spiritual needs and wants would be met. He also called priests, one for every fifty members of the church, to assist him in teaching and leading.

It surprised him the number and types of people who came to learn. Sam's cousin Gideon came when he could, and even Prince Limhi came and listened. Limhi had expressed a desire to be baptized, but the king fretted almost as much over Limhi's safety as he did his own. While adept at sneaking away, the prince worried about arousing his father's suspicions too much, which Alma appreciated. Alma needed to keep the group here at Mormon safe, especially since his family's arrival.

His family. Alma thought of them as he watched the sunset. The sun's descent turned the clouds in the sky vibrant shades of orange and red, causing the water of the lake to turn scarlet. It was what he loved most about this lake, the way the color of the water seemed to change every few minutes. He also loved this water for what it represented, the place of his own baptism and the baptism of Sam, Hannah, Kelila, and Lael.

As always, the second that Sam's name entered Alma's mind, he was lost. He dreamed of nothing else but her, and as if that were not enough, now that she lived in Mormon she seemed determined to haunt all his waking thoughts as well.

She deserves better, Alma reminded himself. Sam deserved a man that she could love the way that Alma loved her, a man who would not treat her as shabbily as Alma had. Unfortunately, her constant nearness tempted Alma to forget all of his noble intentions.

Exhaling loudly, Alma cleared his mind. He rose to a kneeling position as he intended to pray. Before he could speak, his mind was flooded with images of an invading army. The king's army.

The king's men are coming. Gather your people and flee.

Alma jumped to his feet, sliding and running down the side of the mountain. Darkness descended quickly and blanketed the entire valley, making it difficult to see. When he got near the bottom, Alma became aware of people yelling for him. His heart leapt into his throat. Was he too late? Were the guards already here?

Sam ran up to him. He saw the tears that streaked her face. "Alma, quickly. It's Helam."

She took his hand and led him to where a group of people had gathered. They parted to let Alma pass to where Helam lay on the ground. Some in the circle held torches, and Alma's stomach lurched when he saw the blood all over the front of Helam's tunic. "A healer! I need a healer!" Alma called out as he knelt down next to Helam.

Alma looked up at Sam. "I need clean rags. We have to cleanse this wound and stop the bleeding." Sam nodded and ran off.

"Alma." Helam's eyes opened slowly. "I came here to warn you. The king knows we are here." Alma could hear the exertion in Helam's voice, how tired he was.

"Who did this to you?" Alma demanded.

"Am—Amulon."

Helam had come all the way from Lehi-Nephi with this stomach wound? Alma knew what it meant that Helam had exerted himself so much, but Alma refused to accept the reality.

"Don't speak," Alma said. "Save your strength."

"I will not survive."

"Yes, you will. Where is that healer?" Alma couldn't keep the frantic desperation from his voice. Alma watched as the life drained from Helam, seeping into the ground beneath him. Alma pressed down with his hand on Helam's wound. They had to stop Helam from losing any more blood.

"No. Alma, listen to me. I need you to promise to care for my wife. She is a member of the church. She lives here." Helam's voice sounded raspy and spent. "Her name is Dara. Promise me."

Alma hung his head in shame at Helam's words. "I didn't even know you were married. I haven't been a good friend to you."

Helam grabbed Alma's hand and held it tightly, surprising Alma with his strength. "You have been the best possible friend to me. You led me to Christ. You baptized me in His name, and now . . . now I go to Him." Helam smiled at Alma. "My soul is saved, Alma. You saved it."

Alma gripped Helam's hand in return, choking back the tears that burned his throat. "No, my friend. You saved your own."

"Promise . . ." Helam said, his voice trailing off.

"I promise you that I will take care of your wife. She will become part of my family. I will give my life for hers if I have to. I swear it," Alma whispered the words fiercely as his tears fell unchecked.

Sam returned with rags, and Alma applied them to Helam's stomach although he knew it was too late. There was a disturbance to his left. A petite pregnant woman was led through the circle.

"Helam!" she cried out, collapsing next to him. Alma backed up to give Dara and Helam space to say their good-byes.

Alma didn't go far. He turned his head so as not to witness their private moment. While he couldn't make out their words, Alma could hear the soft, loving tones that passed between husband and wife.

Helam called Alma's name again, and Alma rushed back to his side. "Alma, I can see . . . oh, Alma. I wish you could see it. I'm going home." Helam's gaze looked unfocused, the color draining from his face. His breathing got shallower and faster. He turned his head toward his wife. "Dara, I'll miss you." Each word Helam spoke seemed to take a tremendous amount of effort, but Helam pressed on. "Always remember that I love you and our baby."

Then Helam's breathing stopped altogether. His body went limp, and his eyes fluttered shut. Dara wailed, calling out his name as she clung to Helam's shoulders, rocking him back and forth.

Alma felt Sam's arms wrapping around him, and he clung to her, needing her warmth and comfort. After a few minutes, Alma gained control of himself, pulling away from Sam slowly.

The circle of people surrounding them had grown. Alma saw the priests he had set apart in the crowd. He started giving orders to them, making them responsible for the mobilization and safety of their groups of fifty. "Tell the people to pack up their supplies, to take only what they can carry, what flocks they can drive before them, and leave the rest."

"What's happening?" Sam asked, grabbing Alma to make him hold still.

"The king has discovered our hiding place here. His army is on its way. We're leaving."

"But, there are still believers in the city. We can't just leave—"

"There's no time," Alma cut her off. "Helam gave his life trying to save ours. I will not dishonor his actions with our deaths. We must have faith that the Lord will provide a way for them to join us."

"Gideon is a captain," Sam tried again. "His men respect him. He could convince them not to harm us."

Alma looked in the direction of Lehi-Nephi as if he could see the impending invasion. "One man cannot turn the wrath of thousands. If we want to live, we have to run."

CHAPTER EIGHTEEN

Alma didn't have a destination in mind. He just knew they had to get out of Mormon. He stayed at the back of the group as they ran to make sure that no one was left behind.

He kept checking behind him because he expected to see the king's guards at any moment. Vines and leaves lashed out at his band of believers as they fled. Alma knew they couldn't possibly outrun seasoned soldiers. They had some pregnant women and small children. His glance flicked to the center of the group where Sam supported Dara, helping her to run.

Even if they somehow stayed ahead of the soldiers, they would be easily followed. The tracks of hundreds of people trampling down bushes and grasses would be too obvious. Alma prayed as he ran, asking for the Lord's protection of his flock.

Alma then realized that he didn't feel tired. He should have. They had run hard, and it was the middle of the night. But Alma felt fresh. His breathing was even and easy. Looking again at Sam and Dara in front of him, Alma saw that neither one of them appeared tired either. He realized that the Lord was strengthening them. It gave Alma hope.

There was a flash of brilliant illumination followed by a loud explosion off to the right. Several children screamed. Lightning? This was the dry season. How was that possible?

Then the heavens opened, pouring rain on them. "Keep going!" Alma shouted. The people surged forward. A little boy stumbled to the ground, falling face first. Alma scooped him out of the mud and carried him.

As rivulets of water poured down Alma's face, he looked behind himself again to see if there were any signs of the king's soldiers. Instead, he saw the thirsty vegetation reaching up toward the freak rainstorm, springing back into shape as if no one had walked over it. They might be miserable and wet, but the Lord was covering their escape.

Alma allowed himself a small smile. Helam had not died in vain. They were going to make it.

* * *

"How could we have lost the trail of that many people?" Amulon screamed in anger, swiping at a bush with his sword. The guards stared at him with a mixture of annoyance and disgust. Amulon realized that with the light from the rising sun, they could now clearly see his black-and-blue nose. Amulon didn't have time to dwell on his appearance. Vengeance always came before vanity.

Only there was no vengeance to be had. Alma had somehow escaped. Amulon now saw that he had made a serious miscalculation in letting Helam go. They had found his dead body in Mormon. Someone had covered Helam's wound with bandages. Helam must have had time to warn Alma.

Amulon had not been concerned last night to find the empty village. He didn't anticipate that it would take long to run Alma's people down and destroy them. But it had been so dark, and then there was the rainstorm—they had become lost and could find no evidence of the path taken by Alma's followers.

Once the rain stopped, the soldiers had regained their bearings. But still no one could pick up the trail. Amulon faced the possibility that he would have to return to the city and tell the king what had happened. The loss of labor, of potential income from taxes, not to mention the turning of affection, would infuriate the king. Amulon did not want to be King Noah's scapegoat by being the bearer of such bad news.

He could at least remedy one of those situations. Amulon would suggest to the king that they raise the taxes for those still living in the kingdom. That way the king's wealth would not be diminished.

The captain of the unit accompanying Amulon crouched down near the roots of an ancient mahogany tree. Amulon walked closer to see what the captain looked at. As he approached, the captain snapped off a fern frond, bending it several times. Why would the captain bother to do such a thing?

"What are you doing?" Amulon demanded. "Why are you destroying that frond?"

The captain straightened up, staring down at Amulon. "No reason."

Amulon disliked the man's insolence. "What is your name?"

"Gideon."

"Gideon?" Amulon repeated sarcastically. "Aren't you the king's mightiest warrior? His greatest hunter? His best tracker? Why can't you find their path?"

Several of the soldiers moved to flank Gideon and looked angrily at Amulon. Amulon had not realized the respect and affection these men had for their captain. They apparently did not like Amulon's verbal attack on Gideon.

Gideon held one hand up as if to calm them. "I see no sign of their passing. You're the high priest. Can't you just pray and ask God where they went?"

Several of the guards snickered as Gideon continued. "We are tired. We cannot find Alma or his followers. I am taking my men back to the city to rest."

Amulon knew better than to order them back to the search. He didn't have time for arrogant soldiers who didn't know their place. He had to return to Lehi-Nephi, try to save what he could of his reputation, and try to pin this massive failure on someone else to protect his position.

* * *

Amulon realized the mistake he had made in dismissing Gideon.

The king liked Amulon's suggestion and sent out a proclamation announcing the tax increase. There were murmurings from the general populace, but Amulon paid them no attention. They would do as they were told.

Several days later Amulon could not understand what was happening when he heard an uproar in the palace. A man yelled that he was going to slay King Noah. It stunned Amulon when Gideon stormed the throne room with a squad of soldiers.

Gideon strode across the room. He pointed his weapon at the king. "Get a sword. I will not kill an unarmed man."

"Guards!" the king shouted as he jumped up to cower behind his throne. "Arrest this man!"

But none of the other guards tried to stop Gideon or make a move to protect the king. Amulon realized they were all in this together. Gideon had taken control of the army. It meant once Gideon removed the king, he would also take control of the entire government.

"Why are you doing this?" King Noah whimpered from behind his throne. "I am your king!"

"I am a believer," Gideon responded in a low voice. "I know that you kept the truth from us. You lied to us. You led us into sin and iniquity for your own gain. Now because of your greed, you burden this people with taxes worse than anything the Lamanites would do. You must be stopped. I will stop you."

Gideon took the sword from the soldier standing next to him and threw it onto the floor next to the king. "Pick it up. I am granting you the chance to meet your death honorably. But either way, you are not leaving this room alive."

Still the king did not move.

"Pick it up!" Gideon roared.

The king tentatively reached out with one hand and pulled the sword to him. The king stood up, stepping out from behind the throne.

Without warning Gideon struck, slamming his sword down hard on the king's. Amulon realized that King Noah had not been idly boasting about his past military prowess. The king must have truly been a great warrior in his youth since he somehow managed to fend off Gideon's onslaught. It was not an elegant fight, however. It consisted of Gideon swiping and stabbing at the king and the king barely protecting himself.

Gideon was younger, faster, and stronger. The king shook visibly from the strain of blocking Gideon's blows. In a matter of seconds the king would be overpowered.

Amulon couldn't react. He should try to stop Gideon. He should try to save the king. But he couldn't move. Amulon could only watch helplessly as his entire world fell apart.

He had been blindsided by an enemy he did not expect. His worst fears coming true would be the price he paid for his ignorance.

"Stop! What are you doing?"

Amulon saw Limhi enter the throne room. He ran over to Gideon and his father and used his own sword to break the two men apart. "What is going on?"

Gideon glared at the king. "I am going to stop this evil man from dragging these people down to eternal damnation. You know what he has done."

"Yes, I know what he has done. But he is my father. I can't let you kill him."

"I do not wish to fight you, Limhi. But I will if I have to."

"He is my father," Limhi repeated, holding his sword out. "And you are my friend. How can you do this? There are other ways—"

"There is no other way! You know as well as I do that we have no other way of stopping your father's wickedness, and that this is the penalty for the laws he has broken." Gideon tried to circle around Limhi to get at King Noah, but Limhi prevented it from happening.

"And you think you're the one who gets to decide that?"

"If not me, then who? The corrupt priests and judges called by your father? Don't you remember the words of Nephi that Alma read to us? That it was better for one man to perish than for a nation to dwindle and perish in unbelief?"

Alma? Alma was the cause of this uprising? Amulon pondered to himself.

King Noah seemed to suddenly appreciate the opportunity afforded him by his current circumstances. Taking advantage of the two men's argument, the king fled.

Amulon followed after the king, trying to figure out where King Noah thought he could go. He couldn't run. Gideon would outrun him. If the king hid, Gideon would find him. The king had no allies to help him. Even his own son protected him, not because he sided with his father, but because of filial respect. King Noah was alone.

The king crossed the ceremonial plaza, running toward the temple. He dropped his sword, needing his hands to scale the narrow stone steps of the tower. Gideon brushed past Amulon, intent on overtaking King Noah. Apparently, in one way or another, Gideon had won the argument with Limhi and now came to finish what he had started.

Amulon knew that whatever happened to the king would happen to him. Amulon had tied his lot in with the king's. He had a morbid need to see how these events would play out. All his plans, all his scheming and plotting to secure his future, were flying away up the steps that the king climbed.

King Noah scrambled up the steps until he got to the first flat platform. Gideon started up the bottom steps, balancing on his toes to climb the stairs faster than the king had.

Something caught the king's attention. He turned his focus from Gideon to look out over the valley. King Noah put his arm up to block the sun. Amulon could not see the king's face, but he could hear the panic in his voice when he called out, "The Lamanites are coming! I can see them inside our borders. Gideon, spare me! The Lamanites are upon us and will destroy us!"

Gideon hesitated. Amulon thought it might have been a ploy of the king's to extend his life if only for a few more minutes, but the king had never been a good liar. Even Amulon believed the Lamanites were coming. He did not, however, believe the king cared about what happened to his people. It was one thing Amulon had in common with King Noah—they both only cared about themselves.

"Their heads are shaved!" the king called out and a gasp of horror went up from the gathered crowd. They all knew what it meant when the Lamanites came to battle with their hair shorn. It was a signal that this was not a battle to subdue rebellious tributaries or to take captives. The Lamanites had come for one purpose only—to destroy. No one would be spared.

Gideon delayed for only a moment longer and then called out orders to his guards. They had little time to prepare their defenses for battle. Soldiers scattered across the plaza, heading to their posts along the wall. Gideon conscripted men for the battle, sending them to support the seasoned troops.

King Noah countermanded Gideon's commands as he scooted down the dangerous steps. "Run! We can't prevail! Gather your families and run!"

Amulon quickly weighed his options. He could stay there with Gideon's ragtag bunch of professional soldiers and enlisted civilians for a hopeless fight, or he could try to escape.

Running to his home, he yelled for his grandmother. He found her by the cooking fire. Looking concerned, she asked him why he was upset. Amulon said he had no time for explanations and grabbed her by the wrist, pulling her outside.

He fell into the crowd leaving through the back pass of the city, holding tightly to his grandmother so that she wouldn't fall. Amulon had a brief thought for his wives and children, but put it aside. He had himself and his grandmother to worry about.

King Noah was not too far in front of him. Amulon noticed the combined look of terror and guilt on the king's face. Amulon realized that the king knew something about this attack. Amulon said to him, "What reason would the Lamanites have to come to war against us?"

The king huffed and puffed as he ran. He didn't bother to look back at Amulon. "Simple . . . misunderstanding . . . over the . . . tribute."

Amulon wished he had a sword on him so he could strike the king down right then. Only the worst kind of fool would try to cheat the Lamanites out of their required tribute. King Noah's greed would be the death of them all.

The war drums did not head in the direction of the city. The Lamanites followed the fleeing Nephites. Amulon saw that he had made yet another potentially deadly mistake. When faced with capturing a fortified city or running down unprotected stragglers, the Lamanites had chosen to kill those who followed King Noah. Amulon heard the screams and cries of those at the rear of the group as the Lamanites caught them with their weapons.

"Leave behind the women and children!" King Noah shouted. "We will move faster without them!"

Cries came from men in the crowd refusing to leave their families.

Amulon saw that some of the men chose to stay behind. They put themselves as buffers for the Lamanite army. Those families would meet their fate together. Other men ran with King Noah, abandoning their wives and children. Amulon looked at his grandmother. Either he could live or they could both die. It was a decision he never thought he would have to make. He found it surprisingly easy to do so.

His grandmother must have understood Amulon's intent because she clutched him with both hands. "Amulon? You can't leave me!"

Amulon shook her hands off and followed the king. He didn't look back, despite his grandmother's crying his name over and over again.

He didn't know how long they ran, but he realized that King Noah had been right. They were substantially faster without the dead weight.

The king called for the men to stop when they reached an empty clearing. King Noah collapsed to the ground, wheezing loudly. Amulon continued to walk around, not wanting his body to cramp up. Some men walked and stretched as Amulon did. Others sat down on the ground or leaned against trees.

A loud scream reverberated through the forest around them. It was impossible to tell if it had been human or animal or how close it was. Did the Lamanites still follow them?

"This is wrong," a man said while shaking his head. "We should go back." Amulon personally had no intention of going back. To return was certain death. But to his surprise, Amulon saw that several of the men near the one who spoke nodded their heads in agreement as they whispered to one another.

"Our honor and our families are more important than our own lives," another chimed in.

King Noah propped himself up. "We will keep moving. We will not go back."

Amulon read the mutinous looks on the faces of the men that surrounded the king. He could feel the wind shifting. This would not end well for any of them. Amulon started to edge away from the group.

All of the high priests had run with the king and left their families behind. Their sense of self-preservation was nearly as strong as Amulon's. They had always watched and followed Amulon while in Lehi-Nephi. It was no different here in the wilderness. They still followed his lead as they slowly moved toward Amulon and away from King Noah. Amulon thought they also must have recognized the murderous intent of the forming mob.

A large man stepped from the crowd and looked down at the king. "Your father fought the Lamanites alongside his men. King Zeniff sent the women and children to hide to protect them. You have sacrificed our families to save your own skin. And weak fools that we are, we listened to you."

King Noah got to his feet. He shook with anger. "How dare you speak to me this way? I am your king!"

Another man, covered in sweat and dirt from their flight, came to stand next to the man who addressed the king so disrespectfully. "We speak to cowards any way we wish. We are returning to our families. If the Lamanites have killed them, we will have our revenge before we perish as well."

"No one is leaving," the king said. Amulon pushed further back into the underbrush. "You will obey me and do as you are told. I command you to stay here with me."

Amulon could hear the fury and dissension growing in the crowd of men. Someone said loudly, "Gideon had the right idea."

They were going to kill the king. Amulon did not intend to die with him. A group of men surged forward to capture King Noah. Amulon had already started running when he heard a voice say, "Get the priests!"

Despite his exhaustion, Amulon knew he had to keep moving. To slow down, to stop, meant he would die. He could see and hear the other priests on either side of him as they fought their way through the forest vegetation.

The men did not chase the priests for long. When Amulon realized they were no longer being followed, he called out to the other priests to stop. They were safe. The men who pursued them had said they wanted to return to their wives and children. Amulon understood that chasing the high priests would have been a waste of what little time they might have left to try to save their families.

The high priests had stopped on a sloping hill that led out of the valley. From his left, Amulon heard Lib ask, "What is that?"

The acrid scent of something burning wafted up to them. A plume of gray smoke shot straight up into the sky, and even from that distance Amulon could hear a man screaming as he burned. King Noah.

"Just like Abinadi said," Teomner observed.

Amulon turned to glare at Teomner. "What did you say?"

"They burned him." Teomner stared at the smoke pillar. "Abinadi prophesied that the king would meet the same fate he did."

"That's nothing but a coincidence," Amulon snapped.

Teomner looked at Amulon with an empty, hollow expression. "Is it also a coincidence that we are now being driven like wild animals?"

"Yes," Amulon said firmly to close the discussion. He didn't need the other priests to suddenly turn weak and believe the sort of nonsense Abinadi had preached to them. They would all have to be strong, because the only way they would survive would be together.

As Amulon looked over the valley that had always been his home, for the first time in his life he understood why his father had killed himself. Amulon now knew what it was like to lose everything. His position of power, his homes, his wealth, his lands. All gone.

Amulon did have some regret over having to leave his grandmother behind. The Lamanites would surely kill her. He had nothing left. Nothing except the will to survive that his grandmother had put into his soul as a boy.

He would have to start over. Amulon decided he would find a new place to live. He would build up a city of his own. A sinister smile spread across his face at the thought of a city and a land named Amulon. Where he would be king.

CHAPTER NINETEEN

It had taken eight long days for Alma and his people to reach the valley. From her vantage point, Sam saw fertile, dark soil resting next to pure springs and streams. The water was perfectly situated for building furrows and canals to irrigate the crops they would plant. Mountains and dormant volcanoes created the scalloped edges of the valley's walls, making the land seem safe and secure. Sam sighed with relief when Alma proclaimed this to be the place.

"Will we call this land Alma?" someone asked. That made sense to Sam. Cities and lands were usually named after the leader of the first settlement.

She wasn't the only one who thought so.

"We should call it Alma, and Alma should be our king," Ephraim, the former priest of King Zeniff, said.

Sam watched as Alma's face sobered, and she followed his gaze to where he looked at Dara. Dara had her fingers splayed protectively over her stomach as she looked into the valley.

"No." Alma spoke the word softly, and everyone around him fell silent to listen. "No more kings. No more rulers. We will all be the same here. And we will call this place Helam, after the man who gave his life to save ours."

It took the group hours to descend into the heart of the valley. Alma and some of the other men chose a site to build their city on. The men then started constructing temporary huts in that location. The planting would have to start immediately. Sam knew they couldn't afford to miss a season. They needed the food.

The next day the men prepared to burn the vegetation off the land they would use for planting maize. Women picked the fruit from the lands to be cleared. It would give them food, and they could use the seeds to plant gardens and orchards. Alma and some others planned out the construction of permanent buildings. They would build the temple first. They began to pile up the mound of dirt that they would construct the temple over.

Sam helped in the fields. The men constructed a firebreak around the area set aside for planting. The fire was started at the top of the fields, and it raced down, burning everything in its path. The firebreak contained the fire, but Sam worried about the great black and gray clouds filling the sky above them. She hoped they were far enough away that King Noah couldn't see them.

The next week was spent clearing the burned-out field. Trees fell easily, although the men left the stumps behind. It would take too much time and effort to remove them. They would plant around the stumps. Sam enjoyed the hard work of pulling out dead bushes. It distracted her. She didn't spend all her time thinking about Alma or how he seemed to be avoiding her. He didn't speak to her, didn't look her in the eyes. She found herself envying Hannah and her sisters because of the easy affection they seemed to share with her husband, while Sam felt like she had somehow become invisible.

Once the fields had been cleaned up and every family assigned a plot of land to work, the community selected a day for the planting. Everyone was supposed to help get the planting done as quickly as possible. When Sam came to the fields, she found Alma standing at the border. He held his sharpened planting stick and had a bag of corn kernels strapped across his chest. He wore an expression of helplessness.

"Alma? What's wrong?" Sam asked.

With a self-deprecating smile, Alma confessed, "I don't know what to do."

"I do. I'll teach you." Sam tried not to look amused that Alma could build cities but didn't know how to plant corn.

Sam took Alma into the field. She showed him how to use his planting stick to create a hole for the seeds. Sam put several kernels in and covered the hole with dirt by pushing her foot over it.

"How many seeds do I put in?" Alma asked.

"About five or six," Sam replied. She laughed at the sight of Alma studiously counting out the correct number.

"Why are you laughing? Am I not doing it right?"

"You'll get a feel for it once we've been going awhile. You won't need to count them." Sam went on to explain that after the maize had been planted, they would come back to plant beans and squash around the corn. It helped the soil from getting overused. She told him about the nearly impossible task of trying to weed the fields by hand, giving him the advice of weeding while walking up the slope to ease pressure on his back.

This was not all that had to be done. Once the stalks grew tall enough they would have to double over the stems so that the corn ears pointed toward the ground. This would help harden the kernels and keep out the rain. She showed him her deer-bone husking instrument that would open the maize husk, which would then be peeled back and the cob thrown into a pile.

Alma listened attentively, and Sam couldn't help but feel happy. This was the most attention he had paid her in weeks. He took to the planting naturally, doing it as well as he did everything else. He easily outpaced her, finishing up not only his own row, but also the row she worked on before she could reach the end.

"That's what makes you such a great leader," Sam said with a smile. "You're always doing things for others they can't do for themselves."

Although she had paid him a compliment, Alma didn't seem to appreciate it. He gave a cynical laugh. "A great leader. Who am I to lead them? I didn't even know how to plant corn. I'm not certain I can do any of this."

"You are the Lord's servant. Whether or not you think you can do this, you have to. It's all right to ask for help. No one will think less of you for doing so. The people here love you. They would do anything for you." *I would do anything for you.* The unbidden thought startled Sam. She should tell him.

The shielded expression on Alma's face made her glad she hadn't. "The only thing anyone's ever gained from loving me is death."

Alma seemed intent on leaving until Sam grabbed his upper arm, turning him back to face her. "Helam's death was not your fault."

"Of course it was. He died because of me."

Sam shook her head. "No, not *because* of you. He died *for* you. For us. To save us and this church."

Alma sat down on a tree stump. His shoulders slumped inward. "His death weighs so heavily on me, Sam."

The pain in his voice tore at Sam's heart.

"I can't bear watching anyone else suffer because of me. I can't lose someone else that I care about. I'm not strong enough."

Sam knelt down in the dirt next to where Alma sat. She slipped her hand inside his larger one and squeezed gently. "Yes, you are."

"How can you say that?"

"Because I believe in you."

Alma withdrew his hand, making Sam feel cold and alone. "You shouldn't. You shouldn't believe anything I do or say. I told you once that I would give you a better life. Is this it?" Alma threw his hands out wide. "Living in the wilderness away from your extended family and any semblance of civilization? I also promised that I would make you happy. I have totally failed on both accounts. You should have the best of everything, and now I can never give that to you."

"But that isn't what I want. That's never what I wanted. Living in your home in Lehi-Nephi . . . it never felt real. This is real to me." Sam picked up a handful of dirt, letting the grains fall through her fingers. "This is real life. This is what I want."

What Sam really wanted was to be with Alma, to have a true marriage. But as he sat there looking at her with an unfathomable expression, Sam finally understood that it wasn't what Alma wanted. She remembered how he said he planned to release her from their marriage contract. She thought of how he avoided her, how he seemed determined to remove her completely from his life.

Alma didn't love her. The knowledge smacked into her like a giant rock being slammed against her chest. Why else would he treat her this way? Why else would he be so cold with her when he was so warm with everyone else?

After her baptism Sam had resolved that if Alma's feelings had changed, she would find a way to turn them back to what they were. But some part of her had believed that Alma still loved her. Her temper and her pride convinced her it would take very little to make Alma feel that way again.

His words, his face—this felt different. He truly did not want her to be a part of his life. He tolerated her because she demanded he do so. Something in Alma had irrevocably changed with Helam's death.

Faced with this realization, Sam remembered something else, something Hannah had said to her. The words came back to her with vivid clarity.

He either loves someone or he doesn't. It is all or nothing for him.

He had loved her once. Now he didn't. She had refused to let him have all of her heart, and now she had nothing.

* * *

The high priests had been reduced to living like animals.

Amulon still planned to build a glorious city, bigger and better than any other. But the reality of his situation ruined his fantasy. He had no tools for building. No weapons for protection or for hunting. They had no food.

The other priests ate fruit that they found. Amulon refused. He would never eat guavas again.

So he led the priests in late-night raids on Lehi-Nephi where they stole equipment, weapons, and food, as well as any jewels or other precious objects they could find. Amulon was shocked to learn on their first raid that the Lamanites had let the Nephites live. He considered trying to find his grandmother, but his shame at his present circumstances was too great.

Now they were thieves and scavengers and were hunted by guards day and night. They could not stay in one place for very long.

Early one morning they headed to the far reaches of the Nephite lands, to find a new refuge. Orihah and Lib bickered about who would get what portion of meat from the deer they had managed to kill.

Amulon heard something that sounded like a giggle. Definitely feminine. He told Orihah and Lib to be quiet so that he could listen. There it was again. Women were singing.

He followed the sound, along with the eleven other high priests. The sound of the singing and music became louder. Amulon pushed aside a leaf as large as his head to see dozens of young Lamanite women dancing and singing. He wanted to get a better look. Amulon dropped to the ground, using his elbows to propel himself forward as he crawled through the underbrush.

Amulon hadn't realized that they had come so close to Lamanite territory. They had apparently crossed the border into Shemlon.

"Where are the men? The guards?" one of the priests asked before Amulon shushed him. The high priests spread out in a line on the forest floor to watch the dancing women.

"It must be some sort of religious ritual," Shulam, the priest whom Amulon still sometimes thought of as Frog Eyes, whispered. "Something that only the women participate in."

As the priests hid and watched, some of the women left until only about two dozen remained.

"Let's take those women," Amulon said.

"Take them? Why?" Orihah asked.

Amulon raised one eyebrow at Orihah. "Why? Do you want to spend the rest of your days alone? We need women to take care of our needs. We can't go back to Lehi-Nephi to retrieve our wives or children. There's twenty-four of them. We can each have two wives. We can take our tools and supplies and start building a city of our own."

"But if we kidnap those women," Shulam said, "the Lamanites will kill us for it."

"How would they know it was us?" Amulon replied. "We'll take them and leave these lands. The Lamanites will never know."

Amulon saw some of the other priests nodding. He knew they would all go along with his plan. They always did.

The Lamanites had taken someone from Amulon. He would take someone from them in return.

* * *

The months passed so quickly that Sam could hardly keep track of the days. Dara's baby was born, and despite her wish for a son to pass Helam's name to, she gave birth to a daughter she named Zarah.

During the day Dara usually kept Zarah bundled up tightly on her back. But at night she let the baby out, and the women of the family cooed over her, making funny faces and singing to her.

Zarah was now old enough to sit up on her own and make funny little baby sounds. She was their main source of entertainment in the evening. And while Zarah loved them all, she seemed to have a particular love for Alma. Sam completely understood.

Somehow Zarah knew when Alma would return home, and she sat facing the doorway, waiting for him. When he came in, her face would light up, and she would hold up her chubby arms so that he would pick her up. He always did, swinging her around while she laughed.

Sam had never felt such blatant jealousy in her whole life. Not only for Alma's affection, but also for the babies she realized she might never have, babies she desperately wanted. Sometimes at night Sam held Zarah in her arms, rocking the baby to sleep and pretending that Zarah was hers. Hers and Alma's.

But it was only pretend.

The truth was that she hardly ever saw Alma anymore. He usually didn't come home until very late because of all his duties. Not just the religious ones but the secular as well. He pursued the construction of their city the way he had once pursued her, with a fierceness and unrelenting determination. He made a wooden temple and a wooden home for them to live in. Alma told them of his plans to start construction on a stone temple after the next harvest had been collected. Alma went on scouting trips with some of the men to look for limestone rocks to use to build the temple. The trips would take him away from home for days at a time. Whenever he was gone, Sam always felt as if a piece of her was missing.

Alma was on such a trip now. Sam thought of him as she went to get water for the family. The double-handed vase felt bulky and uncomfortable as she carried it. She was not used to hefting it around. Alma usually took care of bringing the water when he was home. Putting the vase down into the stream and pulling it back up only made her think of how this was just one of the many things Alma did for them. It made her miss him even more.

As she walked back to the city and to her home, Sam ran across several other members of the community who all wanted her to stop and talk to them. Sam made her excuses and continued on the path. She knew they would all ask about Alma. She couldn't cope with having to put on a happy smile and pretending everything between them was fine.

Sam sometimes felt like a fraud living here. Not only for her fake marriage, but because she couldn't participate fully in the happiness of the other believers, in the tangible joy that existed all around her. To some extent Sam did feel some of that same joy from her own understanding and growth in the teachings of the Lord. But another part of her grieved constantly for Alma, grieved for what she could have had if she hadn't been so reactionary. So stubborn. If only she could have managed to tame her temper. Her shortcomings had driven him away.

Sam brought the water vase inside, gratefully setting it down.

"I could have fetched the water tonight," Dara said as she held Zarah on her hip.

Sam smiled at her friend, who now felt like another sister. Sam sometimes forgot that Dara wasn't actually a blood relation. "It's all right. I don't mind doing it."

Curious about where her sisters were, Sam asked Hannah. Hannah always seemed to know everything about everyone, and this time was no exception. Hannah told Sam that Lael and Kelila were visiting with a sickly neighbor. While saying this, Hannah came up to take Zarah from Dara. As Hannah walked past her, Sam reached out to plant a kiss on the top of Zarah's soft, downy hair. The overwhelming desire for a child of her own again seized Sam. She suspected that her need for a baby grew daily because of her fear that she might never have one. She blinked back unexpected tears and turned her head away.

Dara folded blankets and clothes that she had washed yesterday and hung out to dry. Sam sat next to Dara to help. The two women traded stories about their day. Dara told Sam tales about the baby that made Sam laugh out loud.

Sam felt very grateful that she had Dara. While she loved her sisters and Hannah, they were a bit younger. It wasn't the same sort of friendship she had with Dara. She especially appreciated Dara's discretion in not asking about Sam's peculiar marriage and their current living and sleeping arrangements. It kept Sam from having to deal with highly uncomfortable feelings.

As if reading her thoughts, Dara steered the conversation toward Alma. She then asked, "When will he be back?"

"I'm not certain." Sam knew her cheeks colored. It was embarrassing not to even know when your own husband was supposed to return home.

"How long have the two of you been married?" Dara asked in a teasing tone.

"Over a year. Almost a year and a half," Sam replied.

"I see," Dara said as she ran her hand along the crease of a blanket she had just folded into quarters. "And how long have you been in love with your husband?"

Sam's mouth dropped, and while she fully intended to say something to deny it, no words came out.

"Probably for as long as he's been in love with her," Hannah volunteered from the corner where she played with Zarah.

Sam regained her voice and sputtered, "Alma does not love me."

Dara and Hannah both laughed.

"He doesn't!" Sam protested. "He might have thought he did at one point, but now he doesn't."

"Are you really so sure?" Dara asked. "Why don't you talk to him? Those kind of feelings don't just go away."

"His did."

Dara gave Sam a sweet smile. "I don't think they have. I've seen the way he watches you when you aren't looking. You should tell him how you feel. His reaction might surprise you."

Sam wanted desperately to hope, to believe Dara's words. But she couldn't. She hadn't admitted to anyone else that she did love Alma. If she kept it inside and never let anyone know, she could retain some control over her life. She wouldn't appear as pathetic or weak as she felt. She just couldn't open her heart that way. She still had some pride. "I won't make a fool of myself."

"My brother, if you don't mind me saying so, is an idiot." Hannah clapped Zarah's hands together, to the baby's great delight. "I told you once that when Alma sets his mind to something, he can't be turned from his chosen path. For some reason he has decided that you would be better off not married to him. You will have to find a way to do the impossible. You have to turn him away from the course of action he has chosen."

Sam couldn't take the rejection again. She had already told him she wanted to remain married to him. She had been vulnerable to him, and he had walked away. She couldn't do it again.

Dara set aside her pile of folded blankets and stood up. She came over to Sam, taking both of Sam's hands in her own. "Don't lose any more time, Sam. If there is one thing you should have learned from being my friend, it is that life is so short and can end so suddenly.

What if Alma was taken from you the way Helam was taken from me? Could you live with yourself if you never told Alma how you truly felt?" Dara let out a deep breath. "I hate to see you throwing your chance for happiness away. Tell him. Please think about it."

Sam doubted she'd be able to think about anything else.

CHAPTER TWENTY

Alma helped to roll the heavy block of limestone across the logs they had laid out. It took far less effort and fewer men when the blocks could be rolled to the temple this way.

When the block and the men reached the base of the temple, Alma called for everyone to rest before they returned to the limestone quarry to retrieve the next block. Alma emptied the contents of a water skin into his mouth. He wiped the sweat from his forehead and sat down.

He heard a woman's laughter. Was it Sam's? Alma looked and saw Kelila walking with a group of girls her age. Kelila sounded just like her older sister.

Alma's stomach twisted as he thought of his wife. He tried to constantly remind himself how he had trapped her into this marriage, how selfish he had been. He told himself that although she might consider him a friend, Sam had never felt anything more for him. Alma figured that Sam stayed with him out of some sense of obligation or gratitude that he cared for her family.

It was more than he could bear to be near her on such a constant basis. To watch her laugh and know that he could never be the reason for her happiness caused him unending torment. Alma spent as much time away from his home as he could. He didn't trust himself to stay strong when he was with her. He would have performed any task, accomplished any feat, to have a second chance with Sam. But he knew he didn't deserve it. He had lost all claim to her.

"Alma?"

Seeing Sam standing there surprised Alma so much that he reached out and poked her arm with his finger to make certain she was real.

He saw her swallow. Then she cleared her throat several times before she said, "I know that you're busy, but there's something I want to tell you."

"What is it?" Alma asked as he stood.

Sam put her hands behind her back and began making circles in the dirt with the tip of her sandal. "I'm not really sure how to say it."

"Just say it." Alma's heart thundered in his chest. Was this it? Was she going to ask him to keep his promise to release her from the marriage? Had she met someone else? An ugly black jealousy reared up inside of him, and Alma pushed it back down. He was being ridiculous. He should just listen instead of leaping to his own conclusions.

"Well, all right. I'll just say it." Sam took in a deep breath. "Alma, I need to tell you that I—"

"Alma! Alma!"

Hundreds of people rushed toward the temple. Something was very wrong. Everyone talked to him at once, and Alma couldn't understand what they were telling him. He realized that many of them had come straight from the fields. They still wore their farming equipment. What would make them leave? He saw from their faces and heard in their voices that they were afraid. Of what?

"Lamanites!"

That he understood. But how could there be Lamanites here? How had the Lamanites found them? Alma grabbed a man close to him and pulled him from the crowd. "What's happening?"

The man was out of breath. "We were gathering the remainder of the harvest when someone noticed an army of Lamanites marching into the valley. We ran here as quickly as we could. What should we do?"

A chorus of voices repeated the question. What could they do? Alma did not have a fighting force here. The believers were not properly trained and they lacked the necessary weapons. There would be no way for them to stand against Lamanite soldiers. If they resisted, they would be killed. He looked at Sam and grit his teeth together. Alma could not allow that to happen.

Alma held his hands up, asking for quiet. "I understand that you're frightened. You don't need to be. Have faith in the Lord your God that He will deliver us."

People started to cry to the Lord, asking that the hearts of the Lamanites would be softened so that they would be spared. Alma called several of his priests to accompany him. He intended to do whatever was necessary to keep the people safe. He prayed in his heart that the Lord would hear their pleas, that they would not be destroyed.

"What are you doing?" Sam ran up to Alma and clung to his arm. "Where are you going?"

"I'm going to talk to the Lamanites. I'm going to keep you safe." Alma gently pulled his arm away. "I'm going to keep everyone safe."

He couldn't have any more deaths on his conscience. Alma would do or say whatever he had to in order to keep this group alive. He would agree to any terms, to any tribute the Lamanites might ask for.

The Lamanites arrived quickly. They had drawn their weapons, but when they saw that Alma and his brethren waited without any swords or arrows, they put their weapons away. The Lamanite that Alma presumed to be captain stepped forward flanked by some of his soldiers. Their red and black warpaint worried Alma. They had come looking for a fight.

"We seem to be running across Nephites everywhere," the Lamanite captain said. "You've spread out like some sort of infestation."

"Yes," a man next to the captain added. "We have managed to find all the Nephites except the ones we're looking for."

Several of the Lamanite soldiers laughed at this. Alma held silent. He didn't understand who the soldiers were speaking of, or what Nephites they were trying to find. It surprised Alma that the Lamanites spoke to him in his own language. While well versed in the languages of the Lamanites, Alma had never known any Lamanites to speak the

Nephite tongue. These men spoke it so well. Who had taught it to them?

It didn't matter. Alma turned his thoughts back to the pressing situation he found himself in. He would wait and see what the Lamanites wanted. He prayed for inspiration and guidance.

"We are lost," the Lamanite captain told Alma. "We need to find our way back to the Land of Nephi. If you will show us the way, I promise that we will spare your lives and your liberty."

Alma pointed to the north end of the valley. He described to the Lamanite captain the route they had taken to come here. He told them that it should lead to the Land of Mormon and from there they would be able to find their way back to Nephi.

The captain thanked Alma and turned to rejoin his men. Relief washed through Alma that it had been so easy.

He quickly realized that it had been far too easy. The Lamanite captain stopped and turned back to Alma. "Now that I consider the matter further, this would make an excellent tributary for King Laman."

"But you gave me your word. You said you would go and leave us in peace. You promised."

The Lamanite captain shrugged. "You are a Nephite. Certainly you knew that I did not mean it."

The Lamanites laughed again, and Alma tried to keep his anger in check. He did not need to make things worse.

"I will now accept your unconditional surrender," the captain said. "If you rebel or resist, I will wipe out this entire settlement. You will send half of all your goods and grains in tribute. My guards will remain here to make certain that you behave and to keep you from escaping. Do you understand the terms of your surrender?"

This was what Alma feared, but he had prepared himself for it. He understood that there was no room for negotiation, and Alma didn't want to annoy the army with a debate. He had no power in this situation. He could only go along with their dictates. "I understand."

"Good. Go and prepare your people. My men will need homes and food. I trust that you will take care of that for them?"

Alma clenched his jaw so tightly he feared he might shatter all of his teeth. "I will."

Understanding that he had been dismissed, Alma went back to the center of the city. It seemed as if the entire community had gathered there, waiting to hear of their fate. Alma climbed up on the bottom step of the temple so that everyone could see and hear him. Alma explained the situation to the people, and what would now be required of them.

One of Alma's priests, a man named Benjamin, stepped forward. "We should fight them. They are not that great in number. Surely we can defeat them."

"The Lamanites are like ants. Where you see one, soon you will see a hundred. Then a thousand. Then ten thousand. It is not a fight we can hope to win," Alma said.

Benjamin drew his sword out. "We should be willing to die to protect our way of life. I am willing to die for my beliefs."

To fight meant certain death for every man, woman, and child in Helam. Alma would not have the blood of innocents on his hands. The Lord had heard their prayers and provided a way for them to live. Alma could not ignore that. "It is easy for a man to die for his beliefs. It is harder to live for them. But that is what we should do."

Alma then put it to a vote—should they fight or surrender? He would not arbitrarily make this decision for them. He would let the people decide their own future. The patriarchs conferred with their families and unanimously decided that they agreed with Alma to do as the Lamanites asked.

"We should thank the Lord for the trials and tests of our faith and do what we can to live the way He would want us to." Alma did not labor under the delusion that the Lamanites would make their lives easy. He knew the hardships that waited for them.

Alma stepped down from the bottom stair. He went into the crowd to comfort and reassure.

"I thought you said the Lord would deliver us," Benjamin said to him as Alma walked past.

Alma stopped. "He did. We're still alive."

* * *

As the Lamanites settled in, Alma could feel the tension and anxiety of the people in Helam. The Lamanite captain ordered a portion of the Lamanite guards to stay behind while the rest returned to Nephi. Reinforcements arrived quickly, and they brought along not only their own families, but also the families of those guards who had remained in Helam.

Initially the Nephites worried. The Lamanites had not kept their word earlier, and the Nephites had no reason to believe that the Lamanites would honor their promise to let them live. But as the weeks passed, the Nephites began to relax when the Lamanites did not treat them cruelly. The Lamanites functioned solely as guards in watching over the people. They did not interfere with the work in the fields, the caring of flocks, the building of the city, nor did they try to restructure the economic system already in place in Helam. The people of Alma were allowed to live their lives as they had before the Lamanites arrived.

Alma knew the transition to living under Lamanite rule was not difficult because the believers had lived their whole lives under the rule of not only a wicked Nephite king, but also a Lamanite king as well. They had always been part of a tributary system. Their lives were not that different than what they had always known, and the people were relatively happy. The Lamanites did not make excessive demands on them.

The only person that had to deal with excessive demands was Alma. The new Lamanite captain, a man by the name of Jacob, held regular meetings with Alma to discuss the administration of the city since Alma functioned as a go-between for the Lamanites and the people of Alma. Alma knew Jacob viewed him as instrumental to keeping the peace in Helam. Alma had been requested to attend an unscheduled meeting that day. Alma understood it was less of a request and more of an order. He felt vaguely uneasy that Jacob wanted to meet with him about something so important that it could not wait.

Alma went to the large wooden structure he and his men were required to build for the Lamanite captain after Jacob determined that all of their homes were too small for his needs. Jacob used it as his home and his headquarters for conducting business.

After a guard announced Alma's presence, the captain said to send Alma in. Upon entering, Alma noticed something strange—a throne built upon a makeshift dais against the farthest wall.

Jacob saw that Alma noticed the throne and gestured toward it. "As you can see, things are about to change in Helam. King Laman has set apart a king to rule over you."

Alma's heart and hopes sank. A king. They had come all this way to escape that sort of tyranny, and now they would be subject to it once more. Alma had feared a day like this would come. He knew it would not take long for King Laman to reward one of his noblemen or one of his sons with a kingdom of their own, and the Land of Helam would be recipient of a new king. Alma recognized that the kingship itself was not inherently bad. If a man ruled in righteousness, he could be beneficial to his people. But Alma did not expect a righteous rule from a Lamanite king.

"He is a man the king respects very much. He was born a Nephite like yourself, but he and his people joined with us. They taught us your language and how to keep records. The king believed it might be easier for your people if you were led by one of your own."

"When can we expect this new king?" Faced with the inevitable, Alma hoped there would at least be enough time to prepare the believers for this new situation.

"He is scheduled to arrive at any moment. It's why I asked you to meet me here. I wanted to make the necessary introductions and to make arrangements for a palace to be built. Obviously this house will not be suitable for the king." The Lamanite captain stopped speaking when the sound of conch shell horns filled the air. "Wait here."

Jacob left, presumably to lead the king to his new home. Alma reminded himself to have gratitude for the blessings they enjoyed. Yes, a king was coming. But they still had their health, their ability to work, their families, the freedom to practice their religion. Things could be worse.

The curtain covering the doorway was drawn back, and Alma realized things were much, much worse.

Amulon. Amulon was the king.

Alma's mind raced with a thousand questions as he tried to understand how this had happened. Where was King Noah? His sons? Had the Lamanites taken control of Lehi-Nephi? How had Amulon schemed his way into this position?

Despite Alma's own shock, he realized that Amulon did not look surprised to see Alma. Amulon wore a smirk as he crossed the room to his throne. Amulon flared out his bright blue cloak before settling into his throne. Amulon made a sound that signified his disapproval. "You know better, Alma. You should always kneel before your king." Amulon signaled to his guards to make Alma kneel.

But Alma did not want to be forced. He understood that Amulon wished to humiliate him. He also knew that Amulon might retaliate against Alma's insubordination by harming the believers. So he knelt.

Amulon laughed, making the quetzal feathers in his headdress shake. "I did not expect you to actually do it. Look at you, so full of humility. The Alma I knew would never degrade himself before me."

"The Alma you knew no longer exists."

With a shrug Amulon said, "Perhaps. But by killing you, I will make sure to get rid of both men."

Watching Alma's reaction, Amulon laughed again. "Oh, you needn't look so worried. I am not going to cut out your heart, although the idea does have merit. King Laman made me king of this land on the condition that I do nothing contrary to his will. His will apparently seems to include not killing Lamanite subjects, which you are now. So," Amulon said as he shifted in his seat, "I've decided to let you die a slow death, hastened by the labors and abuses I will heap upon you. You and everyone else here. I will also take from you what you took from me."

"And what is it you think I took from you?"

The expression on Amulon's face changed rapidly from delight to pure rage as he leaned forward. "Do you know the poverty you reduced me to? What you and your rebellion cost me? The loss of men made it impossible to properly defend Lehi-Nephi, and the Lamanites took control. King Noah was put to death by his own people, and the high priests barely escaped with their lives. For months I lived like an animal in the wilderness, and it is all your fault!"

Alma looked over at Amulon's family members, retainers, and servants that had followed Amulon inside, all of them dressed in a slightly less expensive version of the fine-twined linen that Amulon wore. "You don't seem too poor to me."

"Thanks solely to me and my skills," Amulon retorted. Amulon leaned back in his chair and called for something to drink.

"I see you have no vineyards here. That is something we will have to remedy," Amulon said. A woman took a skin and poured wine into a cup. She handed it to Amulon with her gaze cast down. Amulon grabbed the woman's chin, forcing her to kiss him before he pushed her away.

She was a Lamanite. But the Lamanite guards did nothing to stop Amulon from hurting their kinswoman. The only explanation that made sense was that this woman had to be Amulon's wife. Had that been part of Amulon's scheming to become king? Remembering how Amulon had always enjoyed bragging about his conquests, Alma said, "I see you have a new wife."

Amulon did not disappoint. "Observant as always. We found them in the wilderness and took them as wives. We took them to build up the City of Amulon, but before we could build much of anything, the Lamanites found us. Our wives pled with their brethren to spare us. The Lamanites took us back to Nephi, where I offered my knowledge and skills to King Laman. I increased his wealth tenfold in the space of months. As you can see, he rewarded me for it."

Amulon took a deep drink from his cup and set it down. "Speaking of wives, where is yours? Still hiding in Lehi-Nephi somewhere? I asked the Lamanites to search for Sam when they were retrieving my children and wives from that city, but they couldn't find her. She never did like you very much, did she? I can't say that I blame her."

If Amulon realized Sam were here, Alma could not imagine all the horrors Amulon would inflict on her. Ignoring Amulon's statement and hoping to turn his attention from Sam, Alma asked, "You kidnapped these Lamanite women? You stole their daughters, and the Lamanites let you live?"

"You've never understood or appreciated this about me. This is what I do. I survive. And not only do I survive, but as you can see, I always find a way to emerge at the top. Allow me to demonstrate."

Amulon beckoned a guard over and asked for the man's sword. Amulon threw the sword to the ground, just in front of Alma. "My life is now in your hands, Alma. Kill me. My guards will not stop you or harm you afterward. Strike me down."

Alma's hands seemed to go out in front of him of their own volition. Alma had never felt so tempted. Amulon certainly deserved death, especially since he was responsible for Helam's murder. The law said a life for a life. But to do so would be to turn his back on everything he had come to believe and understand. Alma put his hands back on his lap.

"I cannot take your life. I will not murder you."

"Why not? I would if I were in your position. Does your god keep you from exacting revenge?"

Alma saw that Amulon toyed with him and what little regard he had for the true faith. Amulon had known enough to realize what Alma's response would be, that Alma would not try to kill him. Why did Amulon persist in playing this game? How could Amulon not understand the sanctity of all life?

"Now it is you that does not understand. You knew of the true records. You knew about Christ and the Atonement and, still you do not understand. How could you have been a priest and not believed in God?"

Amulon exploded out of his throne, leaping down in front of Alma. He grabbed Alma by the front of his tunic and pulled him in close. "What has *God* ever done for me? Nothing. Anything I've ever received in my life has been by my own doing. I have survived only by the strength of my own arm. No unseen mystical force had any hand in it."

Amulon released Alma's tunic, pushing him back. Amulon sat back down in his throne. "You may go. I have tired of this conversation."

Alma got to his feet and followed the guard leading him out. At the doorway Alma turned back to look at Amulon. "You do know that if I had killed you, the Lamanites might have sent someone worse. I'm not sure that they could, but anything is possible. I'd rather deal with the evil I know."

With a diabolical grin, Amulon said, "You can't even begin to imagine what I'm capable of. But you will soon find out."

CHAPTER TWENTY-ONE

There had been many times when Sam thought her life to be hard. But all of those times combined paled in comparison to her life now.

The hardships began with the loss of Alma. The day that Amulon had arrived as king, Alma had come home and packed his things. He told them that Amulon believed Sam and the girls to be in Lehi-Nephi still, that if Amulon ever discovered they lived in Helam, he would torture and kill them to punish Alma. He could no longer continue to stay in the same house. He couldn't let Amulon's attention be drawn here. He told the women to always use caution, to avoid Amulon at all costs. He instructed them to hide if they ever saw their new king.

Alma left Hunter behind for protection. He built a hut for himself on the opposite end of the city. Sam keenly felt his absence. With each day that passed she missed him more.

Amulon then increased their already substantial tribute by another twenty-five percent. Few could afford to pay the taxes and feed their family. So Amulon made them work to pay their debts. He set them to building tasks and put Lamanite taskmasters over them. Amulon expected the women and children to work, although many of them were not strong enough to help. When they could not, Amulon ordered them beaten. He seemed to take great pleasure from persecuting the people in Helam. He even encouraged not only his own children, but also the Lamanite children to be cruel to the children of the believers.

Sam saw that the Lamanite guards did not enjoy carrying out Amulon's orders. Especially against the women and the little ones. Part of Sam wished that the Lamanites would rise up in rebellion against Amulon and stop him. But she knew that would never happen.

One miserable, exhausting day, Sam was returning home after her work shift ended when she heard Amulon's voice. The pit of her stomach hollowed out at the sound of that horrible man. Trying to stay calm, Sam ran to hide herself as Alma had told her to. She darted inside the home of a neighbor and unrolled their front doorway curtain so that Amulon could not see into the house. She put her finger to her lips, indicating that her neighbor's family needed to be silent.

Not able to help herself, Sam pulled the curtain back enough to peek out. She saw Amulon arguing with the Lamanite captain.

"You are going to work these people to death. This is not what King Laman would want. We need them compliant and obedient. Not stirred up to anger because of your impossible demands," Sam heard Jacob say.

Amulon gave Jacob a disdainful look. "Need I remind you who is king here and who is not? Everyone will do as they're told."

Sam understood the anger she saw on the captain's face. "This is wrong."

"There is no right or wrong. There is only power. Here there is only my power. You would do well to remember that." Amulon cocked his head to the side at the soft, muted sound of several people saying the same words at the same time. "What is that noise?"

Amulon strode away with Jacob right behind him. Sam knew she shouldn't trail after them, but the sound of many voices speaking in harmony made her also wonder what was happening. She knew Alma might kill her himself if she followed them. She couldn't even explain why she went. But she did.

Next to the temple, in the central plaza, a group of workers who had finished for the day were praying together in a group. They cried out to the Lord for relief from their suffering.

"Stop that!" Amulon said as he crashed through the prayer circle and stood in the middle. "Silence! What sort of blasphemy is this? Saying ritual prayers yourselves?"

No one replied. No one dared.

There was a flurry of movement, and Alma walked up to the plaza to join the people who had been praying. A stab of pain and longing, fierce and swift, overwhelmed Sam when she saw him.

Alma and Amulon began to argue. Sam couldn't hear what they were saying, so she crept closer, making sure to stay hidden. She stood behind the wall of a house, peering around the edge to watch and listen.

"I will not permit these sorts of prayers to be said here!" Amulon shouted, his face turning red with anger.

Sam wondered what made Amulon so averse to their praying. He seemed almost fearful. Of what? It was not just the praying that bothered him. It was something more than that.

"It is no threat to you if they pray," Alma calmly replied.

Amulon wheeled around, his cloak flying up from the fast movement. "I do not feel threatened. What I am feeling right now is disobeyed. I command you to cease your prayers." He turned to the Lamanite guards and said, "I am giving you a command. Whoever you find calling upon their god, put them to death."

Ignoring the gasps, cries, and protests, Amulon left. Sam stayed rooted to her hiding spot so that she could watch Alma. She drank in the sight of him, noting that his hair seemed longer. And he looked tired, as if he hadn't smiled in a good while. He exhorted the people to retain their faith, to be patient and trust in the Lord. He told them that while they could no longer pray out loud, they could pour out their hearts to the Lord, and He would know the thoughts of their hearts.

Sam wondered if Alma had guessed at the thoughts of her heart. If her feelings for him were part of what made him leave. She knew she was being illogical. Alma left to keep them safe. He seemed to be more concerned with that than anything else. But how could she ever feel safe again without Alma in her life? Sam had come to depend and rely on him in ways that she couldn't begin to express. She needed him.

Alma and the other believers drifted away, and still Sam stayed at her hiding spot, this time to think over the words of Amulon. Amulon seemed determined to deprive them of anything that might bring them comfort or happiness.

Twilight had turned into night, and Sam used the twinkling stars and full moon to find her way home. Her thoughts continued to churn. It made Sam furious that something else so important to her was being taken away. Her life felt so out of control, as if she had no say over it. People made arbitrary decisions, and she was forced to live with the consequences whether she wanted to or not.

When she arrived at her house, Sam saw a large figure just outside her home. Sam should have felt afraid, but she didn't. Although she couldn't see his face, she knew it was Alma. He was leaving a full vase of water next to the doorway. He had done this every night since he had moved out. Sam had tried to catch him on numerous occasions, but he did it so silently she never could.

Sam said his name softly, and Alma turned toward her. They just stood there, facing one another, until Alma shook his head. He began to walk away.

"Wait!" Sam called out. "I've been wanting to ask why you still bring the water here."

She wished she could see his face. Sam could imagine the little half-smile she heard in his voice when he said, "So no one else would have to."

Before she could react, Alma disappeared. Alma had just echoed back at her the words Sam had said to him so long ago, when he had asked her why she took the chore of retrieving water for her family when she hated it so much. Sam had told him she did it so no one else had to. She did it because she loved her family.

Could it be possible that that was the reason Alma did it too? Not just to be kind, not out of a sense of duty or obligation, but because he loved her?

Sam went inside, going through the motions of playing with Zarah and preparing their evening meal. Her entire being focused on the possible implications of Alma's words. Was he trying to tell her something? Or was she fooling herself?

She lay on her pallet, unable to sleep. She could only run Alma's words through her mind over and over again, thinking of how tired she was of men in her life making all of her decisions for her. Life seemed to just happen to her. She never felt as though she had control over it. Now she had the chance to make a decision of her own. So she made it.

Alma was always telling them to have faith and to be patient. Tonight she had her faith but not her patience.

Sam got up quietly and wrapped her blanket around her shoulders to ward off the cold. She crept out of the house, taking care to not wake anyone as she slipped outside. Sam headed in the direction of Alma's home, resolving to put aside her pride and sacrifice her dignity. Sam would go to him in humility and tell him the truth. She didn't allow herself to think of the possible outcomes from her actions.

She knew the danger she put herself in, how the Lamanite guards enforced a strict curfew. Not even that fear was enough to deter her. Fortunately she didn't see or hear anyone on her way to Alma's house.

Sam found Alma's home easily. She knew exactly where he lived, having walked past it on many occasions when she had tried to catch even a glimpse of him. It was a small hut, which made sense because only Alma lived there. Sam let herself in, squeezing through the doorway and the hooked tarp that hung down.

Alma slept, snoring slightly. Sam suppressed a nervous giggle. *I can't believe I'm actually doing this,* she thought as she knelt down. She jostled Alma's shoulder. "Alma." She shook him again. "Alma, wake up."

He sat straight up, gripping an obsidian knife in one of his hands. With one quick jerk Alma raised the knife above his head. Sam yelped as she fell backward, scooting away from him until she hit the wall. "Alma, it's me!"

Sam saw Alma's hand lower slowly. "Sam?" He sounded disoriented and confused. Sam wished she had brought a candle or something to illuminate the interior of his hut. With the curtain over the doorway there was very little light. She couldn't make out the expression on his face. Was he happy she was there? Upset? Surprised?

"What are you doing here?"

Summoning her strength, Sam crawled back over to sit next to Alma. She willed herself to stop shaking and tried to control her anxiety. "There's something I have to tell you." Sam cringed. She couldn't keep her voice steady.

Alma reached out so that his hands rested on her shoulders. "What is it? You're trembling. Is it Amulon? Has he found you?"

"No," Sam said, refraining from leaning any closer to him. "It's not Amulon. I came here to tell you . . ." Sam took a deep breath and shut her eyes. She blurted the words out, "I'm in love with you. I want to really be your wife." Now that she had actually said the words, relief made some of her nervousness dissipate.

They seemed to have the opposite effect on Alma. Sam heard Alma's sharp intake of breath, felt him removing his hands from her.

"How can you say this to me? I don't deserve it."

For the first time Sam had a glimmer of understanding for why Alma had pushed her away. She remembered the accusations she had hurled at him and understood why he would feel the way he did. So many of the things Alma had said to her suddenly made sense. He still punished himself for the things Sam had accused him of. She couldn't let his guilt stand in the way of their happiness.

"Because I forgave you a long time ago. And someday you're going to forgive yourself. I want to be a part of your life when that happens." Sam reached out to slip her hand underneath Alma's palm. "Alma, I love you. You said once that you loved me. I hope that you still do. I want us to be a true family."

Alma stayed silent, and Sam held her breath as she waited for him to speak.

When he did, Alma spoke deliberately, each word causing her blinding pain. "There was a time when I would have given anything to hear those words from you. But now . . ." His words trailed off and he pulled his hand away from Sam's.

But now. Alma didn't love her. He might have once, but now he didn't. *Such a fool,* her mind repeated over and over. *Such a fool.* She had come here tonight and handed him her heart, and Alma had rejected her.

Sam shattered into a thousand pieces as wild grief ripped through her. Her pain, her loss, was so great that she couldn't even cry. Sam jumped to her feet and struggled with the curtain, jerking one of the hooks out before she could get through. She ran. She wished she could run from herself.

Sam headed toward the wilderness. She couldn't go home, and she had nowhere else to go. She didn't belong anywhere or to anyone. She had never felt so alone.

She had just entered the forest when a strong hand reached out to grab her arm and stop her. Alma. He had followed her. All the strength went out of Sam's bones. She started to collapse, but Alma grabbed her other arm and propped her against the trunk of a cedar.

"If Amulon knew, if he realized that you were here, if he even so much as guessed, he would hurt you to hurt me. I can't risk that. We can't be together." Alma said each word through clenched teeth.

"We could find a way. I don't care about Amulon. I only care about you." Sam felt pathetic in reiterating feelings that Alma had just said he no longer wanted. She wanted to beg him to change his mind, and she didn't know if she could feel worse than she did right then.

Alma proved she could feel much worse when he told her, "You are a constant reminder of my weaknesses. Of my selfishness. I struggle with this natural man every day, trying to do what the Lord would have me do. But it's hard. And being with you makes it harder."

Sam could feel Alma's warmth emanating from his entire being. She wanted him to hold her. She tried to lean in toward him, but his arms locked and they prevented her from moving. "You're not weak. I don't know anyone as strong as you. It's one of the reasons I love you."

Alma let out a growl of frustration, increasing his grip on her arms. "I don't want to love you. I thought if I could stop loving you, this guilt and pain would go away. But it hasn't."

Despite her declarations, despite her willingness to play the fool for him, despite her wanting even a scrap of affection from him, she saw that this was Alma's answer. He couldn't make things any clearer for her.

"Do you understand what I'm telling you?" Alma's voice sounded full of the same agony Sam was experiencing, but she dismissed it as her imagination. Alma didn't want her. He didn't love her.

"I understand perfectly how you feel. Now let go of me," Sam said as she ineffectually beat her fists against Alma's chest. "No more. I can't take any more of this. I understand that you don't love me."

"No, you don't understand." Alma's voice sounded hoarse. Intense. "I haven't stopped loving you. I've tried not to love you, but I can't stop. You're in my blood, in my breath, in the beating of my heart."

His words were too wonderful, too powerful, too amazing, to believe. "You . . . you still love me?"

"How could I not love you? You're everything to me, Sam."

Alma claimed her lips and crushed her to him. The touch of his lips on hers was so overwhelming that a wave of shock rippled through her. Sam slipped her arms around Alma's neck, clinging to him tightly. Alma's kiss seared her soul.

Sam felt as if she had been engulfed by a raging storm of emotions, and she could only hang on to Alma for stability. He was her anchor, her safe haven. He loved her. She felt such bliss, such completeness. She wanted nothing more than to always be in his arms, to always be with him.

This was where she belonged.

Sam experienced a bereft moment when Alma stopped his fiery kiss. He put his arm underneath Sam's knees and picked her up. Nestling her face into Alma's neck, Sam sighed with the pleasure of being carried in his strong embrace. She hoped he was taking her back to his home.

And that was the last conscious thought she had the rest of the night.

* * *

It took two Lamanite guards to bring out the heavy bag of grain and drop it onto the ground in front of Sam. Sam easily hefted the bag onto her back and tried not to laugh at the guards' expressions of shock. She gave them a cheery wave as she headed to the marketplace with the load.

Alma had seized a moment that morning to sneak away with her. Over the last three months Sam and Alma had become experts at finding secret places and times to meet. Sometimes they had hours and sometimes, like now, they had only minutes. Alma had one arm behind his back, and he pulled his hand out to show that he held a single, white ceiba flower. Like the ones she had worn in her hair on their wedding day.

Sam smiled as Alma tucked the flower into her hair, just above her ear. "I wish I had a roomful of them for you."

"One is all I need," Sam said as she lifted her face up for a kiss. "You're all I need."

A little bit later, Alma told her that as much as he would like to spend the rest of his day just kissing her, he had brought Sam here because he had a message from the Lord that he wanted to share with her. Alma said that the Lord had heard their cries for relief and deliverance. The Lord had said He would ease the Nephites' burdens, so much so that they would not even be able to feel them upon their backs. This blessing had been given so that the people would know that the Lord would always be with them in their afflictions.

Sam and Alma had spread the word to the rest of the community. The people rejoiced with gratitude for this promise, and got to enjoy the total bewilderment of the Lamanites. Amulon ordered the workloads to be increased, and the people submitted to all of Amulon's whims with a patience and cheerfulness that made Amulon furious.

Everyone—men, women, and children—had been given an unnatural strength and endurance. This great miracle lifted the spirits of all the people of Alma. Sam exulted in the fact that she could fully share in the complete joy and happiness she felt all around her.

Especially now, since Sam had a secret happiness of her own. One that she would share with Alma soon.

Setting down her bag, Sam held a hand over the slight bump in her stomach. Sam grinned, trying to imagine what Alma's reaction would be when she told him that she was going to have his baby.

CHAPTER TWENTY-TWO

Escape had been the foremost thought in Alma's mind since Amulon's arrival. But Alma could not think of a plan that would allow all the members of the church to leave safely, and he would not sacrifice a few to save the rest.

As Sam's stomach grew in size, Alma's anxiety also grew. He worried constantly over the safety of his beloved wife and their unborn child. Alma had gone to the Lord in prayer many, many times asking for deliverance, for inspiration on how to lead his people away from Amulon.

The Lord did not answer.

Regardless of how many times Alma asked, there was never a response to that question. Alma heard the voice of the Lord and gained inspiration in other areas such as what to teach the people, or whom to call to the office of priest. But on the subject of their deliverance, the Lord remained silent.

So Alma waited. He remained patient, trusting that when the time was right, the Lord would tell them how to leave.

As Sam neared the end of her pregnancy, she was no longer able to physically sneak out and meet Alma anywhere. She had become fiery and testy with him, informing Alma on a regular basis that she wanted the baby out. Alma knew how uncomfortable Sam was, how she could no longer sleep and how she needed to go to the bathroom about every three seconds or so. Sam complained that she felt like a duck because she had to waddle when she walked. When Alma told her he thought she looked adorable, Sam was not amused.

Because Sam wanted to stay within the confines of her home, Alma came there in secret almost every night. Alma wished Sam did not have to suffer, but at the same time, the baby fascinated him. Alma liked to talk to Sam's stomach and to see the bulge of a little foot kicking a reply. He loved it when the baby had hiccups, and Alma would rest his hand on Sam's stomach to feel them. Sam did not share his enthusiasm for these events. She informed him that he could have an opinion on what her attitude should be when he had someone stuck underneath his ribs, someone who devoted their entire tiny life to making certain that all of his internal parts turned black and blue.

Where other women became ill only in the beginning of their pregnancies, Sam's illness didn't stop when it was supposed to. She had thrown up almost every day. Sam pleaded with the baby, promising it anything if it would just come out.

Alma had started to share in Sam's impatience, particularly since it had gone two weeks past when the midwife had estimated the baby would come. He hoped each day for the news that Sam had gone into labor. But no such message ever arrived.

Alma headed to the house without any gifts. Sam had told him the scent of flowers made her want to vomit. The smells of almost every kind of food had the same effect. She seemed to prefer it when Alma came empty handed.

There was a slight noise behind him, and Alma immediately turned around. There was no one there. But his instincts warned him that something felt off. Was he being followed? Alma darted behind the wall of a home and held still. He listened and waited for another sound. None came. After a half hour had passed in total silence, Alma gave a soft laugh at his irrational fear and stood up. He was distracted and tired, which apparently had made him imagine things.

Sam greeted him with a weary smile. She was alone, and although Alma briefly wondered where the other women had gone, he was glad for this time alone with Sam. Alma planted a kiss on his wife's forehead before he leaned down to kiss the top of her belly. Alma hugged

Sam to him and refrained from pointing out that he could no longer get his arms all the way around her. He had already learned the hard way not to invoke the wrath of a very pregnant woman.

Alma had just released her when several Lamanite guards burst into the room. Alma stepped in front of Sam, blocking her from view. "What do you want?" he demanded.

"What do I want?" Amulon stepped through the doorway. "I've already told you what I want. To make you suffer the way you made me suffer."

Everything inside Alma tensed when Amulon walked in. Alma looked left and right, desperately wishing he had brought a weapon with him so he could fight their way clear. He didn't care that he was totally outnumbered. For Sam and their baby, he would have defeated them all.

Amulon sauntered around the one-room hut, as if taking a tour of the place. A servant followed behind Amulon with a giant feather fan to wave away bugs. Amulon walked toward Alma, and Alma moved back, making certain that Sam stayed behind him.

"It's difficult to miss how despite my best efforts, the people here are so annoyingly happy."

Amulon came so close that Alma felt the wind from the fan behind Amulon. "But you," Amulon said. "You're happier than all of them. I've only known one person to make you that happy." Amulon gave a slight nod to the Lamanite guards. "Take him."

"No!" Alma said, struggling against the three guards it took to hold him. They dragged him back, leaving Sam exposed.

"And there she is." Amulon looked surprised at Sam's condition. Amulon took a step back. Pointing his gaze toward Alma, he asked, "Is it yours?"

Alma again tried to get free of his captors but to no avail.

"Did she finally relent, or did you force her? I would have forced her myself. More fun that way."

Alma bit off the retort that sprang to his lips. Alma knew if he spoke, if he gave Amulon any reason to act, Amulon would kill Sam then and there.

Amulon turned his attention back to Sam. Alma could see the wild fear in her eyes, but Sam stood quietly, regally, refusing to show Amulon how afraid she really was. Amulon's eyes raked over Sam, and he said with disgust in his voice, "I always did find pregnant women revolting. I couldn't stand to go anywhere near your sister once she became so repulsive."

With a cry Sam slapped Amulon across the face. His head jerked to one side from the force of the blow. Amulon turned his head back slowly with a low laugh. He smacked Sam in return, knocking her to the ground. Alma roared in response, struggling so much that two more guards came to help hold him down.

A hot, powerful darkness welled up inside Alma. "If you so much as breathe on her again, I will make you wish you'd never come to Helam. If you're angry with me, take it out on me. Leave Sam out of this."

"But what better way to take it out on you then to hurt the people you love? Bring her with us," Amulon said to the guards. "Perhaps we can cut that thing out of her."

Sam wept large tears, begging Amulon to do whatever he wanted to her but to leave the baby alone. Alma managed to thrash around and get one of his legs free. He kicked one of the Lamanite guards, but he was immediately pushed back to the ground.

Two Lamanite guards grabbed Sam, pulling her up. Sam went limp. Alma worried that something was seriously wrong. He called her name as they roughly hauled her outside, but she didn't respond.

"Sam!" Alma tried again.

"What about him?" one of the guards holding Alma asked. "Do you want us to put him in the prison?"

Amulon nodded. "Tie him up and then take him there."

With a patronizing smile, Amulon knelt down next to Alma. "For whatever remains of your life, you are going to regret that you didn't strike me down when you had the chance."

Alma already regretted it but had no time to think further on the matter, because the blow to the back of his head knocked him out.

* * *

Alma flittered in and out of consciousness. He prayed without knowing he did so, and somewhere between wakefulness and sleep Alma heard a voice. Some conscious part of Alma's mind recognized it, recognized the burning feeling it caused deep within him.

On the morrow . . .

Alma struggled to listen, to understand what he was being told. Tomorrow. He was supposed to do something tomorrow. *What am I to do?* Alma asked in his mind as he tried to focus.

You will go before this people, and I will go with you and deliver this people out of bondage.

Cold water splashed against Alma's face, and he sat up with a great gasp. But he did not find himself surrounded by Lamanites as he expected. The Lamanite guards lay on the floor all around him, and Alma looked up to see Hannah and a handful of his priests. He felt the ropes that bound his arms behind him being cut. "How did you know?" Alma asked.

"Dara forgot Zarah's favorite blanket," Hannah said as she put the container on the ground. "I was returning home to retrieve it when I saw the Lamanite guards going inside our house. So I went and got help, and now here we are. Where's Sam?"

"Amulon took her. I am going to get her back tonight, and we are leaving this place first thing in the morning." Alma rubbed his wrists where the ropes had cut into him.

"How?" Hannah asked. "The Lamanites will never let us go."

"The Lord will provide a way," Alma replied as he took the knife to cut the ropes on his ankles.

Alma gave directions to the priests there to tie up the guards and gag them so that they couldn't call out. They were to awaken the other priests, and each priest would be responsible for their fifty believers in directing them to pack up whatever personal belongings they could. They would need to gather all of their flocks and all of their grain.

"That will take all night!" one of the priests exclaimed.

"Then we had better get started," Alma said with a determination that did not permit any further protest. Alma also instructed the priests that if they came across any patrols they should gag and tie them as they had done in the prison. They couldn't risk anyone raising the alarm. Alma asked the men to give him what weapons they had. He strapped an arrow carrier across his chest and slid his arm through the bow to carry it on his shoulder. He took two small knives that he put into the sash around his waist, and tied on a large sword sheath.

"Are you planning to fight the entire Lamanite army by yourself?" Hannah asked in a timid voice.

"I am only planning to fight one man," Alma said. "I will be back with Sam soon."

"What if you don't come back?"

While he understood Hannah's concern, he couldn't afford to let any more time pass. "Even if I don't come back, you will still go at dawn's first light. But I will be back. I promise."

"Where will we go? The Lamanites will just find us again."

The answer popped into Alma's mind. "We will go to Zarahemla. We will find refuge there."

Alma stopped only long enough to hug his younger sister before he ran out into the night.

Arriving at Amulon's home, Alma slowed down to a trot. He assumed there would be guards outside. He did not see any. Alma wondered if this was some sort of trap, if Amulon expected him to come. Or if it was merely a sign of Amulon's cockiness and arrogance that he would not even bother with guards. Alma crept around to the back and put his ear against the wall to listen. He did not hear anything. It hadn't been very long since Amulon left with Sam. Why was it so quiet?

He realized that it was possible Amulon was not here, that in order to keep Sam from Alma, Amulon had taken her somewhere else just in case. Alma used his knives to pry off a plank of wood from the back side of the house. He carefully slid it free from its bindings and peered inside. A fire burning in one corner was the room's only illumination.

Amulon's Lamanite wife sat next to the fire, humming to herself as she stirred some sort of stew in a pot. She looked over at Alma, and simply stared at him. But she did not cry out or react the way Alma thought she would. She went back to her humming and stirring, ignoring Alma entirely.

Realizing that this woman was not going to scream for help, Alma quickly surveyed the rest of the room. He saw someone lying in the middle of the floor. A man. Amulon?

Then he saw Sam in a corner, her arms wrapped around herself. Alma said her name softly. Sam didn't move.

Alma ran around to the front of the home and entered through the unprotected doorway. The Lamanite woman acted as if she didn't notice Alma when he entered. He went over to Sam, and when he put his hands on her she cried out.

"Sam, it's me. It's all right."

"Alma?" Sam lifted her tear-stained face to look at him. She threw her arms around his neck, hugging him tightly. "We have to hurry. Amulon sent his guards to bring you here. He wanted you to watch . . ." Sam's words trailed off, and she didn't finish her sentence. She didn't need to. Alma knew exactly what Amulon had wanted him to witness.

"I got here in time?"

"He never touched me," Sam replied. Alma's arms tightened around her, grateful for at least that one reprieve. "But when he wakes up and realizes that you've taken me—"

"It won't matter. The entire city is leaving. We are going to find Zarahemla and live there." Alma helped an unsteady Sam get to her feet. "What happened to Amulon?" Now that he was inside, Alma could see that the man lying in the middle of the floor was indeed Amulon.

"I'm not sure, but I think she drugged him." Sam nodded toward the Lamanite woman who continued to ignore them as though she were not aware of anyone else around her. "He told her to get him some wine. After one drink he collapsed."

"Baby." The Lamanite woman said the word in the Nephite tongue, startling them both.

Alma responded in Lamanite. "Yes, we're going to have a baby. Thank you for protecting her."

"Baby." Then she looked at Sam and Alma. She pulled her blouse free of her skirt to show her stomach. A long, wicked looking scar ran across her stomach. "Baby," she repeated again while pointing to the scar.

Had this woman been with child? And someone stabbed her? Or . . . tried to cut out the baby while she was pregnant. Just as Amulon had threatened to do to Sam.

"Did Amulon do that to you?" Alma asked. The Lamanite woman hummed and did not answer.

"I'm going to kill him," Alma said furiously. He took out one of his knives and walked toward the unconscious Amulon.

A shadow detached from the wall behind the Lamanite woman, a small boy who ran growling toward Alma with a knife held over his head. The woman reached out to stop the boy, holding him close while the boy struggled and snarled at Alma. "Mahlon," the Lamanite woman said, repeating the boy's name over and over again in an attempt to soothe him. There could be no doubt that this child belonged to Amulon—he looked just like his father.

Sam grabbed Alma's arm. "There's no one who wants Amulon dead more than I do, but I won't let you become a murderer. You said we were leaving. We will never have to worry about him again. Please, let's just go. All of us."

"All of us?" Alma repeated. Sam pointed to a doorway that Alma had not noticed before. There was a room beyond this one. Alma walked over to it and inside saw several women and children ranging in ages from baby to teenager. Amulon's wives and children. Before Alma could speak, one of the women said, "Are you truly leaving?"

"Yes," Alma replied.

"Then we want to come with you," the woman said.

Alma nodded. "You must hurry."

Two of Amulon's Nephite wives tried to convince the Lamanite woman to come with them. But she refused to acknowledge them and instead held Mahlon tightly and continued humming. There in the firelight, Alma could see the multicolored bruises on the faces of the women and children. Alma looked back at Amulon sleeping and again felt an overwhelming rage.

"I should not let such a man live," Alma repeated again.

"Alma, you are a better man than that. Let's leave," Sam said softly.

For Sam, Alma could curb any impulse, fight any temptation, accomplish the impossible if she so much as asked for it. He could not refuse her now.

So instead of killing him, Alma took Sam's hand and led her away from Amulon, and away from the life they had endured in Helam.

* * *

Alma's instructions had been carried out, and all of the believers, hundreds of them, gathered together in the central plaza with their flocks, food, seeds, tools, and anything else they could carry. The other believers were surprised when several members of Amulon's family joined the group. Amulon's eldest son told Alma they did not believe in the ways of their father and wished to join the church and to be numbered with them.

An uneasy silence settled over the community as Alma waited for the signal. Pink, red, and orange lines formed at the horizon as the sun began its daily journey through the sky.

Now.

Alma stood up and with a wave of his hand let the people know it was time to go. He could sense fear at their openly rebelling. They all knew what the consequences would be if they were caught. But they followed Alma, trusting him in this as they had trusted him in everything else.

As they passed through the gate, Alma saw the Lamanite guards at their posts but slumped on the ground. He walked over to one and nudged the guard with his foot. The guard's breathing stayed even and steady. He did not respond in any way to Alma's nudging. Alma realized that the Lord had caused a deep sleep to overtake the Lamanites.

Alma walked faster toward the south end of the valley. He didn't know how long the Lamanites would stay asleep. He wanted to put as much distance between them as he possibly could.

No one knew exactly where Zarahemla was, but Alma continued with faith that the Lord would inspire him on which direction to go.

They traveled quickly all day through the wilderness. They had to hack their way through the underbrush and hanging vines. Alma worried that it might slow them down too much.

Alma and his followers entered a wide, bowl-shaped valley. Alma saw a passage out on the far southwestern end. He had noticed that as they traveled, he felt weaker as he moved further away from Helam. That blessing of strength and endurance that they had received seemed to lessen with each step they took. He wondered if he should push the others to the opposite end of the valley or if they should stop there for the night. Everyone else was most likely just as exhausted as Alma.

Sam made the decision for him when with a loud gasp she told Alma that her waters had broken.

The baby was coming.

CHAPTER TWENTY-THREE

Alma said that camp should be set up there, and a happy murmur arose from the people.

"For Alma!" someone yelled, and everyone around Alma cheered in response.

Ephraim came up and clapped his hand on Alma's shoulder. "I don't care what you say. We're naming this the Valley of Alma."

Alma was too worried and tired to protest. They could name it what they wanted. They would only be staying here long enough for Sam to give birth.

The men went to work erecting huts for not only their own families, but also for the widows and orphans who had no one to make a temporary shelter for them.

Word of Sam's condition spread through the crowd, and several of the men built a hut for Alma and Sam so that Alma could stay with his wife. The midwife and some experienced mothers came to help with the birthing.

As Sam moaned from the pains that seemed to come every fifteen minutes or so, Alma heard the people outside. Now that they could once more pray aloud, men, women, and children gathered to thank the Lord for easing their burdens and for delivering them out of bondage.

The women inside the hut spoke in low tones to Sam and sponged her sweaty forehead with cool rags. As the night progressed, Sam's pains became faster and more intense. Alma couldn't stand to see Sam in this much agony. He asked the midwife if anything could be done to hurry the process along. She informed Alma that first births usually took a long time, sometimes as long as two days.

Two days? How could anyone be in this amount of pain for two days? "You are so brave, so strong," Alma told Sam as he brushed a kiss across her cheek.

"Stop talking," Sam said. "It makes me want to throw up."

Sam squeezed his hand tightly as another pain came, and Alma told himself that if they could just make it to the morning, then things would be all right. The baby would come. Sam would stop hurting so much. Everything would be fine in just a few more hours.

"Is that a hand?" one of the mothers asked.

The midwife gasped in horror. "The baby is breech."

"What does that mean?" Alma asked.

"It means that I will have to turn the baby so that it can come out properly. If she passes out, you will have to wake her."

"Why would she pass—" Alma didn't get to finish his question because Sam screamed as if she were being torn in two. Alma could only hold her tightly as the midwife pushed and pulled at Sam's stomach, trying to turn the baby. The midwife gave Sam a brief respite before resuming her task. Alma didn't even know how much time had passed until the midwife seemed satisfied with her efforts. She checked and informed Alma and Sam that the baby was now in the right position. Sam had only to push when the pains got worse, when her body told her it was time to push. Then the baby would be born.

It all sounded so simple, but there was nothing simple about the deathly pallor in Sam's cheeks. Alma talked to Sam, trying to keep her awake as the midwife had said to do.

"I'm going to die," Sam whimpered to Alma. She seemed so fragile, so weak, so unlike Sam. It terrified Alma.

"You will not die. I won't let you." Alma's voice shook.

"If the baby is a girl, I want you to name her Miriam. For my sister," Sam said just before another wave of pain hit. This one seemed to last longer than some of the others. After it had passed, she said in a breathy voice, "If it's a boy . . ."

Alma knew Sam needed to conserve her strength. "If it's a boy, you want him to be Sam for your father. I understand," he said impatiently. He wanted Sam to stop speaking as if her death were some sort of foregone conclusion. She had been in his life for such a short time. He couldn't lose her now.

That made Sam open her eyes and focus on Alma's face. With a sweet smile she said, "No. Name him Alma. For his father."

"Don't talk that way. You can do this. Women have been doing it for centuries."

"Spoken like a man who never has to give birth," Sam said sarcastically.

Alma was glad for the return of some of Sam's fire. He kissed his wife again. "Do you know how awful it is to watch someone you love in this much pain? I would gladly trade places with you."

Sam let out a short laugh. "As would I."

The next few hours passed in a combination of quiet and screams as each new contraction hit and overwhelmed Sam. Alma realized that he must have dozed off when he awoke with a start. But it wasn't from Sam crying out. He had heard the voice of the Lord warning him.

Alma jumped to his feet and called out for Benjamin and the other priests. Men poured out from huts all around Alma, some barely dressed but carrying weapons.

"The Lamanites are coming. We have to get out of this valley. Get everyone together and move out now!"

Alma returned to his hut and went to pick up Sam. "What are you doing?" the midwife demanded. "You can't take her! She shouldn't be moved right now. She needs to stay and finish giving birth."

"If she stays here, the Lamanites will kill her. We are all going now. Return to your families and get your things. We have to hurry."

The midwife and the other women ran out of the hut. Alma found Dara, Hannah, Lael, and Kelila and told them what was happening. Everywhere Alma looked there was chaotic confusion of people who obeyed without understanding exactly what was going on. Alma called for the people to follow him.

"You have to leave me," Sam said so quietly against Alma's chest that he almost missed it. "You have to lead this people. You have to find Zarahemla and teach the people there. I am slowing you down. Leave me."

Alma tightened his grip on his wife. "If I have to carry you every step to Zarahemla, I will. I will never leave you."

Sam's eyes fluttered shut. Alma stopped to shift Sam's weight in his arms. He yelled out to the people, urging them to hurry.

"We will never outrun the Lamanites," Hannah said from behind Alma's left side.

"We don't have to outrun them. We only have to get clear of this valley. The Lamanites will be trapped here."

"How do you know that?" Hannah asked.

Alma glanced over his shoulder at his sister. "I just know."

The people ran on, and Alma stood at the entrance of the narrow passage until he had made certain that every single person had left the valley. To the northeast Alma saw something. He squinted against the sunlight and realized that it was the Lamanites. They had found them.

"Move!" Alma shouted. "The Lamanites are here!"

Alma ran, wishing the ground was steadier so that Sam wouldn't get bumped up and down so much.

Sam let out a loud yelp. "Alma, it's now. I have to push now. Put me down." Alma stopped to see where they were. He hoped that this would be far enough. Alma yelled for one of his priests to keep the people going through the pass until they reached the next valley. He said they would catch up.

Hannah took off her cloak and laid it on the ground for Alma to put Sam on. "Go get help," Alma said. Hannah nodded and ran off.

She returned a short time later with Dara and the midwife. "Why didn't you tell me last night?" Dara asked in an accusatory tone. "I wanted to be here for you when this happened."

"I knew," Sam said in between moans and deep breaths, "that Zarah was sick. She needed you."

"You needed me," Dara chided. "Your sisters are perfectly capable of taking care of Zarah for a few hours."

With Dara on Sam's left side and Alma on her right, Sam pushed and rested, pushed and rested. Over and over. Alma despaired of the baby ever coming. This seemed to be taking far too long, even though he was apparently the only one so concerned.

"I see the top of the head!" the midwife exclaimed. "Keep pushing, Sam."

"I can't," Sam said as she leaned her head against Alma. Sweat matted her hair to her forehead. "I'm so tired. I can't."

"You have to," Alma said as he jostled her head up. He held her face in his hands and forced her to look at him. "Remember Miriam. You can't give up. You have to push. I need you to keep going. Our baby needs you to keep going."

Sam clamped down on Alma's hand and yelled something that sounded like curses on Alma's mother as she pushed with everything she had.

"That did it! The baby is here!" the midwife said as she laid the baby on Sam's stomach. "You have a son."

Alma felt speechless as he gaped at this tiny, amazing being—who started to wail with all the strength in his lungs.

Sam promptly burst into tears along with the baby as she took him into her arms. The baby calmed down when Sam started to speak. He looked up at his mother with wide, dark eyes. "Oh Alma, look at him. It's our baby. He's here. Look at his little fingers and toes."

"Look what you did, you beautiful, perfect angel," Alma said as he kissed his wife. "I didn't know it was possible to love anyone this much."

"What will you call him?" the midwife asked.

Sam took the rag that Dara had offered her and started to clean the baby off. "His name is Alma."

"You don't think he should have a different name? One that means born in the wilderness or something?" Dara teased, her eyes also glistening with happy tears.

"No," Sam said as Alma leaned down to kiss his namesake on the top of his head. "His name is Alma."

Suddenly, a loud roar that sounded like a combination of a massive earthquake, a thousand volcanoes erupting, and the worst kind of thunderstorm exploded all around them.

"What is that sound?" Sam called out, trying to cover little Alma's ears.

Alma stood up and looked back toward the mouth of the passage. "That is the sound of the Lord answering our prayers."

* * *

Amulon had awoken to find the sun beginning to sink in the sky, every single Nephite gone and every Lamanite fast asleep. How had Alma done this? Had he drugged them all? Amulon didn't see how it was possible for such a thing to be done. It infuriated him that Alma had managed it, that he had slipped through Amulon's fingers. Amulon refused to let this happen all over again.

Amulon went to the barracks and shook Jacob, the Lamanite captain, until he woke up. "The Nephites have left, thanks to your inability to properly do your job. Get your men. We have to bring them back and punish them accordingly."

"What do you mean they've left?" Jacob asked as he rubbed his eyes. "How can that be?"

"You're supposed to be the head of the military here," Amulon snapped. "Why don't you tell me?"

Amulon stormed out, returning to his home to gather his weapons. Alma would not get away. Amulon had not yet had his full revenge. He did smile over the thought of now being able to kill Alma without worries of repercussions from King Laman. Alma had broken too many Lamanite laws. Alma had led the people in rebellion. The law demanded he be put to death.

While at his home, Amulon realized that many of his children and some of his wives were gone. It made him even angrier that Alma would dare steal his property.

Jacob waited outside with the barely awake Lamanite guards. Jacob, however, seemed fully alert. He studied Amulon with a cold expression. "Your hatred and cruelty have cost the king a profitable tributary. He will not be pleased."

"All the more reason to chase down these traitors quickly and bring them back here. Let's go."

The trail was easy enough to follow. Alma didn't even try to disguise their tracks. He couldn't have with this many people and animals running away. The trackers estimated the footsteps to be less than a day old.

There were only a few hours of daylight left and Jacob insisted that the guards be allowed to stop for the night.

"They've had enough sleep," Amulon said. "We keep going." He couldn't let Alma escape. Amulon had to catch him.

Chasing after Alma was not as easy in the dark. The thick forest vegetation made it nearly impossible to see more than a stone's throw in front of them. Amulon heard the whispers of the Lamanite guards. They had already been spooked by the strange sleep that they had all succumbed to, and now with this unusual darkness closing in on them, many said they thought they should turn back. These were omens that the gods were not pleased.

Amulon told them all to be quiet, to stop acting like small children and remember who was king. He was the one they needed to worry about, not some nonexistent gods. The men ceased their idle talking, but Amulon sensed that they still worried. Superstitious fools.

Just before dawn, Amulon and the Lamanites entered a valley. From the crest that they stood on, Amulon saw Alma and his people. They were fleeing out the opposite end of the valley. Amulon laughed triumphantly and told the Lamanites to give chase but to leave Alma alive. Amulon wanted to kill Alma himself.

The Lamanites ran down the north wall, the sight of their prey giving them renewed strength.

As they approached the center of the valley, Jacob yelled for his men to hold their positions.

"What are you doing?" Amulon screamed. "They're getting away!"

Jacob gave Amulon a disdainful look that bordered on insubordination. "Don't you hear that?"

"Hear what?" Amulon stopped. "I hear nothing."

"Exactly. No insects, no birds calling, no monkeys howling, no animal sounds at all. The forest has gone completely silent."

"So?"

"It means something is wrong," Jacob said as he looked around him. "Something is coming."

Amulon saw several of the other Lamanites nodding their heads in agreement as they started to back away.

"Stop with your inane, idiotic superstitions!" Amulon yelled. "We are going to catch those people and take them back."

"It is not wise to insult another man's beliefs." Jacob crossed his arms. "It is certainly not something someone acting as a Lamanite emissary should ever do."

Amulon was about to tell Jacob what exactly he could do with his Lamanite beliefs when a low growling sound started at the outer edges of the valley and rumbled down the walls until it totally surrounded the Lamanites. The sound became louder and louder until it was deafening.

The ground beneath their feet rocked and churned so much that everyone lost their footing.

"It's a sign!" one of the guards shouted. "The gods want us to turn back!"

"The creatures in the underworld are trying to claw their way to the surface!" someone else wailed. "We're all going to die!"

The earth stopped moving, and the sound tapered off. "It's not a sign of anything. It was nothing more than an earthquake," Amulon said in disgust. He stood up while the Lamanites all cowered on the ground. "Get up." Amulon kicked one of the guards in the stomach. "Get up!"

The rumbling thunderous noise returned and the ground shook even harder than before. Amulon fell over, thinking that he had never known earthquakes to get more intense after the first one. They usually lessened.

The second earthquake ceased, and Amulon again stood. "Get up, you lazy, miserable dogs!"

Jacob was the only one to stand. "The earthquake has to be appeased, and the only way to appease an earthquake is a blood sacrifice. Only we can make the earth stop moving."

Amulon had never heard such complete nonsense. "Fine. Sacrifice one of your men and be done with it."

"I will not be sacrificing one of my men."

But the only non-Lamanite here was . . . Amulon. Panic squeezed Amulon's chest, making it feel too tight to breathe.

Jacob took out a sharp obsidian knife and advanced on Amulon. "Seize him," Amulon ordered, hearing the terror in his voice. "Protect your king!"

Not a single Lamanite moved to stop Jacob. "When I have to explain this disaster to King Laman, he will be pleased with the gift of your heart and the knowledge that your remains were torn apart by wild animals."

The earth again shook, and Amulon's screams of pain blended in with the sound of the earthquake until the loss of his blood made them both go still.

CHAPTER TWENTY-FOUR

Alma and his people continued their journey in a state of relief and happiness, knowing that they were now truly free of the Lamanites and Amulon's tyranny.

They walked twelve days in the wilderness, making frequent stops to rest. Alma constructed a litter for Sam and the baby that his new scribe, Zechariah, helped Alma to carry. Every time Alma glanced over his shoulder at Zechariah, the young man was making puppy eyes at Lael, who studiously ignored him except when Lael believed the scribe not to be looking. Then she made the same sort of lovestruck expression in return. It was obvious to Alma that he would need to discuss this situation with Zechariah and that there would be a wedding in the near future. The prospect of Sam having to organize such a ceremony should have worried Alma. But Alma had only to listen to the way Sam gave orders to her sisters and Hannah while still confined to the litter to have total confidence that his wife could handle a new baby, planning a wedding, and creating a new home.

A new home in Zarahemla. Alma sent scouts ahead of their group to look for the city. The people felt a blissful joy the day the scouts returned with the news that they had seen the white tower of Zarahemla's temple. They were almost there.

As Alma and his followers entered the valley of the Land of Zarahemla, Sam insisted on walking at Alma's side. Alma protested, but Sam told him she felt much better. She wanted to enter Zarahemla on her own two feet. Alma tried to take little Alma from

Sam's back, but she refused. "Just hold my hand, and I'll have all the strength I need," Sam told him with a smile.

Hannah pointed out with delight the temple tower, and a loud cheer went up from the people. They had done it. They had found Zarahemla.

As they came closer to the city, it looked as if the entire Nephite nation had turned out to meet their long-lost brethren. The people of Zarahemla sang songs and played music to greet them. There were so many of them. They were not nearly as numerous as the Lamanites, but there were more people than Alma could have imagined.

A tall, handsome man detached himself from the Zarahemla crowd and walked toward Alma. He carried two small boys with him, and the man set the boys on the ground once he reached Alma. He extended an arm, and Alma grasped it. "I am Mosiah. I am king here. We welcome you."

"Thank you. I am Alma of Lehi-Nephi. I can't begin to tell you how glad we are to be here." Alma realized that the king's forearm felt gritty. He looked down to see dirt on the king's arm. It surprised him.

The king followed Alma's gaze. "You'll have to forgive my appearance. I was working in the fields with my sons, Aaron and Ammon, when I received word of your people coming."

A king who worked his own fields? Who brought his royal sons along with him when he did so? While Alma had felt somewhat discouraged that Zarahemla did have a king, it thrilled Alma that Mosiah was such a humble man. The king's sons peered out at Alma from behind their father's legs. They looked exactly alike. Alma decided that they must be twins.

Hunter bounded over and yapped at the small boys. Aaron and Ammon both began to cry, and Mosiah picked them up. "They don't like dogs," the king explained apologetically. "We will set aside farm land for your people and room within the city for those who want to live there," the king said. "You should come to the palace tomorrow so that we can make the arrangements."

"Thank you," Alma said, wishing that there were words to fully convey how appreciative he felt of the king's kindness.

"Alma!" Alma looked into the crowd and saw someone pushing their way through it.

"Prince Limhi!" Alma shouted back.

Limhi came over to them and greeted Alma. "It's just Limhi now. I gave up any claim to the throne. King Mosiah is a righteous man and a good king. He leads his people well."

"How did you come to be at Zarahemla? What happened?"

Limhi told Alma and his people the story of their subjugation by the Lamanites, of the heavy tribute they had paid. Limhi explained how Ammon and his men had come to Lehi-Nephi. King Mosiah had sent them to find the city at the request of some of the citizens of Zarahemla who had moved there from Lehi-Nephi. Limhi recounted how they had drugged the Lamanite guards and escaped. Ammon and his men led Limhi and his people there to Zarahemla.

Alma remembered the Lamanite soldiers who told them they were looking for Nephites. He realized that the Lamanites must have been following Limhi and his people when they stumbled across the Nephites in Helam.

When Limhi finished with his tale, he said, "Can we perform the baptisms now? I have waited for such a long time."

"Baptisms?" Alma repeated with a laugh. "My people are hungry and tired. Let us build our shelters for the night and have something to eat."

"Yes, yes. Of course. And after that is done, could you baptize us?"

"Limhi has mentioned on more than one occasion that you created a church," King Mosiah said with a mischievous twinkle in his eye. "It will be the desire of many here to join with you, to be instructed by you. But tonight we will rest, and tomorrow we will celebrate and glory in the Lord's goodness to His people."

"And then the baptisms," Limhi interjected.

"Yes, Limhi," the king said with a tolerant smile. "Then the baptisms."

King Mosiah finalized the arrangements to meet with Alma the next morning, and then the king put his arm around Limhi to lead him away to allow Alma to care for his people. Without Alma even having to give the instruction, everyone started to clear the area to begin building their huts. Many of the men from Zarahemla offered to help build the shelters, and the women from Zarahemla brought enough food to feed the entire Lamanite army.

Alma heard a feminine voice calling out Sam's name. He turned to see a woman with Sam's black hair running toward them. "Jerusha?" Sam said in a whisper of disbelief.

The two women embraced, tears running down both of their faces. Sam had spoken of her sister Jerusha, the one who had left Lehi-Nephi with her husband and his family to find Zarahemla. It seemed that they had found it.

Sam and Jerusha spoke at the same time, and Alma could barely understand them, but they seemed to have no trouble knowing what the other one said.

"We begged the king to make contact with Lehi-Nephi for so long," Jerusha said. "He finally sent Ammon, and they were able to find Lehi-Nephi with the maps that my husband made for them. But when they returned and you weren't among them, I can't tell you how much I worried."

By then Lael and Kelila had run over to hug the older sister they hadn't seen in years. After exclaiming how much bigger and older her younger sisters had become, Jerusha asked, "Where's Father?" It fell to Sam to tell Jerusha what had happened to their father, and all that had happened to them since then. Alma could see the joy and the sadness in Sam's tears as she talked with Jerusha.

Jerusha ran over to Alma and threw her arms around him, nearly knocking him over. "I am forever indebted to you for taking care of my sisters."

"I love them," Alma said. "I will always take care of them."

Jerusha looked up at him. "I know you will. Sam could not have chosen a better husband." Alma could only barely hide his mirth at the suggestion that Sam had chosen him. He exchanged a secret smile with his wife, who he knew shared in his amusement. Jerusha released Alma and went back to sit next to her sisters. "The entire extended family is here, you know. We will have to have a celebration of our own."

"I'm always ready for a party," a deep voice said behind them.

Kelila and Lael ran over to hug Gideon. Gideon made a show of counting the family members. "Excellent. Everyone's here and alive. That's always good. But how did you manage such a feat without me?"

"I'm not certain how I manage to remember to breathe without you here to remind me to do it," Alma replied with a smile and only a small touch of sarcasm.

Gideon grinned. "I see you have a new addition." Gideon made silly faces at little Alma, who only yawned in response. "I assume you were wise enough to name this handsome fellow Gideon."

"His name is Alma," Sam said.

"Ah. Such a pity. I suppose he will have to make do."

"I know what it is to have your father's name," Sam said as she walked over to put her hand in Alma's. "Little Alma will consider it an honor to carry the name of a man as wonderful as his father."

Alma's heart swelled with love and appreciation for Sam. He leaned down to kiss his wife when Gideon's loud coughing interrupted them.

"Limhi says you're to baptize half the city tomorrow. I hope to be among that number." Gideon took Alma's arm. "All jesting aside, we are all so happy to have you here. I can't wait to learn more from you and the scriptures. Until tomorrow."

Alma watched as Gideon said his good-byes to his cousins, and he felt Sam leaning against him. Her head rested on his upper arm and Alma basked in the warmth that seemed to emanate from Sam. Alma couldn't be certain, but he thought he detected the faint scent of vanilla.

"You will have so much to do here."

Alma nodded, and rested his own head on top of Sam's. "With you standing at my side, I can do anything."

His words were as true as any others he had ever spoken. With Sam and the baby, his own little family, Alma knew he really could do anything.

The joy Alma experienced in that moment at his spiritual and eternal riches and blessings overwhelmed him. Alma leaned back slightly to see his son, who gnawed on his baby fist. Alma rubbed the soft skin on his son's cheek, and realized that faith worked both ways. Babies were a reminder of the faith the Lord had in men, that despite all his shortcomings and weaknesses, the Lord still believed in Alma and gave him one of His children to care for and raise. The Lord trusted that Alma would teach this precious soul, and it was more than Alma could comprehend. Alma had always taught his followers to have faith in the Lord, and it amazed Alma the amount of faith the Lord must have in him.

Not just in teaching his own son, but in teaching all men the redemption to be found in Christ, the redemption in family and the redemption of forgiving yourself and letting go. Alma let the past—all his concerns, guilt, and doubts—float away on the wind, and for the first time in his life he felt truly free. It gave him a lightness of being, a gratitude for the love of Christ and His Atonement, and a burning desire that all his brethren would come to know and understand the same truths.

Alma grinned, excited at the possibilities the future held for him.

As Sam had said, there was much to be done.

ABOUT THE AUTHOR

 Sariah S. Wilson grew up in California. She graduated from Brigham Young University with a degree in history and currently lives in Cincinnati, Ohio, with her husband, Kevin. She is the oldest of nine children and is the mother of two sons and a newborn daughter. You can contact her via her website, www.sariahswilson.com, or drop in at sixldswriters.blogspot.com where Sariah blogs with five other LDS authors.